HEMLOCK CREEK SUSPENSE

BOOKS 1-3

HEATHER DAY GILBERT

Series: Gilbert, Heather Day. Hemlock Creek Suspense; 1-3

Subject: Romantic Suspense Stories; Genre: Suspense Fiction

Author Information: http://www.heatherdaygilbert.com

OUT OF CIRCULATION

1

_____

Rearranging the new books, librarian Katie McClure reflected on just how completely her dreams had run aground.

Growing up, she'd always planned on joining the FBI, where her father had worked for fifteen years. But a permanent foot injury and her dad's early death had negated that plan.

So much for doing anything memorable or spectacular. It seemed God had a funny sense of humor, derailing her noble aspirations and sticking her in the podunk West Virginia town she grew up in.

"Miss Katie, where's the latest Georgia Ray book? I've read five in the series and can't find the next one."

Katie snapped out of her funk, directing the young patron to the correct Juvenile Fiction shelf. The girl's mother, searching for her own reads in Adult Fiction, shot her a grateful smile.

Returning to the New Releases shelf, Katie caught sight of a tall man she'd never seen at the Hemlock Creek Library before. He seemed out of place in his urban button-down and slim dress pants. His wavy, nearly-black hair set off crystal-clear blue eyes. He winked in response to her gawking, and she mentally kicked herself. Seriously. Her life was so boring that instead of bird-watching or stargazing, she'd resorted to nearly salivating over some handsome man perusing library shelves?

Sighing, she decided to reorganize the week's display books by color, starting with red. She'd worked up a small grouping of her favorite reads when she glanced toward the Reference section. Something caught her eye.

A man in a mask.

She didn't hesitate to scream. "Everyone hit the floor!" Why wait around to see if the man had a gun?

Her boss, Reba, shot her a quizzical look from the floor behind the front desk. Katie pointed toward Reference, breathing slowly and pondering what she could use as a makeshift weapon, should the masked man move her way.

Sure enough, black combat boots marched straight toward her. Probably hadn't been the smartest move to shout and draw attention to herself, but she had to do something to protect the library patrons—especially the children.

She slid a chunky, oversized book from the shelf, hoping to hurl it at the fast-approaching man. She was utterly exposed in the middle of the floor.

Out of nowhere, the dark-haired stranger crept her way, positioning himself in front of her. "It's going to be okay," he whispered.

As the masked man rounded the corner, his unnaturally golden eyes narrowed, taking in Katie's would-be protector before fixing on her. A shorter masked man with a submachine gun trailed behind him, glancing around nervously.

A thick, foreign voice filled the air. "Ms. McClure—"

How did he know her name? Had he targeted her?

She closed her eyes, breathing a prayer she couldn't even put into words. Seemingly in direct response, police sirens wailed and tires screeched to a halt on Main Street.

The men exchanged glances, then bolted for the side door that gave way to an outdoor reading area.

Everyone stayed frozen for a few moments. A slight whimpering sounded from the Children's Section, followed by a mother's soothing murmurs.

Katie tried to de-escalate her ragged breathing. The man had known her name. But why? What had he wanted from her?

As police officers burst through the doors, the dark-haired man lightly tapped her shoulder, pulling her back to reality. He stood, thrusting out his hand to help her to her feet.

"Thank you." She tried to keep her balance, but stumbled into him, accidentally reaching for his waist to right herself. Her eyes widened as she realized he had a concealed gun tucked under his shirt. Guns weren't allowed in the library, but then again, it comforted her to know that if there'd been a shootout, he would have been armed. Who was this guy?

"So sorry." Her face reddened, and in return, the man dazzled her with a brilliant smile. For the thousandth time, she wished she could be more like her older sister. Molly didn't have a stumbling gait like her own. Molly's hair was a glossy auburn, while hers was a bright, flaming red. Molly always knew exactly what to say to men. Molly had boyfriends in droves, but refused to marry anyone with a salary under $120,000.

After an intense but brief conversation with the police officer in charge, Reba made an announcement on the library speakers. "The intruders are gone. Please gather in an orderly fashion in the conference room so the police can take statements."

"Ace Calhoun," the man intoned, drawing Katie's attention back to him. His voice was deep and had a decidedly Northern clip to it. "Nice to meet you. Good thing I was passing through today. I thought I'd get a taste of small-town life, but I'm guessing what happened here isn't a daily occurrence?"

She shook her head, still in disbelief. "Not at all." She took his proffered hand, giving it a weak shake. "Katie McClure. Thanks so much for trying to protect me." She kept her eyes on his chiseled face, but couldn't stop thinking about his concealed gun.

He seemed to read her mind. "Don't mention it. I'm just visiting from Manhattan. I came down to attend the Executive Protection Conference. I'm a bodyguard." He subtly patted his belt holster.

She nodded mutely, unsure how to respond.

A young police officer walked over to take their statements. It was more than possible that Ace didn't want the cops to know he was packing heat in the library, so she left out that tidbit as she explained the course of events.

When their statements were complete and the officer strode off to speak with other witnesses, Ace smiled. "I really need to get going, but nice to meet you, Katie McClure. Here's my card."

He pressed a business card into her hand, but she pocketed it and watched as he walked toward the library doors. Pushing through the turnstile, he ambled out onto the street without looking back to notice her final wave. She doubted she'd ever see him again—maybe he was her guardian angel.

Ace Calhoun was on a mission—a mission he hadn't wanted to accept. But his boss wouldn't take no for an answer. "You have to do this job. You owe me one favor, then you're off the hook."

Pretending to be a bodyguard wouldn't be hard. He knew his way around weapons and bulletproof vests. And his orders—to charm a couple pretty sisters and gain access to their home—couldn't be easier.

But he hadn't expected company.

Those masked thugs had made it clear they were looking for Katie. Who had tipped them off? This would throw a massive kink into his plans.

In his calculated fashion, he'd already begun laying the groundwork. He had chatted up the oldest sister, Molly, at The Greenbrier Resort where she worked. Not only did she look like a model, she had been extremely receptive to his overtures.

And today he'd tracked down Katie McClure at the Hemlock Creek Library. She was taller than he expected—maybe 5'11. She had long red hair, just as described. What his boss hadn't mentioned was her liberally freckled skin, her button nose, and her grape-green eyes that peeked out from under straight red bangs and followed his every move.

In fact, she was a little more than he bargained for, with her hawk-like observational skills. Although she projected an innocent vibe, she had to be equal parts savvy, given how quickly she had raised the alarm for the masked men. And she hadn't mentioned his concealed Sig to that cop, even though she was aware of it.

One thing was certain: Katie McClure, wobbly as she was on her legs, was no pushover.

In a tradition they had maintained since Dad's death, Katie, her mom, and Molly gathered for a family dinner. Katie's brother, Brandon, had moved to Arizona before Dad died, while she was only in high school.

While Katie had always admired her dad's dedication to the FBI, Brandon had loathed it and resented Dad for all the hours he'd spent at work. The McClure women knew he had never forgiven his father, but they didn't know how to broach the topic when he visited every Christmas.

Katie was working on a salad when Molly burst through the front door, making her expected late entrance. Katie suspected her sister's alleged "overtime" consisted of chatting up wealthy old men.

Dropping her oversized purse and elegant trench haphazardly on the couch, Molly balanced precariously first on one leg, then the other, removing her strappy gold heels. Then she unbuttoned her blouse, stripping down to a fitted Pima tank top. Finally, she padded into the kitchen, her red toenails sparkling with each step. Molly McClure knew how to make an entrance.

Katie glanced down at her own clothing ensemble—Dad's oversized oxford shirt and her favorite beat-up jeans. Well, it had been a long day.

"Katie!" Molly dropped kisses on her sister's cheeks in an affected European fashion. "Mom told me what happened! Heavens to Betsy, are you all right?"

Katie nodded. No use going into details with Molly the Melodramatic, who would make the entire event seem like some kind of personal attack.

But wasn't it? They had known her name.

Lost in thought, Katie carried the salad to the table, while Molly busied herself cutting garlic bread. When the oven timer buzzed, Mom rushed in, gave Molly a peck, and set her bubbling veggie lasagna in the center of the table.

After they settled into their seats, Mom said the blessing and Molly launched into colorful descriptions of guests at The Greenbrier. Katie finally tuned in when she heard the words "New York City."

"...And this suave, smiling man from New York City came right up to the desk and produced this platinum card. Jessica flirted with him relentlessly, but I'm telling you, those Yankee men have that air of...*je ne sais quoi*. Longish black hair, arctic blue eyes, big muscles...dreamy."

Molly had to be talking about the mysterious Ace Calhoun she had met at the library—able to impress the female staff at The Greenbrier with a single smile. Being a bodyguard must be a lucrative profession, if he was able to afford such a high-class resort.

Molly shot her a look. "I'm telling you, sis, he was perfect. Come to think of it, he's your type."

Her type? Since when did burly Yankee bodyguards constitute her type? Molly was only looking on the outward appearance, which—granted—was very pleasing. Katie wondered what Mr. Ace Calhoun's heart looked like, which was the only thing that mattered. Still, she had to concede she'd been impressed with his noble attempt to keep her out of harm's way.

"I've met him," she said shortly.

Molly's gold-flecked eyes widened. "You're kidding me! How?"

Katie calmly forked up a bite of Ranch-drenched salad and took her time chewing it. This was too fun, keeping Molly in suspense. Instead of playing her usual role as homebody sister, she was now a woman of the world. In the know.

"We met at the library."

"At the *library*?"

Katie tried to ignore Molly's tone, which was loaded with

sarcasm. "Yes. Occasionally people do come and go from the library, and sometimes—though rarely—those people are from out-of-state. Just passing through."

Molly looked like she wanted to jump out of her seat. "Yes, but you said you'd *met*. You must have talked to him. What did he say?"

Not much, come to think of it. But she'd never admit that.

"Actually, he tried to protect me from those thugs. He got between me and their guns. Then afterward, he told me he was a bodyguard from Manhattan, attending a conference. I didn't realize it was at The Greenbrier. Pretty swanky conference, if you ask me."

Molly rolled her eyes. "Of course it is. I'm sure he's a top-tier bodyguard."

Katie snickered. Her sister was just making up that *top-tier* terminology, something she tended to do.

Molly's eyes flashed. "What are you laughing about? I suppose you're feeling special that he talked to you. He talked to me too, you know."

That much was inevitable. Most men fell over themselves to get Molly's attention. It was the way it had always been, even more so once guys noticed Katie's limp. She was not the popular sister.

Mom intervened. "Girls, girls. Have either of you talked with Brandon lately?"

Molly poured herself a refill of sweet tea. "I called him last night. He said he's been flying the helicopter more than guiding whitewater tours this month. I guess they have a new guy trained on the rafts."

"I wish he'd just come home. It's not like we don't have whitewater in West Virginia." Katie stabbed a piece of lasagna, sending veggies and noodles sliding on her plate.

Mom placed a hand on Katie's. "I know you miss him. When it's time, I believe God will bring him home to us."

Molly nodded. "You should call him sometime, sis. He asks about you a lot."

Katie knew she should. Besides, for once she had something interesting to talk about.

After cleaning up, they cozied onto the couch to watch their customary episode of *Gilmore Girls*, but Katie found herself yawning repeatedly. Even Lorelai's clever one-liners weren't making her laugh tonight. She finally stopped fighting the urge to conk out and stood up.

"I need to hit the sack. Reba wanted me to come in a little early tomorrow, just to regroup. I'm wiped out."

Molly frowned. She stretched her legs before grabbing for Katie's discarded blanket. "I don't know why the library isn't a crime scene or something. Why do you have to go to work after what you went through? You should take a sick day."

The idea was tempting, but Katie was no longer the kind of girl who took sick days. She'd been confined to bed far too long in high school after her foot injury. It made her value each day she could be up and around.

After giving Mom and Molly a hug, she walked outside toward the back door of her garage apartment, following the solar lights along the connecting pathway. The automatic light came on, illuminating glints on the ground that made her look twice.

Glass had been carefully swept under a bush and her porch broom was askew. As her gaze trailed up, it became obvious a glass panel on her door had deliberately been broken. What if someone lurked inside, waiting for her?

Gathering her wits, she walked as quickly as she could back to the house. She went straight to Dad's office, opened a drawer, and loaded the nine millimeter Sig he'd always carried. Mom's eyes widened as Katie emerged, holding the gun by her side.

"Wha—?"

"Call the cops. Somebody might be out there."

Molly gasped and slid onto the floor, cowering on the carpet. "Don't you *dare* go out that door."

Katie wasn't that stupid. "I'm not. I'm sitting here with the gun to protect your sorry hide."

Molly's slow grin assured her she wouldn't go into hysterics. You never knew what kind of drama Molly would bring to a situation.

"Thanks, John Wayne."

It took the police nearly ten minutes to arrive. When Katie saw them pull up, she unloaded the Sig and replaced it in the case.

She met them at the door and led the older police officer to her apartment. He motioned to the other officer, turning on his flashlight. Guns at the ready, they proceeded to comb over the three rooms. After what seemed like thirty minutes, they finally turned on the light and gave the all-clear.

She hesitantly walked in. It quickly became apparent what had occurred.

Everything had been turned over or ripped apart. Drawers were emptied, their contents strewn about.

Katie righted her favorite wicker chair. What was this all about? Was this the work of the same gunmen from the library? What were they after?

The police asked her those very questions, but she had no answers to offer. By the time she trudged back to her old bedroom in Mom's house, she could barely hold her eyes open. There was no way she'd sleep in her apartment tonight.

Mom hugged her, mentioning that Molly had finally returned to her own townhouse in Lewisburg so she could work in the morning. They both knew the real reason was that Molly would be scared out of her mind to stay here tonight.

Reloading the Sig and placing it under her pillow, Katie dropped fully-clothed into her white canopy bed. What little sleep she had was riddled with nightmares.

Ace munched on a flaky, buttery croissant and washed it down with pitch-black espresso. He planned to visit the McClures' home later this morning.

Today he sported his turquoise polo shirt that always garnered female compliments, as well as several generous sprays of a newly-released cologne called *Hedonist*. A fragrance counter saleswoman had offered him the used sample bottle after he had sweet-talked her a bit. He hoped Katie McClure was so easy to tempt.

He had decided to focus on Katie. She seemed more level-headed than her sister. Chances were, Katie would be privy to any secrets the McClures hid. Anyway, he couldn't very well pump *both* sisters for information under the guise of dating.

Thinking of Katie's green eyes and serious demeanor, he found himself wishing he could make her laugh. If he could, maybe he could get close enough to accomplish what he was here for.

This whole job was utterly distasteful. What would his granny have thought? Granny was the one person who had believed he could make something good of himself. She took him to church and told him God made him for a special purpose. He used to believe that, until someone framed him and he wound up thrown into the slammer. When God let him go to prison, he'd decided it was better to trust in himself, not in some God he barely knew.

Luxuriating in the shiny charcoal Lexus he'd rented with his boss' money, he couldn't deny that crime did seem to pay. Leather seats, sunroof...this was living the life.

He shook his head, focusing on the task at hand. Today he would take the next step in winning Katie McClure over.

Breakfast was tense, the break-in still fresh in their minds. Mom had made Katie's favorite—French toast—but they both took only a few bites. As Katie sipped her strong coffee, the doorbell rang.

"I'll get it." She figured it was the police with more questions, and she had nowhere to go. Reba had decided to close the library today.

Mom nodded and Katie slowly made her way to the door. Her foot was always stiffer early in the morning.

Opening the door just a crack, she was dumbfounded to find Ace Calhoun standing on their front porch.

She forgot her manners. "What are you doing here?"

Ace smiled, and the effect wasn't lost on Katie. She had to admit he looked just as natural in jeans and a T-shirt as he did in his trendy outfit from yesterday. He actually looked like one of the local "good ol' boys".

"I wanted to check in with you before I left. Your sister gave me your address."

She shook her head, tightening her lips. Of course Molly had been handing out her home address willy-nilly to good-looking guys. "Thanks. I'm home today because they closed the library."

"That's probably wise. I'm hoping the police have a lead on those guys?"

"Not yet." She didn't want to mention the break-in last night, since it was none of his business. "Are you flying out of Lewisburg?"

"Yes...in one of those tin-cans I flew here in, no doubt. But I need to get back to Manhattan. Bodyguarding waits for no one." He laughed.

Mom walked up behind Katie and put her hands on her shoulders. "Excuse me, but did I hear you say you're a bodyguard?"

Oh, no. Surely Mom wouldn't...

Ace nodded earnestly and produced an I.D. that read Kern Personal Security. Mom flipped it over, pulled it out to examine the back, and seemed satisfied.

"And you two know each other...how?"

Katie sighed. This friendly chatter could mean only one thing. Mom was going to invite Ace in.

"He's the guy from the library. The one who tried to protect me. He's flying out today—"

Mom placed a hand on her heart and interrupted her. "You don't say! Well, you just come right on in here and have some French toast, young man. It's the least I can offer for your bravery."

"I just ate, but I'd be happy to have a bite or two. Thank you."

Katie refilled their coffee and Mom heated the French toast for Ace. When she set the plate down, he scanned the table.

"What do you need?" Mom asked.

"Maple syrup?"

Katie pointed to the bottle of Mrs. Butterworth's. "Don't you see that?"

He hesitated, then reached for the bottle. "Oh, sure. I'm just used to real maple syrup."

She snickered, but Mom shot her a look.

"So, you're a bodyguard in New York," Mom probed. "I guess you've run into plenty of scoundrels."

Ace nearly choked on his bite. He took a big swig of milk. "Yes, more than I ever wanted to."

Her stomach sank. She knew exactly what was coming next.

"Ace, I tell you what," Mom continued. "We have a little problem here and I don't know what to do. Katie's apartment next door was ransacked last night. The police are looking into it, but I know we'd feel a whole lot better with an armed guard around. Now, I can't offer you much money, but I have some left in our retirement nest egg and I'm sure the whole family will go in on this."

Surely he'd say no. Manhattan would pay a lot better than small-town folks ever could. She held her breath.

Ace glanced at her, then back at Mom. His gaze intensified. "I hate to hear that. And while I do have other work pending, I can have them call someone else in." He extended a hand. "Ace Calhoun, at your service."

She couldn't believe this city-slicker was willing to hang around Hemlock Creek. Yes, he knew how to carry a gun, but did he know how to deal with heavily-armed thugs like those library invaders? Something in his suave smile threw her off-guard, and she couldn't quite bring herself to trust Mr. Ace Calhoun.

Ace couldn't believe how easily he'd tricked Mrs. McClure. Yes, she had excused herself to call Kern Security for verification, but his boss had made sure his story checked out.

Katie was a different story. Those green eyes tucked under a fringe of red lashes were definitely more piercing than trusting today. As she stalked out of the kitchen, he noticed her limp was more pronounced than it was yesterday.

Ace followed her, easily overtaking her stride. "Did you injure yourself somehow?" He motioned to her foot.

The glare became more serious, hostile even. "No. I have a permanent limp."

She said it almost like a dare.

Before he could respond, the front door opened and Molly whisked in. "Hey Katie, how's—" She nearly dropped the purse dangling at her elbow when she caught sight of Ace.

"Well, hello." She grabbed his hand, her smile brightening. "Nice to see you around."

"Thank you. I'm going to be in town a while longer. Your mom actually hired me to protect your home until the police catch these guys."

"Oh, mercy." Molly fanned herself and winked at Katie. "Maybe I need to move back in."

He caught a barely-perceptible flash in Katie's eyes. Did she feel possessive of him? That was a good thing. But her words fell flat.

"He won't be staying here, I imagine. Maybe down at the Kingsbury Hotel."

"Is that the one I saw near the gas station? I'd be happy to move over there." Anything to stay close.

"With that Lexus and your...Manhattan job, I would think you could afford The Greenbrier a few more days," Katie mumbled.

"Katie!" Molly looked appalled. She shot Ace an apologetic look. "She's a librarian, you know. They spend too much time buried in books and not enough time practicing *politeness*."

Katie shrugged, walking up the hallway. Molly wasted no time, her warm eyes focused on Ace's.

"So. How do you like West Virginia? You know, I've heard West Virginia girls are the prettiest in the United States." She smiled widely.

He stayed noncommittal, ignoring her brazen overtures, even though her looks were definitely hard to ignore. "I'm sure that's true."

Katie returned, awkwardly balancing a bucket, broom, and cleaning supplies.

He grabbed the wobbling bucket before she could protest. "Where are we going?"

She glared. "*You're* not going anywhere. I'm going over to clean up my apartment."

Molly gasped. "You're not moving back out there, are you, with some home invader running loose?"

"I don't know. But I'm not leaving my things flung around like that."

"Let me help," he said. "It's the least I can do, and if those men come back..."

Conflicting emotions played on Katie's face. She finally gave in. "Okay, I could probably use an extra set of hands. Cleanup isn't Molly's thing."

Molly stuck her tongue out at Katie, but didn't deny what she'd said. "I'm going to find Mom. Let us know if you need anything. Especially if *you* need anything, Ace." She winked.

Ace trailed behind Katie, secretly pleased he'd gained access to her apartment. Maybe he could do some unobtrusive snooping.

Now if only Katie would respond to him as warmly as her

sister. He determined to crank up his friendliness factor...or would that even work?

Watching Ace throw himself into cleanup duties, Katie felt somewhat repentant for her distrustful attitude. The man truly did seem committed to helping, and for the love of everything, he was *so* easy on the eyes. She pretended not to notice, but the way his muscles strained at his T-shirt sleeves attested to why he was a bodyguard. Not to mention he was packing a handgun that looked bigger than her dad's. Even though she hadn't gone shooting much since her dad's death, part of her was still impressed with a man who could handle a gun.

He caught her gaze. "It's a .45. That's a large-caliber—"

"I know what it is," she snapped.

"Sorry, I just assumed you didn't shoot. Most women I've met don't."

"Well, you aren't in Manhattan anymore." She didn't know what had possessed her tongue. She had never been this snippy in her life. She tried to soften her response. "I don't shoot these days. But I used to."

He nodded. She appreciated that he kept silent and didn't push the issue.

"So, tell me about your family, now that you've met mine," she said.

He unearthed a pair of her low heels, depositing them on the couch as carefully as if he were returning eggs to an upturned nest. "Not much to tell. I was closest to my granny, and she died when I was a teen. My dad was always busy at work...my mom wasn't really invested in my upbringing, I guess you'd say. I don't have any siblings."

She nodded. "And how did you come to be a bodyguard?"

He shrugged. "I watched my dad. He owned a gun store. He didn't teach me about weapons, but I watched him show them to others." Those intense blue eyes rested on hers. For one moment, Katie glimpsed the rejected little boy in the grown man.

Bustling around to soften his painful candor, she shoved all her clothes into a big trash bag to sort later. No need for him to go through those. As the weight of the bag increased, she found herself stumbling while she dragged it along.

He moved to her side, so quickly she didn't have time to react. He spoke softly near her hair. "I can get that for you."

Ignoring his understated woodsy scent, she pulled the stuffed garbage bag up with both hands, nearly toppling herself. "It's no trouble."

He gave her a slightly crooked smile, obviously amused. "Of course it's not." He plopped down on the couch, watching her.

"What are you doing? You could...put all the big spoons back in my drawer in the kitchen or something."

"Doesn't seem like you need my help." He stretched his arm along the couch.

"Of course I do! Why did you come over here in the first place?" The bag seemed to grow heavier as she stood.

He leaned forward, intense. "Then say it."

"Say what?" Exhausted with her façade of strength, Katie finally dropped the bag.

"Say you need my help. It kills you, doesn't it?"

She gasped. Who was this man, to come into *her* apartment and try to figure her out? To be so glib about her weakness? She would never ask him for help.

"Just because you're our bodyguard doesn't mean you're allowed to mouth off like that. I can get this place cleaned up just fine on my own, which was my original plan." She started to whirl around, but her slower foot caught in a quilt on the floor and she tumbled onto the couch—uncomfortably close to Ace.

She expected him to take advantage of the situation, but instead, he stood and offered his hand, like a gentleman. She swallowed her pride and took it, allowing him to help her to her feet.

As they continued to work in silence, she kicked herself for her outburst. She had not been herself since this New Yorker invaded her hometown. Or rather, since those thugs invaded the library.

The urgent, nonstop barking of the dogs next door broke into her thoughts. Without thinking, she rushed out the door to see what the unusual ruckus was about. She could feel Ace hot on her heels.

Wheeling around the side of the apartment, she caught sight of a man in a black hoodie, loitering in front of the McClure house. Ace protectively stepped in front of Katie. When the man noticed them, he fled up the sidewalk. Ace broke into a sprint. "I'll try to catch him," he shouted.

She shivered, even though it was a warm August day. She prayed Ace would catch the stalker and wouldn't get himself killed in the process.

Ace hadn't kept up with his daily jogging since he'd been in West Virginia, so a sudden, unrelenting stitch in his side slowed him down. By the time he rounded the street corner, the hooded man had vanished.

Who was that guy and what was going on? No way his boss had sent in some kind of hit team, knowing Ace hadn't even finished the job yet.

Still, he had to get moving on his plan. His boss wouldn't tolerate heel-dragging. And in a way, these stalkers had already helped him—opening the door for him to step in as the McClures' bodyguard. Perhaps Katie, motivated by fear, would open up to him.

But that wouldn't be easy. He'd seen anger flash in Katie's eyes when he'd challenged her to admit she needed help. Yet she hadn't cracked. He probably should have focused his intentions on her sister Molly, who would have been more than willing to answer his questions without much effort on his part.

And yet something about the plucky redheaded librarian drew him. Maybe it was the genuine grief in her eyes as he described his childhood. Maybe it was the way she was different from other women, almost immune to his magnetism.

But Ace had to admit that he wasn't entirely immune to hers.

3

Mom met them at the door and listened as Katie told her about the stranger.

"Could have been nothing at all," Mom said. "Now you all come in here and get some lunch. You've been working hard."

Mom always looked for the best possible interpretation of any circumstance. Katie wished she'd inherited her mom's optimism, but instead she'd developed a tendency to suspect the worst. Then again, without that cautious instinct, she wouldn't have boldly shouted for everyone to hit the floor in the library, and who knows? Maybe she'd saved someone from getting shot.

Regardless, she determined to give things a cheerier spin when talking to Ace. The poor man probably thought she was one of those "mean girls" who had nothing nice to say to others.

Just as she was about to compliment the chicken salad on croissants, Ace piped up.

"Mrs. McClure, these sandwiches are wonderful. As good as any New York deli."

Mom smiled, pouring him a glass of sweet tea. He took a

gulp, then unintentionally pursed his lips before slowly swallowing. Katie had to laugh. The debonair Yankee couldn't hold his sweet tea!

He coughed. "Excuse me, but could I have a glass of water?"

Mom looked befuddled. "Something wrong with your tea? I just brewed it fresh."

Katie silently refilled his glass with water as he struggled to explain. She tried to wipe the smile from her face but found it impossible.

"It's just...sweeter than what I usually drink. I drink unsweetened tea, black coffee...pretty bland stuff, really."

As Katie handed him the glass, he gave her a grateful look. She felt pulled in by those dark-lashed eyes, but briskly looked away. There was a hurt behind them she wanted to know more about. But he wouldn't be around long enough to explain, if the cops could just figure out how to track these men down.

The fact that the guy in the hoodie ran when he saw them was definitely suspicious, but should she tell the cops about him? They might think she was starting to see things, overreacting after the library incident and the home invasion. She decided to keep quiet, hoping it was just a random person loitering for a moment on their sidewalk.

At least they had Ace around.

The day slipped by quickly, with no further incident after the iced tea debacle. Ace had no idea that much sugar could be dumped in tea, and he couldn't figure out how anyone could get used to drinking it that way.

Standing next to an exhausted Katie as they surveyed her now-clean apartment, he felt a fresh sense of pride and accomplishment. He'd done something *right*. And yet his spying and snooping was so wrong. The price of freedom, he told himself for the hundredth time. Once he got done with this job, he'd never see his boss again.

But he would never see Katie McClure again, either.

Glancing at her, he was again surprised by how tall she was. Even as she drooped against the counter, taking the weight off her bad foot, he sensed her hurt ran deeper than an external injury.

"So...did you always want to be a librarian?" he asked.

She blinked rapidly, but didn't look at him. "No."

"You don't like your job?"

"That's not what I said." She brushed bangs from her eyes and fixed him with a weary look—one that was old beyond her years. "I like being a librarian. I'm good at it, and I love the people. But I had other plans. I wanted to be in the FBI like my dad."

He raised his eyebrows, unable to respond. Having done his homework, he was already aware that Sean McClure had been in the FBI and that he had died of an unexpected heart attack at the age of fifty-one. But a woman who wanted to choose an FBI career? He had never run into anybody like Katie.

She frowned at his incredulous look. "What? You don't think I could have done it? Back then, it would've been easy. I practiced shooting. I started taking judo when I was eight. I used to run five miles every morning. I could have done it, Mister...Doubter."

Her prickly exterior faded a bit, revealing a glimpse of a girl who'd desperately wanted to prove herself until her opportunity was snatched away. He lightly touched her arm and was surprised when she didn't recoil.

"I understand what it is to fail to meet expectations—those others put on you or the ones you put on yourself." He shifted his gaze from her teary eyes to the window, struggling to maintain his cool. "I'd better get going. It's already late afternoon."

She followed him outside. "Thank you. But wait—what if they come back at night?"

He had already thought of this angle, but was waiting for her to recognize it.

Fear darkened her eyes. "I know how to use Dad's gun, but haven't gone target shooting for a long time. Maybe...maybe you'd better stick around closer. You can stay in my apartment, if you'd like, since I've moved back over to the house for now. It would save you money, especially since we can't afford to pay you Manhattan wages. That way you could keep an eye out, if you wouldn't mind."

He shrugged, trying to hide his excitement at this inside opportunity. "Of course. It's a great suggestion that makes all kinds of sense. I'll run back to The Greenbrier and check out. I can pick up some food on the way back."

"Goodness, don't bother. Mom always makes enough to feed an army. She'd be happy to have you over."

As Ace slid into the Lexus, he adjusted the rearview mirror and glanced at his smug look. He felt like kicking himself. Faker. Liar. Worthless.

Granny's voice filled his mind. "God knew you before you were even born. Follow after Him and He will lead you on right paths."

That was his problem. He had stopped following God. He wouldn't know a right path if it rose up and punched him in the face.

But he was pretty sure it didn't look like this con-job he was pulling on the McClures.

After telling Mom about Ace's willingness to stay in the garage apartment, Katie trudged into her room and flopped on the bed. She wanted to go for a walk in the woods behind their house, but didn't dare expose herself to whoever might be lurking around.

When she was a teen, Dad had felled several trees to make a clearing in the woods. He surrounded the opening with honeysuckle bushes, forming a haven of sorts. Recognizing Dad's rare effort to build something lasting for his family, they had all pitched in, stringing Christmas lights from tree branches and setting up a fire pit to make it comfy.

Brandon had built a picnic table, and she and Molly had painted it blue. Now the table was covered in a blanket of leaves, sitting unused since last summer.

It always seemed enchanted, that wonderland showcasing not only the apple green leaves of spring, but the deep golds and russets of fall. When she lost herself in the woods, Katie always gained new perspective.

But now the thought of some man lurking around their home chilled her. What if someone attacked her? She couldn't run or kick. All the joy she used to take in developing her strength and skills had vanished right along with her ability to walk straight.

At least her room overlooked their woodland paradise. She gazed at the trees, fully clothed in summer green. Suddenly, she froze. The man with the black hoodie stood out against the natural backdrop, his binoculars fixed on her.

On his way to The Greenbrier, Ace's cell phone buzzed. He tapped his hands-free headset and his boss' rough voice nearly blasted his eardrum.

"You found anything yet?"

It was early in the game. Why was he already asking?

"Not yet. These things take time and finesse."

"You better finesse your way right into that stash, Ace. I tapped you for this job because I know how the ladies love you. It should be no problem to extract information from one of those girls."

"I know. I'm working on it." Ace felt like laying on the gas, but it was impossible to do that on these curving mountain roads. "By the way, you want to explain why there's another crew down here working on the McClures? Are those your people?"

Dead silence reigned. Maybe the wireless signal went out? He glanced at his phone. Still had bars.

"Are you *kidding me*?" His boss sounded like he wanted to punch something. Or maybe shoot something.

"It's no joke." Ace filled his boss in on the thugs' appearance at the library. When he mentioned the ransacking at the McClures, his boss lost all control. Ace could almost hear him spitting into the phone.

"You gotta get in there and find that money first. I'm betting Anatoly sent his men down. That Russian—" His boss launched into a string of profanities, some of which were even fouler than the ones Ace had heard in prison. He concluded with, "You'll have to watch your back. But you're finishing this thing. Or you'll be locked up again—I'll make sure of it."

Ace stifled a groan. He was too far gone now. Quitting wasn't an option. He couldn't leave the McClures exposed to those Russian mobsters, and there was no way he was going back to prison. All he had to do was find the stash and he could wake up from this nightmare. His boss' minions would probably settle things with the Russian henchmen once he handed the money over.

The 1.5 million that Sean McClure, FBI agent, had stolen from Anatoly.

He still found it impossible to believe that Sean had risked his family and life to make off with bank heist money. How had he worked it out? Why hadn't his FBI superiors discovered it?

In the years that had elapsed since Anatoly's heist, the mobster had doubtless grilled all his men about the theft, maybe bumping a few off along the way. And yet why had he only recently realized Sean McClure might have taken the money? What had tipped him off?

His boss continued, words tinged with a threatening edge. "I'm coming down in a few days. I want to talk face to face and make sure we understand one another."

After setting up a time and place, Ace hung up and groaned. Tonight he would search the apartment and maybe the garage. His boss had just shortened his timeline. Showing up clueless and empty-handed wouldn't go over well at their meeting.

When he parked, he noticed a text had come through from Katie. She must have gotten his number off his business card. He stared at the screen.

Katie: *Hoodie Man in woods. Do I call the cops!?!*

The text had been sent seven minutes earlier. He texted back, choosing his wording carefully in light of Katie's obvious fear:

Ace: *Is he still there? Don't worry. I will be there soon. Just stay inside.*

Her reply came quickly:

Katie: *He's gone now, from what I can tell. I have the gun. Mom is working on supper. I didn't even tell her.*

He smiled and texted back:

Ace: *Good girl. I'll be there soon. Will knock five times.*

At The Greenbrier, he raced into his yellow-wallpapered

suite and began snatching clothes from drawers and tossing them into his open suitcase. As he packed up his bathroom things, he met his own deceitful eyes in the mirror. Had Sean McClure been like him, trapped in an impossible situation? Or had he willingly opened Pandora's box when he decided to steal heist money from a Russian mobster?

Didn't matter. Ace would find the money, if there was money to be found. If not...

He hated to think what Anatoly's men might do to the McClures.

Katie trailed behind Ace as he combed the woods. Dad's lightweight Sig felt natural in her hands. She had to make time to go shooting, to remind herself of the weight of the trigger pull and the feel of the gun's slight kick. But even now, she was confident she could hit her target, should the need arise.

She was impressed how methodically Ace searched for Hoodie Man. When he finally pronounced the woods abandoned, she took a deep breath of air, trying to slow her shallow breathing.

She dropped onto the picnic table bench, carefully placing the Sig on the bed of leaves in front of her. Ace followed suit, sitting across from her.

He took a long look at her, scanning her face intently. Was he staring at all her freckles? A blush crept up and she propped her face in her hands to hide it, leaning on the tabletop.

Thankfully, he took the hint and glanced up at the sky instead. "Storm moving in, I think."

"For a city boy, that's pretty astute. Usually I can smell them coming."

He grinned. "I remember sticking a hand between our window bars, catching raindrops before they hit the pavement. It does actually rain in the city, you know."

She laughed. "I guess it does."

His focus casually shifted to her lips. When his eyes met hers, they held some kind of unasked question.

Her sister would have rushed to fill the silence, joking and flirting. But she wasn't Molly. And so she waited.

The hush continued, stretching interminably. Finally, he broke it.

"So your dad was FBI, right?"

She nodded.

"Was that hard on you?"

She shifted, fingering the cool metal of the gun. How did she explain that although Dad's long hours hadn't affected her, his bravery had? He had been willing to put his life on the line to protect the people of the United States.

And why had God taken a man like that so early? Sometimes she felt like God enjoyed snatching things from her—her ability to walk properly, her father, her chance for an exciting future...but she couldn't let her mind go there.

"Some jobs require long hours. Dad had one of those jobs. We understood."

His clear eyes filled with pity, something she simultaneously hated and craved. As large raindrops splattered her nose and cheeks, she grabbed the Sig, happy to close the conversation. "We'd better head inside. I'll bet Mom has a warm supper waiting."

4

Katie observed the normally chatty Northerner as he fell silent during their evening meal. Maybe he didn't care for chicken and dumplings, or maybe he was disappointed they hadn't nabbed the man in the woods.

She smiled as he drank the unsweet tea she'd made for him. She had been so tempted to throw in just a tablespoon of sugar—unsweet tea seemed so unnatural—but resisted. Apparently it hit the spot, because he'd asked for another glass.

"Thank you for the meal, Mrs. McClure." Ace rubbed his forehead, like he was exhausted. "I think I'll head over to the apartment and gear up to keep watch tonight." He scraped his plate, placing it carefully on the counter before walking out.

Katie helped Mom clear the table, then cut a slice of key lime pie to take out to Ace. A taste of Mom's famous pie was sure to cheer him up.

He stood outside the apartment in the waning light, tacking a piece of plywood over the open door pane. "I stopped by that hardware store in town and ordered glass for this. Should come in next week. It's standard size."

She was taken aback at his thoughtfulness, which he seemed to be downplaying. "Thank you for doing that." She motioned to the piece of pie. "I'll just put this inside." She scooted around him, through the open door.

His all-black luggage was piled in the corner of her small living room. She snickered when one whopper-sized suitcase caught her eye. For such a brief bodyguard conference, he'd packed even more clothes than a woman would. She could imagine what her brother would say about that.

She set the pie plate on the counter next to his gun, realizing it wasn't the .45 he'd carried earlier today. This one was a nine millimeter, she felt sure. She wondered if it was a Sig Sauer, like her dad's. Gently picking it up, she examined the frame for the brand...

"Put that down!" Ace's deep command echoed in the small apartment. Startled, she returned the weapon to the counter. How dare he assume she was doing something stupid?

She tried to explain. "I just wondered what it was."

Ace gave her a hassled look. "It's a gun, and you shouldn't be handling it."

Anger boiled up. Words exploded from her like fireworks. "I know good and well it's a gun, you dimwit. I just wondered if it's a Glock, a Sig, or a Ruger. I told you I know how to handle guns—you saw me with one today."

Ace crossed his arms. "And you told me you hadn't gone shooting for a while. You can't be casual with firearms, as I'm sure you know."

Now he was lecturing her. Katie raised her chin and tried to stomp out the door, but her awkward gait morphed into a step-drag canter. Regardless, she did succeed in brushing past Ace like he was yesterday's trash.

Once in her room, Katie burst into tears. She already knew she was incapable of doing most of the things she wanted, but to be talked down to like that was insufferable.

She wished she could pull a judo flip on Ace or throw a vase at his head.

But a deeper part of her wished she could say the words that would calm his stormy eyes and make him smile. It *had* been foolish to handle someone else's gun. Maybe she should apologize in the morning.

When Molly showed up for her belated supper, Katie emerged briefly to say hello, then skulked back to her room. Like any good sister, Molly followed her. She probed and prodded until Katie gave in, recounting the day's events.

As Katie finished sharing about the gun-touching incident, Molly shocked her by laughing outright. Auburn curls tumbled around her face. "You know what your problem is, don't you? Why, Katie Beth McClure, you're smitten with that Yankee!"

Katie blushed as a wave of realization hit. Why hadn't she seen it? Truth be told, she was downright fascinated with Ace Calhoun.

Molly continued to dispense her sisterly advice. "Right now, the sparks are flying. But you need to figure out if you all have anything in common. He's from New York City, you're from West Virginia. He totes guns, you shelve books. You know Dad and Mom didn't have a lot in common, but Dad was a Christian and so is Mom." Molly's hazel eyes fixed on hers. "You need to get to know that boy, sis."

Later, as Katie snuggled into her soft, worn sheets, she reread a few chapters of *Little Men*, one of her favorite books by her favorite author, and one that never failed to make her feel calm and happy. As usual, she savored the interactions with Professor Bhaer and his wife, Jo. If only she could find a man like that, someone who loved her just as she was, yet challenged her to be better than she ever thought she could be.

Shockingly, Ace Calhoun came to mind. She snickered.

Well, the man certainly didn't hesitate to challenge her, that was for sure.

She hesitantly prayed that she could have more chances to get to know Ace Calhoun...and that God would help her bite her tongue in the process.

After an uneventful night, Ace joined Katie and Mrs. McClure at the kitchen table for French toast. Must be someone really liked it. He remembered Granny's pancakes, light and fluffy as cotton candy. As he sipped his second cup of black coffee, he turned to Katie, determined to smooth things over from his outburst last night. "You want to go shooting sometime? As you know, I have an extra handgun."

A wide smile stretched across Katie's face, triggering a nearly electric response in him. She had no idea what a knockout she was.

Leaning toward him, she briefly rested her hand on his, obviously pleased. "I'd love to!"

He tamped down the guilt that rose like bile in his throat. Last night, after going over every inch of Katie's apartment, he'd decided to take a more aggressive tack in gaining access to the McClure home. This shooting scheme was just another step in his plan, a way to ferret out where Sean McClure could have hid the bank money.

He'd found no clues as he'd examined Katie's apartment —right down to the diaries in her bedside table drawer. Apparently, she hadn't nosed into her dad's work much. Her diaries were full of written-out prayers, asking God why she had a limp, why her dad died young, and why she couldn't find a man who would love her for who she was.

In other words, her dream man looked like his exact

opposite. Wasn't he just using her for his own ends, like a phony?

This morning, as he stared at Katie's welcoming, Julia Roberts-wide smile, he faltered. He wished he could be that dream man.

The man his granny had prayed he'd grow up to be.

Katie wasn't sure where Ace's magnanimous suggestion to go shooting came from, but she'd take it. First, because she used to enjoy shooting immensely, before *the unfortunate event*, her private nickname for that injurious volleyball game. Second, because Molly had been right. She felt a spark of interest in Ace Calhoun that she'd rarely felt with any other man.

She peeped over her favorite sunset-colored mug, watching him carry on an easy conversation with Mom. There was something about him—not just the chiseled nose and chin, or his striking combination of blue eyes and dark hair. There was something deeper about Ace, something not easily visible on the surface.

She couldn't imagine having a job that would cover a stay at The Greenbrier. Sure, Molly got her in for meals now and again with her employee discount, but she would feel ostentatious paying for even one night at the lavish hotel. And yet here sat a man who took it as a matter of course, who rented a Lexus, and who had more than one handgun.

Her cell phone rang, startling her. Mom grinned and gave her a quick wink. So she wasn't unaware of her daughter's scrutiny of the hired gun.

As Katie picked up, Reba's weary voice filled her ear. "Could you come in today?"

"Um..." Katie glanced over at Ace. What would he do? Stay here and guard Mom? But who would guard her? Oh, well.

She couldn't live in fear forever. "Sure. I can come in around ten."

"Oh, honey, that'd be great. We're getting swamped already with all these summer reading activities. Kids bouncing off the walls today." Reba abruptly hung up.

Taking in Mom and Ace's anxious stares, Katie made a public service announcement. "I'm going in to the library today. I'll be fine."

Ace glanced at Mom as if they had some secret understanding. "I'll come along," he said.

Mom nodded. "I have to go into town today anyway, so I won't even be around. It's more important that you get back to your normal life."

How many times had Katie heard that in high school? She never understood how she could get back to her normal life when she was living her new "normal." But she knew better than to sass her mom, who only meant well. She turned to Ace.

"Okay, but you'll just need to stay out of the way. They're really busy." She tried to channel some of last night's irritation with Ace, but found it had almost completely dissipated. The man was winning her over, no doubt about it.

"Will do." He stood and carried their plates to the sink, then returned to tote the milk back to the fridge.

Katie had to admit, this city boy was no slouch around the kitchen. That was more than she could say about most of the guys she'd dated.

He was going to find that money in the next couple days if it killed him.

As Ace brushed his teeth, he reflected that Katie seemed to be softening toward him. He would try to keep those positive feelings flowing. Maybe he'd launch a barrage of compliments, or touch her elbow repeatedly as he earnestly spoke to her. Those tried-and-true flirting techniques had yet to fail him. But in case of emergency, there was always the old fallback—fake an injury.

It was despicable, this plan. But there was no way around it. He had to gain access to Sean McClure's things, and the only way in was through Katie.

❦

The library was hopping, as both children and parents disregarded the unwritten keep-it-to-a-whisper rule. Katie jumped right in, entering data from the summer reading forms and guiding children to bookshelves.

Ace seemed content to sit on an extra rolling chair and observe. Reba had only hesitated a moment to let the bodyguard bypass the *No Guns Allowed* restriction posted on the library door. She didn't want to take any chances with a library full of children running around, and Katie was thankful she could focus on her work instead of worrying about masked men.

When she finally glanced at the clock, it was nearly one and they hadn't taken a lunch break. Ace must be starving; he was such a large and well-muscled man. She tried to keep her eyes from wandering to his biceps, which filled out his fitted blue dress shirt in a most impressive way.

She gathered her purse and keys and walked over to him. "I'm so sorry. I totally lost track of time. I have an hour lunch break."

He stood, halting his apparently tireless visual rounds of everyone in the library. He met her gaze. "Sounds good."

"You want to run home and get something to eat? Mom

always has sandwich supplies and chips. Or if you're into healthy, I'm sure there's fruit and hummus."

He shot her a radiant smile, and she nearly lost her balance. "I'll eat anything. I'm easy to please."

Reba reluctantly agreed to let them go, her eyes lingering on Ace's holstered guns. Katie prayed there would be no repeats of the other day's armed guest appearance while they were out.

Ace seemed unusually chatty in the car. "Those kids were cracking me up. One of those little boys kept circling the front desk, his eyes glued to my guns."

"It's not every day they see someone like you sitting around. I mean, you do cut an impressive figure." Her cheeks heated and she tried to will the blush away.

He was watching her, but she forced herself to keep her eyes on the road. It was awkward being confined in her small car with such a fine specimen of a man. She struggled to land on a topic of conversation, finally saying the first thing that popped into her head.

"So, were you close to your grandma?"

He stretched his legs, then adjusted his seat so he could keep them fully extended. "I was."

She could tell he was hedging, dancing around something he didn't want to share. Should she keep probing?

Hoping to keep him talking about himself for a change, she said, "So tell me about her. Was she one of those cozy knitting grandmas or one that goes out line dancing?"

To her relief, he laughed. "I don't think they line dance up my way. But she wasn't a knitter, either. To be honest, the main things I associate with my granny are good cooking and going to church."

Katie tried to hide her surprise. "We go, too. You're welcome to come along."

She glanced over and took in his serious look.

Finally, he sighed. "I don't believe in that stuff now."

Something pricked Katie's heart. Yes, she believed in *that stuff*, but did she really believe all of it? If she dug deep and examined her blackest thoughts, she had been angry with God for years. Even as she sang songs in church, read her Bible, and prayed, there was a splinter of doubt that always needled her...that feeling that God had enjoyed keeping her from the life she wanted.

"You look pensive," he said.

"Sorry."

"It's not a bad look. But I do prefer your smile."

She smiled in return for his compliment as she pulled into the driveway. "Thanks. And, Ace?" She pulled out the key and looked full into those disarming blue eyes. "I understand where you're coming from."

As Katie dropped her brown sack purse to the couch, Ace noticed a white envelope protruding from an inside pocket. He pointed to it.

"Love letter?" he joked.

She drew her eyebrows together. "I don't know what that is. Reba already gave me my paycheck."

Pulling the envelope out, she gasped. "It's from them—I just know it. It says *To Miss McClure*."

What? That purse had been sitting right there, on the librarians' desk, the entire time. How could anyone have slipped something in? Was Reba in league with Anatoly's thugs? Or had they taken advantage of his one bathroom break and shoved it in then?

Katie ripped into it before he could stop her, tearing the entire end off the envelope. He hoped they hadn't laced it with anthrax or some chemical weapon. Katie's hands shook as she pulled out a crumpled piece of notebook paper and read:

"We're done playing games, Miss McClure. Anatoly wants what's rightfully his. Your family will stay in our sights until you bring us what your daddy stole. You send us a text message at this number when you find something: 212-589-3316. It's untraceable so don't even bother. If we don't hear from you in four days, we will come and find it ourselves."

She slumped to the couch and Ace grabbed the paper, hating that they had threatened her. And now she knew—

"What Dad stole? What are they talking about? And who is Anatoly?" Tears welled in her eyes.

He had to play dumb, but at the same time, this was an opportunity he couldn't afford to pass up.

"I think Anatoly is a famous crime boss in New York—I've read news articles on him." He tried to sound casual. "I remember he pulled off a huge bank heist years ago, but they couldn't pin it on him because the money was never found." He watched for a reaction from Katie. Did she know more than she let on?

She seemed oblivious. "But what would my dad have to do with that?"

He hesitated for effect. "Your dad was in the FBI. Maybe he was in charge of Anatoly's case?"

She shook her head, straight red hair slipping over her shoulders. "Dad never mentioned an Anatoly."

Time for a direct prod. "But did he keep records of his cases somewhere? Didn't you say he had an office?"

She sat up straighter. "Yes, he had one—it's right down the hall. Maybe we should see if he kept any files."

He extended his hand, helping her up. This threatening note had turned out to be a windfall for him. "Okay, but first let's eat something. You're still shaking."

In the kitchen, Katie slowly assembled one turkey sandwich for herself and two ham and Swiss on rye for him. She loaded a large bag of chips, apples, two water bottles, and a package of Oreos into an antique-looking picnic basket.

She fixed him with a determined look. "Let's eat in the woods at the picnic table. I don't care if they're watching us—I have to get out of the house."

He nodded. "I'm locked and loaded."

"Hang on." She went down to her dad's office. When she returned, she racked the slide on the Sig, fitting it into her belt holster.

He carried the picnic basket as they made their way into the still forest. Shafts of sunlight filtered onto Katie's thick red mane, lighting it afire as she cleaned the table. The silent near-reverence of the clearing felt liberating. It chinked at the invisible armor he'd draped around his heart. He forgot about his mission. He forgot about everything except the light touch of Katie's pale fingers as she handed him his sandwich, a lustrous gleam in her eyes.

An uninvited thought hit him with such surety, he couldn't shake it. Grandma would have loved Katie. She would've called her a "sweet young woman" and urged Ace to pursue her.

It was as if he were being prodded from the grave. Or maybe from God.

He shook his head. Fanciful thinking, indeed. He had one job, and one job only: find the money for his boss so he could move on without a prison threat hanging over him...or even worse, an unspoken death threat. He was fairly certain he'd be taking a long walk off a short plank if he didn't find that money.

As they began to eat, he gently led the conversation in the direction he wanted. "I know that note must have rattled you. Not to cast aspersions on your dad, but he was an FBI agent, and they do know how to keep mum." He waited a moment to let that insinuation sink in.

As it did, her eyes widened. "I know my dad wouldn't lie."

"But what if he tried to protect his family by not telling anyone? What if that money is sitting around somewhere?"

Was he laying it on too heavy? Did he seem too eager?

She sighed. "I suppose I could check some other places, just to be sure. I don't want those cretins 'keeping my family in their sights,' or however they put it."

He nodded. "I can help you."

"Thanks." Her gaze flitted from the trees to the house, then to her half-eaten sandwich, then finally rested on him. "I hate this feeling. What if someone's watching me right now?"

He leaned across the table, touching her hand. "I'm here."

She offered him a brave smile, but continued. "I mean, anything could happen. I can't get away, Ace. I can't run. I hate being so...inept. Of course I'm the perfect target for these goons."

The Oreo seemed stuck in his throat. Her fear was grounded—she couldn't run if those mobsters chased her. He had to distract her.

"Didn't you say you're off work tomorrow? We could go shooting, then nose around some of those possible hiding places. Better to feel like you're proactive, rather than reactive, I always say."

She rested her elbows on the table, obviously relieved. "I shouldn't have to work unless Reba gets desperate. Tomorrow it is. We can go to the range my dad liked." She stood and began tidying up, her long hair swishing like she was in a shampoo ad.

"And maybe after work today, we could check out your dad's office," he added, as if it were an afterthought.

Her gaze sharpened for a split second. He candidly met her eyes, but his insides twisted with the weight of his own treachery. Docile as Katie McClure seemed, he was betting there was a serrated edge to that smooth demeanor. An edge that would push her to take risks for her family.

Risks such as putting her trust in a fake bodyguard like him.

5

Their search of Dad's office hadn't turned up anything. Katie hadn't wanted to let on about the note, so she told Mom they were looking for more ammo—which wasn't entirely untrue. They had emptied every drawer and file, working into the evening. Finally, after a late supper, they had agreed there was nothing to be found and headed to their respective rooms.

The pitch-dark night sky seemed to amplify every little noise outside her window. She was positive someone was creeping around, but the dogs next door were silent, so she finally turned on her box fan around three in the morning and drifted into turbulent dreams.

Reba had asked her to come to the library for a half-day, but she and Ace could hit the shooting range after that. She didn't want to admit it, but being around the buff bodyguard made her feel secure.

Stepping out of her morning shower, she thought about the threatening note she had handed off to him. If she contemplated the scrawled message inside, an icy wedge of fear stabbed at her.

A song from her childhood came to mind—a Bible verse set to music. "When I am afraid, I will trust in Thee." She hummed it to herself, over and over, trying to displace the anxiety. Yes, even more than Ace, she had to trust in God. But that didn't mean she had to drop her guard. Shooting practice would come in handy, giving her confidence to conceal-carry the Sig, at least until the threat blew over.

But she knew it wouldn't blow over until Anatoly's thugs got their money.

Donning her favorite khaki jacket and brown pants, she twisted her hair up and glanced at her reflection. All she needed was a pair of black glasses to scream *Librarian*. If only she could glam it up like Molly. She had a brief image of herself at The Greenbrier restaurant, dressed to the nines, across from Ace in a tuxedo. He would look a little like Cary Grant, she decided.

A knock on her door pulled her back to reality. "You ready?" Ace sounded impatient. "I already got breakfast but we're running late."

She sighed. Ace didn't phrase things like a Southerner. He didn't soften his bluntness or coddle her. He never called her *honey* or *sweetie* like most men did. And yet somehow that made him seem more trustworthy.

She grabbed her purse and slipped into brown ballet flats. She would try not to think of oversized thugs and threatening notes. Today she would focus on the children at the library and rest in the quiet presence of the strong man who watched her every move.

Ace hated to waste more time at the library, but searching the house without Katie would never fly. He could only hope the half-day passed quickly so he could get down to the business he came here for.

He covertly observed Katie as she drove. Her face seemed to radiate a peaceful glow. How did she find that peace in the middle of the storm raging around her? She and Mrs. McClure were still eating regular meals, but his own appetite had dwindled after a late-night follow-up call from his boss. The gist of it was find the money...*or else.*

He wiped sweat from his forehead. It must be ninety degrees in this piece-of-junk car, but it was probably all she could afford. Unbuttoning the sleeves on his yellow Brooks Brothers shirt, he haphazardly shoved them up to his elbows.

The heat served to fuel his frustration. If only Katie would work up her confidence and move to a larger city, she could have a decent-paying job that utilized her obvious people skills. That limp seemed to control her life. No one should let anything control them...trap them.

And yet here he sat, trapped. Controlled by a cruel and wicked man. He stretched his leg and kicked the door, not accidentally.

She shot a glance at him. "You okay? Sorry it's so hot. The A/C hasn't worked for years so the car vents just blow hot air around. You want to open windows instead?"

"Sure." He tried to mellow his tone, but couldn't. What was she doing sitting here with him, trusting him? Why hadn't her mom been more wary of a strange bodyguard, no matter how perfectly his credentials had checked out?

Because Ace was too slick, that's why. His boss had chosen him because of that.

The wind tugged strands from her updo, whipping them around her face. What a contrast she was with the Manhattan up-and-comers he had dated. Those meticulously-coiffed women would have run screaming from this clunker that doubled as a wind tunnel.

Yet Katie merely hummed along, oblivious to the wind...and to how completely she had mesmerized him. He couldn't tear his eyes from that soft freckled skin, those plush lips, and that wild hair.

He had to get it together. He had to finish this job.

She slowed as she pulled into the library parking lot. "My space is taken," she said, turning the wheel and crawling up the rows. "Good grief—all the spaces are taken. I hope there wasn't some event going on that I forgot about."

He pointed to an open area behind the dumpster. "Reba probably wouldn't mind if you parked there, would she?"

Only after she had maneuvered into the tight space did he realize her car would be out of eyesight from the library window. It probably wouldn't be a problem, but he'd be sure to leave early after work and sweep the area.

"Thanks for the help." She grabbed her bag and shot him a warm smile. "Time to go impress some kiddos with your big guns." She winked.

A nearly chemical surge caught him off-guard. In so many words, Katie McClure just let him know she found him attractive. A lesser man would prey on that vulnerability to get what he wanted. And today, Ace was that lesser man.

Children begged for another story as Katie finished reading the final chapter of *My Father's Dragon* aloud. She pointed them to the next book in the series, in sore need of a stretch and a snack.

"Thank you so much." One lingering mother patted her back before hustling her children to their next summer activity. Katie returned to her chair, noticing Ace wasn't positioned in his usual spot. Maybe he had taken a snack break himself.

She imagined what it would be like without her loyal bodyguard around. Presumably, as soon as the cops caught up with those thugs, Ace would high-tail it back to New York City. He had given her note to the police in hopes they could analyze the handwriting and trace the phone to track down Anatoly's henchmen.

Grabbing her purse, she headed to the bathroom to re-twist her hair and apply lip gloss. She should have done that upon arrival at the library, but the kids had nearly attacked her, begging her to start reading early. It did feel nice to be loved.

Leaning in toward the mirror, she tried to observe her reflection dispassionately. Clear green eyes, now easily visible because she'd pinned back her bangs. A brand-new flush to her usually pale cheeks. An upward tilt to her lips and only a slight crease in her forehead, which told her that even though she was stressing over that death-threat note, something was keeping her afloat.

That something was Ace. She wanted to kick herself. It needed to be God, not some dude. But what a dude he was. She couldn't wait to get home and change, pick up the Sig, and hit the range. Ace could probably share all kinds of shooting tips with her.

She moved to dodge a woman entering the bathroom, then froze as a boom louder than thunder ripped through the air.

This time she wasn't the one who gave the warning. "Hit the floor!" Ace's deep shout bounced over rows of books as he jogged toward her. She let the bathroom door close fully, but wasn't able to take a step before Ace tackled her, pinning her to the ground.

"Shh. Wait."

"What was that?" She tried to slow her breathing, even though she felt like she was hyperventilating.

"I said *shh*." He released his grip on her wrists, so tight it would probably leave bruises. "Stay put. Sounded like an explosion."

"An *explosion*? I have to check on the children! And Reba! And—"

"You'll do no such thing. I am phoning the police. You aren't going to move until I figure out what's going on." He pulled her to a sitting position. His eyes were dark with concern. "Will you stay here until I come back?"

"You can't leave me! You're my bodyguard!" She probably sounded like a whining child.

He pushed her hair aside and leaned in toward her ear. The proximity of his breath, his masculine smell, and his deep, reassuring voice nearly unleashed her brimming tears.

"I'm not going to leave you alone, Katie." His rough fingers lightly grazed her neck as he shifted her hair back over her shoulders. "I promise."

She settled against the wall, determined to be strong. Some kind of FBI agent she would have made, nearly crumpling into tears in the face of a loud blast.

As Ace went to check things out, she began to pray there would be no more explosions.

For the first time, she allowed herself to entertain the possibility that the bank heist money could have fallen into Dad's possession. If it had, didn't she have a responsibility to find it and stop this madness?

Maybe it wasn't even Dad's doing. What if his partner, Jim Chrisman, had been dirty? He could have hidden the money somewhere. Strangely enough, Jim's life had also been cut short, undetected late-stage cancer taking him a year before Dad. She remembered Jim's jokes about her red hair every time he came to go fishing on Dad's boat.

There was an idea: they could search the boat. She hadn't been to the marina in years, but Mom maintained the membership for Brandon, since Dad had left his boat to him.

She was tired of being a target. It was time to go proactive, like Ace had said.

Staring at the smoldering, twisted remains of Katie's car, Ace wished he could beat himself up.

Bomb-sniffing dogs had swept the parking lot and the library and it became apparent that only one charge had been set—directly under Katie's car.

He now realized it was no accident that all the parking spots had been taken this morning. He cringed, imagining Anatoly's men as they hunched in multiple cars, observing Katie and him. After he'd obliviously walked her into the library, those punks had probably planted that C4 charge and later remote-detonated it.

At least they had blown the heap after the kids left the library, and before they had walked to the car at closing time. That told Ace they weren't ready to kill Katie yet. They still believed she would find the money.

After sharing his suspicions with the police sergeant, he walked toward the library, but the sergeant motioned him up the hill. "They've been evacuated. That way."

Ace followed the man's pointing finger up the incline the building was situated on. On Main Street, a cluster of library evacuees huddled in front of the bank. He easily spotted Katie's towering red head and rushed to her side.

"What happened, Ace? Before they moved us over here I looked out the window—where's my car?"

There was no way to soften the truth. As he explained that her car had been the target of an explosive charge, she began to shake violently.

Instinctively, he pulled her close and smoothed her forehead as he would a feverish child. "Shh. It's okay. It's going to be okay." He tried to ignore how perfectly her body snuggled into his side. She was tall, but the right kind of tall.

A coconut scent wafted from her hair and he tried to focus. "I'll get you home, don't worry."

She pulled back, resting her still-shaking hands on his chest. But determination filled the steady gaze she leveled on him. "No. We're not going to go slinking home. I'll phone Mom and see if someone can pick us up, but we're going to get your rental car and take a little trip to our storage unit and some other places. It's high time we started hunting for that money so I can protect my family."

6

Mom picked them up in her small Toyota, wiping at her eyes the entire trip home.

"It's okay. I'm okay." Katie kept up a stream of reassurances, but Mom's uncharacteristic silence hung like a weight in the car. When Esther Sue McClure's bubble of cheer was popped, the only way she could deal with it was to retreat into herself. It had happened only once before that Katie remembered, for the entire year following Dad's death. She had prayed Mom would never have to go through such grief again.

But then again, maybe Dad's decisions had brought these mobsters to town. Had he stolen that money, regardless of the heartache it might cause his family? She couldn't believe that.

She felt an urge to call her brother. Maybe Dad had mentioned something to him? It had been too long since she'd seen Brandon's familiar red-bearded face on Skype. She would call him tonight.

But for now, she and Ace had work to do.

After a brief lunch, Katie called Mom's best friend to

come and stay with her a while. If anyone could offer wisdom in a tough situation, it was Jeannie Young. Jeannie had lost her son in Afghanistan, yet amazingly, her faith in God had only grown stronger since.

She pocketed keys to the storage building and boat. Mom shot her a questioning look from the couch.

"I thought I'd show Ace the marina while he's here, take a break from all the library stuff." It wasn't the whole truth, but Mom didn't need to hear about Dad's possible corruption right now. "My cell phone is charged if you need me. I'm feeling fine, Mom—I promise."

Mom offered a resigned nod. "Yes, you might as well get out of the house."

As Katie sank into the cozy Lexus seat, Ace remained quiet. His eyebrows furrowed as if the weight of the world sat on his shoulders.

She was beginning to feel like the designated situation-lightener. "Don't worry. You did your job and made sure I was all right. And I am."

He shot her a dubious look. "But you shouldn't be. Someone blew up your car, Katie. Doesn't that bother you?"

She sat back, stung by his harshness. "Well, of course it does. But what can I do about it, besides what we *are* doing?"

He ran a hand through his hair, creating dark, disheveled spikes. She was possessed by the strangest urge to reach over and smooth it back down.

He continued. "What I mean is, aren't you worried about losing your life? You only get one shot at it, you know."

So that was what was on his mind. "I know where I'm going when I die, so I'm not scared. Of course I want to live a long time—don't we all? And yes, we only get one go-round on this life. So I want to make the most of it." She paused, letting the reality of her words sink in. Yes. She wanted to make the most of this life God had given her, not cower around wishing she could be Molly or anyone else.

He didn't say another word as she directed him to the storage facility. Once there, he pulled into the empty lot and parked outside the barbwire fence. She took Mom's key and unlocked the gate.

When she opened the double doors to their unit, she peered into the jam-packed space and apologized. "Sorry this is so full of junk. Knowing Mom, we probably still have bins of baby clothes in here."

It was stuffy as all get-out as she tried to maneuver deeper into the building. Ace hung back, propping the doors open and taking a long, measuring glance around. "Tell me where your Dad's things are."

Stumbling around bed frames, lamps, and camping supplies, she finally managed to locate Dad's boxes. She swept her arm out. "His things are from about here on over."

He nodded and pointed to the left. "How about you take that half, I'll take this?"

They pawed through box after box for over an hour. She wished she'd packed something to drink in the parching heat. She was about to suggest they hit the nearby Wendy's when his phone rang.

He checked the caller, then motioned to his car. "I have to take this."

As he strode outside, she couldn't help but wonder. Was it some kind of private call from a girlfriend?

Minutes slowly ticked by. The combination of stifling building, thirst, and repressed shock from the morning's car bombing began to weigh on her. Things began to get dark around the edges and she felt herself slipping from the box she sat on.

Abruptly, Ace's strong hands gripped her, shifting her

entire body into his massive arms. "I'm taking you out to the car." He carried her to the leather car seat, where he positioned her with her head over her knees.

As he started the engine, air-conditioning hit her face full-blast. She gasped and nearly clobbered her head on the dashboard.

"Take it easy," he said, gently pushing her head down again. "You nearly passed out. I'm going to find something to drink for you."

He seemed to know where he was going, whipping around the winding mountain roads like a native. Good thing she didn't get car-sick, like Molly. Pulling into the Wendy's drive-through, Ace barked orders for four waters. At the next window, he practically threw a twenty-dollar bill at them, then grabbed the bottles and passed one to her. She eased into a sitting position.

"Drink this, slowly. And breathe deep," he said.

She did as told and started to feel a bit refreshed. Not to mention, utterly humiliated. She was so weak.

"I'm so sorry—" she started.

"Don't apologize. It was my fault. Paid too much attention to my phone call and not enough to you."

"Who was it?" Why did she feel the need to pry?

"My boss." He didn't elaborate, just sucked down half his water bottle.

"So sorry—I'll bet you need to head on back to New York. And here you are stuck in West Virginia." She should dip into her savings to help Mom pay him for his services.

He took another gulp of water and turned to her. Those blue eyes pulled her in, like specks of ocean in land-locked Hemlock Creek. He stretched out a hand and cupped her cheek.

"You have more color. That's good. I didn't realize you had

so many freckles until you blanched out back there." He gave her a half-smile. "Let's go back to the building and finish up. You're a trooper for doing this, especially when we're getting nowhere." His voice roughened. "And by the way, you have a habit of apologizing for things you don't have any control over. I don't want you ever to apologize to me again."

"Never?" She grinned. "Must mean I'm perfect."

He gazed at her just a second too long. "It's not that much of a stretch."

⁓⁓⁂⁓⁓

This was getting too stupid. How dare his boss call him in the middle of the day, knowing he was probably with Katie? Not only that, but he had simply repeated his earlier threats, as if those hadn't come through loud and clear with the last call.

Katie *was* a trooper, going back into the storage building. The relentless heat had completely plastered his oxford shirt to his back, forcing him to strip down to his T-shirt.

And for what? A search for money that probably wasn't there.

Now they'd taken another half-hour to rummage through the remainder of Sean's boxes and even his T-shirt was soaked. Katie looked okay but was still peaked, even as she sipped at her water. He needed to get her out of here.

He stretched and made a proclamation. "That's enough. We've been through every box. There's nothing to find here."

She handed him the building keys in an exhausted silence, then limped out to the car. He followed, turning on the engine so she could sit in the air-conditioning while he locked up.

She was speaking on the phone when he returned. She wrapped up her conversation, turned off the phone, and explained. "I called Reba. She's hanging in there, but she's closing the library for the rest of the week. So we can take our time checking Dad's boat. Thanks so much for doing all this." She smiled, at first hesitantly, then that blinding-wide smile that made him feel like a hero.

Couldn't be further from the truth. Her hero was a villain.

Dad had been a member of the Sutton Lake Marina since Katie had turned twelve. His Cabin Cruiser boat, the *Vixen*, was the one thing he had splurged on for himself with his earnings. At least she hoped it had been his earnings.

She treasured memories of summer nights she'd camped on the deck in her sleeping bag, picking out constellations as the boat lightly bobbed beneath her. Back then, she'd felt like she could do anything, be anyone.

After her accident, she'd stopped visiting the *Vixen*, mostly because she felt off balance and feared she'd pitch overboard like a klutz.

Again. Fear. She had begun to see it for what it was, to name it. This frantic race to find the bank money was driving her to overcome those fears...that, and the confidence of having Ace Calhoun by her side.

As they stepped onboard, she took the steadying hand he offered, glancing at his face. His Yankee candor seemed to have been replaced with reticence since the explosion. It was like he had gone inward, and she really wished she knew how those gears in his head were churning.

She fiddled with the rusty lock on the cabin door, finally jiggering it open. They stepped into the small space that smelled faintly of mildew. Mom had never cared much for sailing, so it hadn't been cleaned for a while.

"We need to get looking or we'll melt in here." She propped the door open, then gestured to the cabinets by the small refrigerator. "You check the right side, I'll check the left. Or should I say, you check starboard and I'll check port."

He cracked a smile. "Well, aren't you all nautical?"

"I'd forgotten how much I love this. I used to wish I could live on a houseboat, like MacGyver."

"You watched that show?"

"Just the re-runs."

"I didn't know you were a retro TV girl. I'm a big *A-Team* fan, myself."

They fell into a companionable silence as they began to plunder the cabinets.

Bypassing cans of Spam and pork and beans that were probably three years expired, she pulled up a zippered pouch. "Hey, what's this?"

He was by her side in a moment. His cologne made it hard to concentrate, and she couldn't ignore the way his damp T-shirt draped his muscles. Seriously, the guy could probably beat up three men at once.

After unzipping the pouch, she pulled out folded bank statements and handed him half of them. She felt somewhat traitorous sharing them with someone outside the family, but it was for the greater good.

They read over the papers, finally coming to the conclusion that nothing looked amiss. No out-of-the-ordinary deposits or strange payments had been made.

"It's hopeless." She yanked out another drawer. The heat was so smothering, she had the ridiculous—and inappropriate—urge to strip to her unmentionables and jump in the lake. "Let's go on deck and get some air," she suggested instead.

Outside, Ace didn't hesitate to sprawl out on the warm wood deck, and she carefully lowered herself to join him. But it only took a few moments to realize the blinding sun was going to scald her pale skin. Ace probably couldn't feel it—he had that skin color that seemed to maintain a perpetual tan. She struggled back to her feet. "We might as well get going. Mom's probably working on supper soon and I don't think there's anything here."

"Let's jump in first."

Had he read her mind? It was so hot...

"We can't go home all wet—" she started.

But he had already begun stripping off his T-shirt. He laid his holstered guns on the deck, then boosted himself over the back railing and began to doggie-paddle in the dark lake. He grinned up at her.

"Come on in—the water's fine!" He splashed water on the deck.

How could she resist?

She carefully slid off the port side and did a butterfly stroke to him. She'd forgotten how swimming seemed to erase her limp.

Good grief. She would have never guessed a couple weeks ago that she'd be swimming in Sutton Lake with a personal bodyguard. Especially not with one who looked a whole lot like Superman.

"Are we friends?" The question popped out before she could stop it.

"Of course." He floated languidly, drops of water flecking his sleek chest.

"Good." His companionship had almost been like a security blanket these past few days.

She dove into the cool water, paying no attention to the sopping blouse and pants that weighed her down. She felt like a carefree kid again.

Boldness filled her and she voiced something she'd been curious about. "So...Ace is an interesting name. Is that your real name?"

He swam closer, his look unreadable. Why had she felt

compelled to ask that? She did a few strokes backward, wishing she could vanish.

But his lips curled into a smile. "Yes, believe it or not, it's real. My dad was heavy into baseball. 'Ace' is a term for the best starting pitcher on a team."

"So did you play baseball?"

"Only a little. I wasn't the best at it and I surely wasn't a pitcher. My dad came to one game and as I recall, he left early."

Such disappointment for a little boy. These candid glimpses into Ace's childhood explained who he was more clearly than his often-enigmatic actions.

His smile widened. "But Granny told me 'Ace' can also mean a champion; a master. She prayed that way—that I would become a champion for God."

"I like that." She swam closer. "Sounds like you actually do believe in God."

"I did, as a kid. Asked Jesus into my heart and all that. Granny's prayers carried me along for a while, but then when I was a teen, it became blindingly clear that God didn't seem to be on my side. Then Granny died. It was kind of downhill from there."

She wished she had pithy words of wisdom and restoration to offer, but she had been struggling for years to believe that God loved her and wanted the best for her. So many times it didn't seem like it. Maybe Ace needed to talk to Mom's friend Jeannie—and maybe she did, too.

Ace looked at the sky, then at his waterproof watch. "It's getting late; we'd better get back. I know your mom will be worried."

The moment was lost. But he was right—Mom would worry if they didn't show up soon.

After he climbed back onboard, he helped pull her up. Strangely, she didn't even feel self-conscious about her clothing-laden weight, possibly because she was hyperaware of the secure feeling of her hands in his. His long fingers were surprisingly rough, which appealed to her more than she would have guessed.

They lowered onto the deck benches for a few minutes to dry off so they wouldn't soak the Lexus interior. The waning afternoon sunshine felt just right. She wished she could live in this bubble of light and warmth forever.

Reality intruded as her cell phone buzzed.

"Hello?"

"Katie, where are you?" Molly's voice had a desperate edge to it.

"We're fine. I'm just showing Ace the *Vixen*."

"What? So let me get this straight: your car was bombed into oblivion, but for some reason you two decided to be-bop on over to Sutton Lake? Good grief, sis. You could've let me know. Didn't you get my texts?"

"I didn't see them—we were busy. And you know me, a real be-bopper." She tried to control a snicker. "We're heading home now. Don't wait up for supper."

Molly huffed. "We won't. I have to get going but I wanted to see my thankfully-still-alive sister before I went out tonight."

"Who you going out with?"

There was an unusually long pause. "Someone you wouldn't know."

Katie's eyebrows shot up. It wasn't like Molly to be cagey about her illustrious dates. "I wish you'd stick around and tell me more about him."

"No time. Maybe another day. But stay safe, okay? That bodyguard better be earning his keep."

As she hung up, Ace stood, helping her to her feet. Near the car, he surprised her by crossing to her door first and opening it. He hadn't done that before.

"Why, thank you." She smiled. "I see you have excellent manners."

"Could be your Southern ways are rubbing off on me."

A zing of hope shot through her chest. She tried to tamp it down, but she couldn't erase a very clear picture that formed in her mind. Ace Calhoun, wearing a plaid shirt and jeans, tromping out to the Christmas tree farm with her family on their yearly tree hunt. Where did that come from? How could he ever fit in here?

As she watched him struggle to squeeze his still-damp body into his dry dress shirt, Ace grinned, and that last domino of hesitancy she had toward him toppled.

The truth was, she'd never met a man who fit so well with *her*. But was he so far gone from God he wouldn't ever come back? She'd always wanted to marry a strong Christian— stronger than her, at least.

It almost felt like something was propelling her toward Ace, something bigger than what she could see or understand. She would begin praying about her mixed feelings in earnest. But one thing she was increasingly sure of: Ace Calhoun was a decent man.

Ace ignored the long red strands of hair whipping around Katie's head. He ignored her contented smile and that glow she seemed to bask in, even after a tedious day in which her car had been blown to smithereens by C4 explosives, to say nothing of the hours she'd spent searching for hidden money with him, nearly passing out in the process.

The storage building had been a bust. The boat had been a bust. He was trying not to show his disappointment, but sometimes it seemed Katie saw right past his smiles into some part of himself he preferred to hide.

What would she think if she ever knew his real motive for staying here?

Stealing a glance at her as she leaned into the seat, relaxed and nearly dozing, he gripped the wheel harder. The truth was, his biggest motive for staying in Hemlock Creek sat right beside him.

7

A much-calmer Mom welcomed them at the door. She didn't bother to ask about their damp clothing. "Come in, come in," she said. "Ham biscuits and gravy coming right up."

The comfort food hit the spot, but Katie feared the exhaustion of the day must have shown on her face.

Mom kissed her head. "You're my sweet baby girl. I'm so thankful you weren't hurt." A warm teardrop slid onto her hair. "Oh, and your brother wants you to call. I didn't tell him what happened to your car."

Funny—she and Brandon always had some kind of uncanny connection, even though they didn't always see eye-to-eye. Even miles apart, he seemed to have an instinct for when she was in need of some big-brother boosting.

"Don't let me stop you," Ace said. "I need to get back over and get some shuteye myself."

She nodded, unable to articulate her gratefulness for his presence at the library, his willingness to go on her wild goose chase for the money, and his talking her into an impromptu but much-needed swimming excursion.

As Mom hummed, scrubbing out her cast-iron skillet,

Katie slowly and deliberately covered his hand with her own. When his eyes met hers, questioning, she took a deep breath. "Thank you," she whispered.

For once, it seemed he had nothing to say. He just sat there, his covered hand resting on the wooden tabletop.

Finally, as Mom swung around to wipe down the table, he murmured, "You're one in a million, Katie McClure."

Katie swiped on a bit of powder before Skyping Brandon, lest her natural blush become apparent. She wanted to talk about Dad, not about her bodyguard, who had admittedly set her heart aflutter.

He picked up quickly, giving her a close-up view of his full red beard but not much else.

"Hey, bro—pull that phone back a little!"

He laughed, rearranging his phone camera. "Just wanted to give you the full river-guide mountain-man effect, sis."

"Scary."

"Well, you're looking good. But what's the deal with Mom hiring a bodyguard? I feel like she's only telling me blips of information, like I can't handle the truth."

Knowing her brother's tendency to get overheated, she started at the beginning, explaining the library intrusion, the apartment break-in, the stalker, and finally, as the pièce de résistance, the car bomb. With each event, his eyes widened and his ruddy face grew a shade darker. When she stopped for breath, he exploded.

"I swear I will come back there and I will kill those people! They bombed your car?! I swear I will contact some of Dad's FBI friends! I'm hopping the next plane!"

She used her most soothing voice, trying to talk him down and redirect his attention.

"No need to come back—that's what the bodyguard is for. Plus, the police are on the case. And I actually wanted to ask you about the FBI stuff. Did Dad talk much to you about his friends, or maybe any particular cases?"

Brandon paused, taking a swig of his ever-present can of Dr. Pepper. The flame in his cheeks died down a little. "Let's see. All he ever really mentioned was his partner Jim, because he was always coming over to go fishing, you know? I mean, Dad didn't talk about specific cases. But I do remember him saying they should've done an autopsy on Jim. I think he didn't buy that late-stage cancer explanation for his death. Dad wanted to look into things, as I recall. But it was too late, because Jim had already been cremated, like his will directed."

Dad's suspicions could have been founded. What if Anatoly had killed Jim because he was connected with that bank heist case? And what if...Katie gasped, forgetting she was on camera.

"Sis, what's going on? You're white as a sheet."

She described the note to him, and he jumped to the same conclusion she had.

"So this Anatoly might have killed Jim, then taken out our own dad. For a bank stash that's gone missing." His green-gold eyes darkened. "Sis, I feel like I need to be there with you. Where's Molly? Is she safe?"

"She doesn't seem to be a target right now for some reason. Seems like they've honed in on me."

"Yeah, that doesn't make sense. But if I were there, I could divert attention...then meet those punks with a rocket launcher or something."

She laughed. "Brandon, this isn't one of your shooter video games. This is real life. And I have a bodyguard."

He leaned in, winking. "Now *him* Molly told me about. Tall, dark, and handsome—that about cover it?"

Sighing, she decided to play along. "Yup. Undeniably handsome and nice."

Brandon crinkled his nose, something he did when he was unsure of the situation. "You be careful. Maybe you can't even trust him."

"I can. He's already protected me from danger a couple of times. Why would he do that if he was some kind of mobster?"

"I don't know. But I watch a lot of murder mysteries. It's always the last one you suspect."

"No one's been murdered. Well, at least no one we're sure of."

"Let's keep it that way," he said.

As the morning light trickled in through the white wooden blinds, Ace groaned. His boss was showing up at three this afternoon. Ace had arranged to meet him at the overgrown, ramshackle warehouse he'd noticed on the way to the storage facility.

Before then, he had to wheedle out of Katie any remaining hiding places and search them. Then he could say with confidence the money was nowhere to be found in the McClure household. Surely his boss would take his word for it and leave them alone.

Wouldn't he?

There were no guarantees. This whole business was dicey, from start to finish.

He took extra care as he got dressed—placing one gun in a hip holster, one in an ankle holster, and a small Ruger .380 in a belly band, just in case. He slid a throwing knife into a leg sheath, then slipped on his neck chain that concealed another knife. He would be ready if his boss had any funny business in mind.

He put on a looser-fitting oxford shirt and pants, hoping to project a relaxed vibe while covering his mini arsenal. Striding out into the pale morning light, he followed the path to the McClures' front porch and knocked. Smells of fresh coffee, cinnamon, and nutmeg assailed him as the door swung open.

Molly, dressed in a fitted skirt that accentuated her curves, stood inside the door. Her red platform heels boosted her to his chin height. She draped her arms around him in a loose hug. He automatically stepped back so she wouldn't bump into the weapons on his chest. Could the woman scream *available* any louder?

"Aren't you looking dapper this morning?" She grinned, taking stock of him from head to toe. "And what are you two up to today?"

Katie emerged from the kitchen, hair tossed into a loose, off-kilter knot. She wore what looked like a boy's Pac-Man T-shirt and acid-washed jeans. Could the sisters be more different?

Katie sipped at her steaming mug. "I thought of one last place we could check. Come on in and have some breakfast. Mom picked up some real maple syrup this time around." She winked.

He nodded, thankful for her lighter demeanor. Molly's heated stare was making him uncomfortable. Since when did a beautiful woman's attention bother him in a bad way? Since Katie, that's when.

As they joined Mrs. McClure at the table, Molly lathered butter on her French toast and jabbed her fork in the air. "Well, you two be careful, whatever you're doing. It's ridiculous that some freak is trying to kill my sister. I swear to you, if I knew how to use guns, I would be dangerous!"

"Probably why Dad never taught you," Katie murmured.

He nearly choked on his coffee. He'd never met a librarian with such a wicked sense of humor.

After Molly swirled out of the kitchen with her usual flair, Mom stood, excusing herself. "I'm going to a Bible study with Jeannie this morning. It's been too long since I've made time for one."

"Maybe I'll go with you sometime...after things calm down," Katie said. She really did need some accountability.

Mom nodded, giving them a winsome smile. "Stay safe today."

The moment they were alone, Katie lowered her voice. "I stayed up last night thinking about hiding places. Dad sometimes went to the attic, I remember. It's just a crawlspace, really, but there might be something up there."

He nodded. "Good idea. We'll check it out. By the way, I have to head over to town later to pick up that glass panel for your door. Shouldn't take me long. I've lined up for a police patrol unit to sit outside your house starting at two-thirty. They'll stay until I get back."

Leaving her *alone*? He was just casually taking off? She drilled her gaze into his. It didn't take him long to get the message.

"Katie, I wouldn't leave you alone unless I was sure you'd be okay. You have the Sig. You'll have a patrol car outside."

"What if they come through the woods, into the back door?"

"Sit in the living room, where you can get out fast. Lock all the doors. Your mom should be back by then, right? So you won't be completely alone."

She may as well be. Mom was barely better than Molly in

an emergency. She had a habit of passing out when her kids bled. The time Brandon sliced his finger with a razor, Katie had been the one who drove him to the E.R.—on her learner's permit. And forget about guns. Mom had no interest in handling one, though she was admittedly handy with her Emeril kitchen knives.

"It's okay," she said, mentally talking herself down. She was not going to be paralyzed with fear. After all, someday Ace would have to leave them—maybe someday soon. If only those cops would track down Anatoly's thugs, maybe the McClures could start to get back to normal.

He gave her a concerned look, but she ignored it.

"We'd better check the attic while Mom's gone." She clomped down the hall, not caring if she looked as unwieldy as a lame elephant. Grabbing a stepstool from Dad's office, she placed it under the attic door and tried to grab at the dangling rope pull. It was just a little too high.

"Allow me." Catching up to her, he offered a slight flourish and a bow.

She shrugged, stepping aside.

He climbed on the stool, pulling the rope and easing the built-in ladder down to the floor. "Are you able to climb up?"

Heat rose in her cheeks. "I'm not handicapped. Just lame. Of course I can get up there." In reality, she had never gone upstairs before and had no idea if her bum foot would hold her weight.

Noting his apprehensive look, she continued. "In fact, I'll head up first." Clinging to one step at a time, she slowly made her way to the top. Once inside the rectangular opening, she screwed in the light bulb to illuminate the tight space. Moving to the side floorboards, she motioned to him, trying not to ponder how she'd ever get back down.

After placing a couple guns on the floor, he climbed up. She tried not to notice as he contorted to squeeze his wide upper body through the narrow opening. Once he was settled on the opposite side, his clean, cedar scent drifted her way. His dress shirt looked rumpled and his hair did, too.

He smiled, his face only half-lit by the dim bulb. "Let's get to work," he said.

But his lingering smile said something else.

They had gone through three bins stuffed with Christmas paraphernalia Mom had probably forgotten she owned. There was only one left.

Ace dug into it, retrieving a worn leather baseball mitt and baseball. "What's this?"

She leaned in for a closer look. "This was probably the baseball stuff Dad gave Brandon. But Brandon never used it —he was born to play soccer, he said. Tough head and all that."

He laughed, fingering the laces. "This is really old-school. Wouldn't my dad love to see this!"

A brainstorm hit her. "I can ask Brandon, but I know my brother, and he couldn't care less about those things. I think you'd be welcome to take it all."

Resting the mitt and ball in his lap, he plunged an arm into the tissue-paper packed bin, retrieving a plastic bag containing a pile of baseball cards. "These too, you think?"

"Oh sure. Hang on—let me text Brandon."

She did, and just as she suspected, received a quick reply:

Brandon: *No problem, give them to the bodyguard. Just symbolic of how little Dad cared about my preferences. Now someone else can enjoy that junk.*

Not exactly eloquent, but honest. "They're all yours," she said.

Nodding, Ace began to pull the tissue paper out. "Looks

like this is it...whatever this is at the bottom..." He extracted an oversized purple stuffed panda bear.

"Poopsie!" she exclaimed.

"Excuse me?"

"I mean, that's Poopsie. My purple panda Poopsie. I wondered where he went!" She grabbed the stuffed animal, dust sifting into the air around them. "Dad won him for me at the fair one year. Molly was so jealous that she didn't get one. She made Brandon win her a real goldfish instead, then it wound up dying a week later."

He laughed. A timer on his watch beeped and he anxiously glanced at it. "Sorry, but I need to get moving. The police unit will be showing up any minute now. And I want to help you get down the stairs, even though I know you can probably do it yourself. Am I right in thinking you want Poopsie to accompany you?"

She grinned. "Sure thing."

By the time Mom came in asking about the police car, the attic was closed up and Ace was heading out the door. He waved, promising to return as soon as he could.

It was only then she let it sink in: there was no bank heist money in the house. Maybe there never was any money. What kind of daughter was she to suspect her father stole it in the first place?

8

The crumbling roof on the faded stucco building looked ready to collapse. Ace was glad he was the first to show up, so he could better examine the layout. Kicking open the splintered wooden door, he saw he wasn't the first to use this place for nefarious purposes. Beer cans, cigarette butts, and a moldy mattress decorated the interior.

After checking the large room, he situated himself toward the back, near a window with no glass. He could bail out that way if he had to, even though it would be quite a drop into the creek below. He had just finished checking his guns when the door burst open.

His boss was alone, or so it seemed. Peering out the front, Ace could only see one black car. Probably had a driver inside, maybe one or two extra gunmen at the most.

"Ace Calhoun. My favorite ex-inmate. How ya doin'?"

He hated the false charm this man always showed. From his too-toothy grin to his all-American good looks, he was a total fake.

Fake enough to fool the FBI, in fact. And his partner, Sean McClure.

"Jim." He nodded.

"You been enjoying time with that McClure redhead? Always a bit of a spitfire, that one. Kind of nosy about my visits to her dad's boat. Good ol' Sean, wouldn't he roll in his grave if he saw me alive? He was so sure someone had whacked me."

Ace's stomach turned at the casual way Jim Chrisman spoke of his deceased FBI partner. He was becoming more and more convinced that Sean hadn't been in on the theft.

Jim continued. "You searched that boat, didn't you? I told you where I put it. You check there?"

Ace uncrossed his arms and dropped them to his sides, ready to draw and fire if he had to. "Sure did. One of the first places I looked. It wasn't in the built-in bench."

He braced himself for Jim's wrath, but it didn't come. Instead, an ominous silence fell. The calm before the storm?

Jim smiled even wider. "No problem. I take it you've searched the house?"

"In its entirety."

He stood watchful, waiting for Jim to give some kind of signal. It would be easy enough for his boss to cut his losses and have him killed right here.

Jim stalked closer and Ace recoiled. The man laughed. "Cool your jets. Didn't I spring you from jail? I'm your savior. Now you *are* gonna pay me back. Out of the goodness of my heart, I've decided to give you a couple more days. I'm staying over at The Greenbrier, keeping a close eye on that piece of work, Molly. That one grew up *real* nice."

Ace wanted to punch his lights out.

Jim smirked. "That hurt your feelings, Calhoun? Well, try this on for size. You don't hand me the money in two days, and I'm gonna get cozy with the grieving widow McClure. Esther Sue always did have a soft spot for me, and I'm sure she'd be glad if I came out of'—here he offered air quotes

—"'government hiding.' I remember all those nights we sat around the family bonfire, unburdening our hearts to one another." He grunted. "Ours could be a marriage made in heaven. By the way, she *will* marry me, whether she wants to or not. Now, I can't actually say what might happen to those sisters if they get in my way. And the brother...well, he never liked his dad much. Maybe he needs a new one?"

Before he could stop himself, Ace slammed both fists into Jim's chest, sending the shorter man reeling. "You're going to stay out of their lives," he breathed.

Immediately, two armed men entered the room, blocking the door. Jim coughed.

"Don't get fresh with me. I will not get out of their lives, or out of yours, until I have that stash. I know it's around because I hid it myself. No way Sean could've spent all that, and it's not in his accounts. You are going to get to it before Anatoly does, or you'll die trying."

There was no choice. Either he would be the bad guy or Jim would, and he couldn't stomach Jim getting anywhere near the McClures.

"Two days," he agreed.

Jim rubbed at his chest, obviously sore. "I'll see you back here at the same time. And, hey—at our next get-together? My men won't be so shy." He waved his goons out the door, stalking out behind them.

Ace stayed frozen in place, barely breathing until the car pulled away. Then he strode out, slamming the rotting door and unlocking his Lexus.

The Lexus his boss was paying for.

He had to retrench and find that money. As he saw it, he had one last-ditch option, and it was a bold one.

The light was about to shine into the darkness and blind them all.

Mom had busied herself with laundry, doubtless convincing herself that there was nothing dangerous afoot. Katie sat on the couch, Sig at the ready, observing the police car out the front window. She really needed a glass of sweet tea and a sandwich, but she wasn't about to leave her watchful post.

The welcome sight of Ace's sleek grey Lexus nearly brought tears to her eyes. "He's here!" she shouted to no one in particular. After struggling to get up and get her foot moving, she made her way to the front door to meet him.

But he didn't knock. She moved to the window and caught a glimpse of his back and arm as he pulled the apartment door closed behind him. What was he doing? Maybe he was going to install the glass in the door, or maybe he was hungry.

She texted him:

Katie: *We have plenty of food over here if you want some lunch.*

She continued to stand by the window as the police unit slowly pulled away. Leaning on her good leg, she watched the apartment door for a solid ten minutes before giving up. No text. No sign of Ace.

What had happened?

After unloading and storing most of his weapons, Ace stripped to his T-shirt and threw himself onto the couch, letting his endorphin high slowly ebb away. He pictured waves on a Caribbean beach, a pastel-painted cottage he could rent with his payout from this job. Or a relaxing weekend in Connecticut in the fall, taking in the sights.

Only thing was, Katie's flaming hair and smiling face intruded into each vision.

He had to get real. There was only one way for him to get out of here alive, and that was to find the money.

Reading over Katie's text, he made a decision. Uncomfortable as it was, embarrassing as it was, he had go through with it.

It was time to come clean to Esther Sue McClure.

He made minimal eye contact as he ate his late lunch of a grilled cheese sandwich and tomato soup. Katie seemed to want to talk, but what could he say? That he'd just returned from a meeting with her dad's fake-dead partner? That a crooked FBI agent had gotten him out of prison early so he'd be in his debt?

Anxiety seemed to emanate from Katie, from her nervous finger-tapping to her frequent glances out the window. Of course she was worried—she hadn't found the money for Anatoly's men. Just like he hadn't found it for Jim.

Esther Sue finished her sandwich and stood. "I need to switch my laundry over. Excuse me."

Ace stood as well, trying to ignore Katie's startled look. "Mrs. McClure, would you mind if we talked some about my payment and things?" It was partly true.

Esther Sue ran a hand through her light hair. "Of course, dear. Let's talk in the office, shall we?"

He felt bad about leaving Katie in the dust, but she didn't need to know the truth. Yet.

Mrs. McClure shut the office door tightly, then sat in her husband's leather chair. She crossed her hands, fixing him with an inquisitive stare. "Now, how about you tell me what's really going on?"

He was taken aback. "What do you mean?"

She gave a half-smile. "I grew up with three brothers, honey. I know when a man's trying to hide something."

A picture flashed through his mind—that of Mrs. McClure sitting at the fire-pit with her husband and Jim Chrisman. Would she have known if Sean was lying to her? What about Jim? He had to ask.

"Mrs. McClure, I need you to tell me everything you know about Jim Chrisman."

Her pale blue eyes widened. "Good gracious. Well, not to speak ill of the dead, but he always seemed too good to be true—slick, you know. Though maybe that made him a good FBI agent. But his jokes always seemed to have an edge—a sharp, pointed edge. I remember he really burned my biscuits the one time he decided to be sarcastic about the way Katie walked. I'm afraid I lost my temper and told him if he didn't apologize, he'd never set foot in my house again. He said he was sorry, but it left a bad taste in my mouth that a grown man could be that cruel."

Ace nodded. Everything that man did left a bad taste in his mouth. Shifting forward, he said, "I need to be honest with you."

She rested her arms on the desk. "Please do. I'm listening."

How many times had Granny said that same phrase to him? How many times had he unburdened his soul to her like she was some kind of priest? Here he was, back in the same position, seeking absolution.

"Mrs. McClure, I came here with less than honest intentions. I'm not a trained bodyguard, but I can handle firearms and I'm fairly popular with ladies. I was instructed to infiltrate your home and search for money that was concealed here before your husband's death. Dirty money, hidden by none other than your husband's partner, Jim Chrisman."

She sucked in her breath, but didn't speak. He continued.

"It's not something I chose to do, believe me. It's something I had to do to keep my freedom. I won't elaborate on my situation, but suffice it to say, someone powerful holds the strings to my future." He thumped his fist on the desk, dark anger brewing as he remembered Jim's smug look. "Brace yourself, Mrs. McClure. That someone is Jim Chrisman. Sean was right to want to look into his death, but maybe not for the reasons you thought. It wasn't a murder, but a faked death."

She fell back in the chair, one hand flying to her chest. "No. Does that mean...?"

He answered her unasked question. "I don't know if someone killed Sean. Jim has never admitted as much. But the thing is, he's after the money, along with the mob boss who stole it in a bank heist."

"How much money are you talking about?"

"1.5 million dollars."

She vehemently shook her head. "No. There is no way Sean had that money. Our bank account was depleted paying for his funeral expense. I've been living on his life insurance, but I have to get a job soon. I haven't told the kids yet."

He stood, pacing the room. "Jim said he hid it on the *Vixen*. He's convinced it's there, but I've checked."

"So that's what you were doing on the boat." She drew a deep breath. "You've been using my daughter, haven't you?" Her eyes swam with sudden tears.

He bowed his head. "Yes. I have."

She gasped, noisily yanking three tissues from the nearby box before bursting into a rainstorm of tears. "I...thought—I thought you were good for her."

He wished the floor would open and swallow him up. "I honestly hope I can be. I've realized I care more for Katie's safety than for my own. I want to get Jim and the mobsters away from your family. That's why I had to ask you outright."

Esther Sue examined him, sniffing and blowing her nose. Finally, she nodded. "I believe you. But I can't help you. Sean told me nothing about money or that bank case. Just that he wondered about Jim's death." A fresh burst of sobs ensued.

He nodded slowly. It was decided, then. As always, he had a plan of action. Not a safe plan, but it would be worth it if the McClures were finally left alone. He would get the gears in motion tomorrow.

But today, he had a shooting date with a certain redheaded librarian.

9

Katie tried to hide her surprise as Ace emerged, remnants of a smile on his face. What had he talked to Mom about? Surely he wouldn't have asked to...no, that was ridiculous. They hadn't even had one real date yet.

"Let's go shooting," he said.

"Is that wise, do you think? Is Mom okay?"

"I hate to burst your bubble, but it seems like you're the only one those goons are stalking, my dear. And I'll be with you, so you'll have nothing to worry about."

Warmth infused her. Yes, she was safe with Ace.

"Okay, let's get going. I'll tell Mom goodbye."

"No need. She went back to her room and I told her where we're headed. She said to be careful."

"That's my momma." She packed up the Sig. "After you, my knight in shining armor."

After two hours shooting at the range, Ace was convinced Katie had underestimated her skills. It was very possible her aim was even better than his. She had fired all his guns, even the larger .45, and had managed to keep them steady—barely a kick. This West Virginia girl could certainly hold her own in a firefight.

As they slid into the Lexus, he gave in to an idea that had been kicking around for days. "What do you say we go out to eat—on me? Anyplace good around Hemlock Creek?"

Her green eyes danced. "Sure, over in Lewisburg there are quite a few places. Are you looking to get all gussied up or just go somewhere casual?"

He smiled, briefly covering her hand with his. "Actually, I was hoping we could both get dressed up. I've seen Molly looking glitzy, but not you. I have a feeling you'd outshine her."

Her hand drew back a bit. Unlike most of the women he'd known, Katie didn't wear her feelings on her sleeve. He couldn't read her easily. She seemed to like him, but what if she was being all Southern-friendly, simply tolerating his presence until he left?

Tolerating him—like his parents had. The thought crushed him.

He shifted into gear and tried to focus on the winding roads. Glancing in his rearview, he noticed a blue SUV that was zooming up too close to his bumper. Did all these locals drive like demons?

Long fingers wrapped around his hand where it rested on the gear shift, distracting him, pulling him back. "Thanks for taking me shooting. I needed the reminder I'm not helpless. And yes, I know just the restaurant we can go to."

Her honeyed voice, soft with light Southern accents, melted something inside him. He sensed the kind of unconditional acceptance he'd only known with Granny.

As he turned to meet her eyes, the SUV rammed straight

into his bumper, sending the Lexus skidding...directly toward a 400-foot drop off the side of the mountain.

Katie could only think to scream one word: "Right!"

He jerked the wheel that direction. The car flipped around into the other lane, pinning his door against the solid rock on the inside of the mountain.

The SUV sped around them as she tried to control her frantic breathing. This was no accident. After a moment's silence, she managed to croak out a few words.

"Such a close call. I'm so sorry."

He shot her a dark look. "*Do not* say sorry. It's not your fault. I should've suspected they were up to no good, driving so close."

Grasping the wheel, he lightly pushed on the gas. When the car revved, he maneuvered it out of the ditch and into its respective lane. He drove a couple minutes before finding a pull-off area, where he turned the car back toward home.

"Thank the Lord no one else was coming," she said.

He stared straight ahead. "The Lord had nothing to do with this."

She shook her head. "Yes, He did. He protected us."

"You're so sure, aren't you?" His voice held no reprimand, just incredulity.

Hesitating, she responded honestly. "Not always. Sometimes I wonder why He lets those horrible things happen. But I'm starting to believe it's always for a bigger plan...kind of a greater good."

He nodded, dark bangs falling in his eyes. "Granny felt that way too. And to tell the truth, I kind of believe it myself. It's the only way to make sense of the stuff that happens. But then another part of me wants to rail against a God who would do that."

"He's not the bad guy," she said.

Silence blanketed the car. It was like she'd struck a nerve, but why?

Their near-fatal wreck had only crunched the bumper, but as a side effect, it steamrolled any illusions Ace had been operating under.

Anatoly's men would not give up. And they weren't going to be patient.

Daydreams he'd had about a leisurely dinner with a fancied-up Katie were quickly replaced with battle plans.

He would take the fight to the oppressors. He would end this thing. And in the process, he would wound and possibly even break the one person he now cared for the most—the person he might even love.

He prayed God would forgive him for what he was about to do to Katie McClure.

As the doorbell rang, Mom went to answer it, leaving Katie alone with Molly as she prepared for her date.

Molly secured her sister's low, patent-leather heel. "This too tight?"

She shook her head, glancing at the mirror to take in her curled hair, her jewel-green sheath dress, and the sparkling diamond bracelet Molly had lent her. A trifle from a rich suitor, no doubt.

Molly smiled. "Don't be so nervous. You look choked with fear. You should date more often, stay in the swing of things."

Katie gave a short laugh, unwilling to explain she was still shell-shocked from a near-fatal crash. Molly would only freak out and report back to Mom. She tried to act glib. "No, thanks. Have you seen the guys who tend to ask me out?"

"Good point." Molly stood. "So what's up with Brandon?"

"What do you mean? I just talked to him the other day—he's keeping busy with work."

Molly hesitated. "Oh, nothing."

Katie gave her sister a look. "What are you—"

Mom knocked lightly at the bedroom door. "There's a handsome young man here to see you, Katie Beth. Best not keep him waiting."

Nodding, Katie glowered again at Molly and stalked toward the door. The heels threw her off balance and made her limp a bit more, but at least they fit comfortably.

Ace stood just inside the front door, practically hidden behind a huge bouquet of sunflowers.

She beamed. "My favorite! How did you know?"

"Just a guess. Seemed to fit you," he murmured.

Molly, close on her heels, exclaimed, "I've never seen anything so beautiful! Great taste, Ace." She took the flowers when Katie handed them over to her, blowing a kiss to both. "Have fun, you two."

Mom emerged with her camera. "Wait—hold those flowers, Katie. You two stand together."

Feeling like she was heading to the prom, Katie did as requested, trying not to burst into laughter at Ace's whispered instructions. "Give me a librarian pose," he said. "Pretend the flowers are a box of books. Now, smile, you top model, you."

When they finally took their leave, she was glad darkness had fallen so she couldn't see the damage to the rental car. One more reminder of their target status.

He opened the door. "You look amazing. Wait—that's a

boring word. You look...striking. Staggering. Stupendous. And other 's' words."

She laughed, sinking into the seat. "I hope only good ones. You're on a real roll tonight."

"I plan to make you laugh loud and often, Katie McClure. Let's pretend like we're not in danger and enjoy ourselves. Although rest assured, I'm packing heat." He shut her door and strode around, settling into the driver's seat.

His fitted navy suit and light blue tie made him look like a millionaire. She held her breath as he turned on the interior light and leaned toward her, so close his breath brushed her cheek. He spoke quietly. "Just know that no matter what happens, nothing will change the way I feel about you."

Those incredible lips moved closer and he pressed a soft, open kiss on her cheek. If she turned her head, her lips would meet his...

He abruptly flipped off the light and started the car.

The man was completely unreadable. How could she ever fall for someone so mysterious?

And yet she already had.

Digging into the crab dip appetizer with her slice of garlic bread, Katie seemed unaware of the thrall she held over him. When a stray breadcrumb stuck to her lip, he automatically reached up and brushed it off with his thumb.

"Um...I think I got some of your lipstick," he said, trying not to focus on those red lips.

Blotting at her mouth with a napkin, she sighed. "Molly tried to fix me up with long-wearing lipstick but it's useless, given how I like to eat." She gave him that mega-watt smile.

He wanted to touch those nearly-naked lips again, slower. He wanted to embrace her for the woman she was—the woman with the hopeful spirit and wide-open heart. He wanted to kiss her all over that beautiful face, to crush her lean body into his, taking away all her fear.

Instead, he took a long gulp of water, which promptly went down the wrong pipe.

As his hacking intensified, she walked over to pound him on the back. "Do I need to do the Heimlich? I took First Aid in high school."

"I'm...not...choking," he said between coughs. "Just...wrong pipe."

Taking a couple more sips of water, he finally regained a modicum of control. He gave a forced smile to the handful of customers and to their waiter, who stood at the ready.

Katie returned to her seat, grinning.

"Am I really that distracting?" she joked.

Yes. Yes, she was.

⚬⚬⚬⚬⚬⚬

When their steak arrived, Katie turned the conversation back to Ace. "So tell me all about New York City. And please chew each bite carefully so we don't have a repeat of your earlier episode."

He laughed, then went on to describe the soaring buildings near his postage-stamp apartment, the running trails he took in the park, and his favorite modern art gallery. As he spoke, she was swept up in a vision of the life she'd always wanted. Big-city. Big danger. Fighting crime at the highest level.

Was that what Dad had wanted, too? Maybe that explained why he had traveled so much. Or why he would have been tempted to steal that money. Her mind wandered as he continued to speak.

"...but the street vendor on my corner sells the most

amazing gyros," he said. "Plenty of meat and thick pita...Katie? Something wrong?"

"What? No. That is, I was just thinking of how I'm not the only one who turned out like my dad. Brandon loves new adventures and traveling places, too."

His eyes pulled hers in. "I would love to take you to see Manhattan."

She laughed it off. "I'd just be deadweight. I would probably fall onto the subway tracks as I tried to board."

"No, you wouldn't. Stop being so hard on yourself. How about this—I promise I'll take you to New York City someday."

She could tell he was in earnest, but what did that mean for them? Was he proposing a long-term relationship? Why didn't he come out with it frankly, the way he said everything else?

"What are you saying?"

He held her gaze. "I'm saying I want to travel with you. I want to give you adventures outside West Virginia."

Now she mirrored his seriousness. "Sorry, but I don't travel with men, unless they're related to me."

He spoke so softly, she barely caught it. "Or if you're married to them."

"Yes." She leaned across the empty bread plate. "Unless I'm married to them."

10

A strange car was parked outside and the house was aglow with lights when they returned. Though Ace was anxious to see if anything had happened, he needed to take care of something first. Something personal.

"Wonder what's up?" Katie reached for the door handle.

He stretched out a hand, clasping her arm. Chill bumps covered it.

"Are you cold?" he asked.

"No, not really." She raised her eyes to his. They were barely visible in the reflected light from the porch.

Hypnotized, he ran his hand up to her head, gently tugging her face closer. Time seemed to slow as he traced her lips, then lowered his mouth to hers.

She didn't respond. Had he misread her?

But then her hand gripped his sleeve. The pressure from her lips grew stronger, insistent. Confident and womanly.

He was swept into a world where everything seemed to make sense, to fit together. There was nothing to do but respond to the force that could both master him and repair him. Tears actually filled his eyes.

A sharp rapping on the window put an abrupt halt to their enchantment. Straightening up, he wiped off the foggy glass and cracked the window.

A skinny, bearded redhead stood there, giving him a murderous glare. "Let me guess—you're the Yankee bodyguard."

"No way." Katie leaned over. "Brandon?"

⁓⁓⁓

As Mom served an impromptu tray of cheese, crackers, and grapes, Brandon explained his unexpected appearance.

"After I talked to you, I started thinking about things, sis. If those mobsters wanted money, and if Dad didn't take it, that meant they wouldn't give up. So I did the one thing I knew you hadn't—I contacted the FBI and told them everything."

Ace dropped heavily onto the couch. Katie followed suit, taking off her heels.

"They'll be here in the morning. I'll meet with them and figure out a plan to find these Russian gangsters." Brandon hitched up his cargo-style jeans. "Hey, Mom, I could really use some Dr. Pepper."

Mom smiled, ruffling Brandon's overgrown hair. "It's in the pantry. I always keep some, just in case."

As Mom locked an arm in Brandon's and headed for the kitchen, Katie focused on the silent man by her side. From the sour look on his face, she figured he was really upset by their interruption in the car. She hadn't wanted the kiss to end, either, but where would it have led?

Why did she have to be attracted to someone who was such a mess spiritually? He said he'd believed in Jesus at a young age, but his growth had been stunted when his godly grandma died. Was God using their time together to point

Ace back to Him? If so, she wasn't the best person to guide him.

Her brother's deep voice filled the kitchen. Brandon was someone else who was messed up and disillusioned by life. And yet he'd contacted the FBI, probably because he didn't believe Dad had taken that money. Kind of ironic she had switched perspectives with her brother on this one. Usually he had nothing good to say about Dad's work, and she had to be the one defending it.

Ace nudged her elbow with his. "Sorry. I was a little lost in thought. But that was...unforgettable...out there in the car." His eyes were a quiet blue blaze, focused on hers.

She felt like hugging him, hard. She wanted to kiss the joy back into his life. She needed to tuck her hand into his safe, strong grip.

"Tomorrow is the day," he murmured.

"What day?"

"The day you have to contact Anatoly's men with news. I copied the note before I gave it to the police. By the way, I plan to call in another police unit for you tomorrow."

"Why? Won't you be here?"

Brandon sauntered back in, carrying a huge bowl of homemade popcorn. "Look what I talked Mom into making for me. You gotta try this, Ace." He extended the bowl.

As the men fell into an easy conversation about whitewater rafting, she zoned out, focusing on the words Ace hadn't said. The words that would rip her apart when they were finally spoken aloud.

He was leaving.

Thanks to his reckless consumption of Dr. Pepper, Ace spent his final night in the garage apartment pacing and worrying. He knew what he had to do, but the logistics of his plan were tricky. How could he ever explain things to Katie?

He had replayed their kiss so many times. Her reticence had morphed into a certainty that staggered him. He wasn't worthy of such a gift—such unfettered approval. She didn't know the truth. And yet he wanted another kiss, another chance to prove he was the man she thought he was.

He finally crashed on the couch, but his alarm went off at five. Peering out the window, he saw a car and a black van out front.

The Feds were here.

Katie cut into her boiled eggs, meticulously removing the yolks she didn't care for. "You want these?"

Ace shook his head, but Brandon charged into the kitchen and swiped them. "My fave."

"Did you see that the FBI's here?" she asked.

Brandon nodded, popping a coffee pod into the coffeemaker. "Heading out after I eat. You two hanging around today?"

She crunched into a crisp piece of bacon. "I thought we could check the *Vixen* one more time. What do you think, Ace?"

When he turned to her, she stopped chewing. Her mind and her mouth froze when she registered the remorseful look on his face.

"I can't stay. I have to fly back today. Work."

That was *it*? That was all the explanation, all the farewell she got? How could he casually throw their relationship away? Because it was more than a friendship—his kiss last night had made that clear.

Mom padded in, wearing her favorite moccasin slippers. She took in her daughter's face. "What's going on?"

Katie could barely articulate the words. "Ace is leaving today."

Mom teared up, placing a hand on Ace's shoulder. "Oh, honey, we are going to miss you around here. Won't be the same without you."

Brandon chimed in. "Yeah, dude, I know we just met and all, but I feel like I know you. Which is more than I thought I'd be able to say about a New Yorker. Oh—I hope you enjoy those baseball cards. To tell the truth, I didn't even really look at them when Dad gave them to me. Just not my thing."

Seeing her family rally around Ace made it even harder. They all liked him. He wasn't some outsider, coming in and looking down on their way of life. He was like one of them.

Her words came out plaintively, like a whimper. "But Molly won't even get to say goodbye." Why did that suddenly bother her?

He took her hand, setting her emotions roiling. "I'll be in touch, I promise. Maybe I can come down during my Christmas vacation? It's not like I'll have any family events going on."

She couldn't choke out a response.

Mom hugged him. "Of course. You're always welcome here, Ace." She gave him a cryptic look Katie didn't understand.

Had their kiss meant nothing at all to him? He was just going to say goodbye and walk out of her life?

Brandon shoved his fourth piece of bacon in his mouth, then stopped cold, taking a long look at her. "Sis, you okay?"

She stood, unable to comprehend why someone she had grown so close to could abandon her like this. That wasn't love. That wasn't even like.

She fumbled down the hall toward her room. Slamming

the door, she let her thoughts scream even louder. What did it matter if Anatoly's men tried to blow her away? She was never leaving this one-horse town anyway.

Ace whisked around the apartment, jamming everything into his capacious suitcases and trying to shove thoughts of Katie from his mind. He had to do this...in fact, he was doing it for *her*, but she would probably never know. He couldn't stick around here.

As he loaded one gun and strapped it on, there was a knock on the door. He opened it to find Molly, looking downright dangerous in her stilettos and black leather jacket.

"Sit down," she said, shoving her way past him and nearly impaling him with a long fingernail. "We have to talk."

Crossing her legs at an angle as if she were posing for a glamour shot, Molly launched into a diatribe, complete with emphatic hand motions.

"You're a handsome guy, Ace—and you know it." She smiled at his surprise. "Takes one to know one, bub. What I have to say, before you so rudely take off and leave my pining sister in the dust, is that Katie doesn't just fall for anyone. After that foot injury, she closed up a corner of her heart. Then when Dad died, she put up a No Trespassing sign and wrapped the entire thing in police tape. No men have gotten in. Ever." She paused, scrutinizing him. "But here's the deal: she must see something in you that runs deeper than looks."

He took a couple deep, calming breaths, trying to figure out which way Molly was going with this. She didn't slow down, nearly boring holes into him with her stare.

"What I'm telling you is that if you walk away from this, it will crush her. She doesn't even know how in love she is yet, but I can tell. Sisterly intuition. And here's something else. I can tell you're a good match for her. She's happier when she's with you, and she's more...*herself*." She stood and started pacing, sharp heels clicking on the floor. "And so help me, if you leave her in the lurch, I..." She made a wringing gesture with her hands.

He couldn't stop himself. He laughed outright.

Fire blazed into her cheeks. "How *dare* you laugh about my sister?"

He held up a hand, rushing to explain before Molly's anger got the better of her. "I'm not laughing about Katie. I believe I love her too, crazy as that sounds. That's why I have to go."

She raised one eyebrow, but waited for him to explain.

11

A knock sounded on Katie's bedroom door and she cracked it.

Ace stood outside, an inscrutable look on his face. "I wanted to say goodbye before I pack my car. I did tell your sister goodbye and she's waiting in the kitchen to talk with you."

She looked at the half of his face she could see. She tried to memorize his features, while at the same time pretending not to care. "Thanks. Thanks for everything. Bye."

"I'm sorry this is so abrupt," he said. "I'm going to talk with the FBI guys for a few minutes, tell them what's happened, then I have to get rolling. They'll make sure you're protected from here on out."

She couldn't bite back her bitter words. "Washing your hands of us, are you?"

He put a hand on the door, opening it so she could see his entire face. His eyes were filled with concern and a deeper emotion, but she wouldn't be so stupid as to call it love.

"I'm not. I promise I'm not. I'll never get you out of my head, Katie McClure."

She slammed the door.

Minutes dragged into an hour as he talked with the FBI agents. Now the whole story was out. Jim's fake death. His deal with Jim to save himself from prison. His placement in the McClure home and his subsequent failure to find the bank heist money.

It was almost time for the FBI to take over, but not quite. He had one last job to do. He owed it to Katie.

She watched the van doors close as Ace climbed in. Brandon was already talking with other agents in the living room. It was quite a force they'd brought out, she'd give them that. Probably out of respect for her dad...and he was worthy of respect, since it was obvious he'd never absconded with illegal funds.

What a fool she'd been, falling for Ace. Searching for money she knew her dad didn't take. And yet...

Yet he had protected her tirelessly. He had told her things she figured he hadn't told anyone else. He'd opened up to her, hadn't he?

And if she was honest with herself, he had been the invigorating breeze that had blown many of her cobwebs of self-doubt away. She had seen God's hand of protection, remembered what it felt like to be loved for who she was.

She had to tell him that.

Propelled by the obscure emotions she was still processing, Katie pulled on her low boots, then scrawled a note for Mom and dropped it on her bed. She headed out the back door and snuck around the back of her apartment to avoid scrutiny by the FBI agents. Creeping toward the Lexus, she could see a couple bags lying on the back floor, as well as a blanket and pillow.

An idea began to simmer, then it quickly combusted into a blaze. It was perfect. This would be her greatest adventure yet. She smiled at her own boldness, her spontaneity. How very un-librarianesque of her.

She would tell him she loved him, let the chips fall where they may. Maybe he would choose to skip the flight and stay, like the ending of a romantic movie. But then again, maybe she'd have to catch a cab home from the airport.

She didn't care.

She needed closure. And probably one last kiss.

Mrs. McClure stood on the porch, waving as Ace thudded the car door shut and buckled himself in. No sign of Katie. It was probably for the best.

Using his newly-developed mountain driving skills, he made good time, maneuvering the curvy roads like a pro. Glancing at the canopy of green trees arching near the side of the road, his stomach clenched. Such a wild elegance here in Hemlock Creek. It was an unaffected natural beauty of the most powerful kind. He pictured Katie's hair, blowing in the wind. Her eyes, sparkling with amusement and candor. She embodied that unaffected beauty that brought out his most protective feelings.

If only he had more to offer her. If only his life hadn't been derailed by an unwarranted prison sentence. He could have been an upstanding citizen with nothing blotting his record.

Now he had more than a blot, he had made a deal with the devil. At least it would soon be over.

The car slowed. Had they already arrived at the Lewisburg airport? Katie didn't dare raise up from under the blanket until Ace had gotten out. She didn't want to alarm a man who always carried a gun.

Even with the air-conditioning on, the wool blanket she'd hid under felt stifling. Though it carried the comforting smell of its owner, she had to get out from under it. When the car door slammed, she barely shifted, breathing in his scent one more time before exposing her mouth and one eye.

This was probably a dumb idea. She might very well scare him out of his mind, since he'd been in hyper-vigilant bodyguard mode for so long. She wouldn't pop out and open the door...she'd just ease out.

The trunk slammed and she heard him walking away. No! She'd waited too long!

She struggled to sit up, stiffening in fear as she peeped out at the view.

This wasn't the airport. Vines tangled around a large, dilapidated building that was surrounded by trees. One large maple tree was actually growing out of the roof.

A black car was parked off to the side of the building, and Ace was heading straight for it, pulling his rolling suitcase behind him.

Had he found the money and contacted Anatoly's men? Was this some kind of drop?

Had he betrayed them all?

Barely rising above the window ledge, she held her breath, watching two larger men exit the black car. They were holding Uzis, but they didn't look like the same men from the library.

A man emerged from the front seat, smiling like the

Cheshire Cat. Sandy blond hair, deep tan, ridiculous Hawaiian shirt.

She'd know him anywhere. Jim Chrisman. She gagged, nearly losing her breakfast. So Dad's partner hadn't had cancer, and he wasn't murdered, as Dad had suspected. In fact, he'd never died in the first place. And Ace must have known all along.

A dark blue SUV raced up from the far side of the parking lot, screeching to halt in front of Ace and the others. Three armed men jumped out, also toting heavier artillery. They formed a loose circle around the initial collaborators.

As Ace stared at the newcomers, she couldn't miss the look of panic in his eyes. When he slowly raised his hands in the air, she dropped to the floor, pulled the blanket over herself, and started praying furiously. She had no weapons, and Ace had no chance.

He had never been so nervous, even though he was the one who'd secretly invited Anatoly to this rendezvous. He carried only one pistol and they could mow him down faster than he could blink, despite the bulletproof vest the Feds had loaned him.

The FBI lurked somewhere, listening to this exchange through his earpiece. They knew his suitcase was stuffed with empty Dr. Pepper bottles, so the moment he opened it, he'd be toast if they didn't get to him first.

But he was banking on one thing: Anatoly wasn't the kind to cut a deal. Jim might try to wheedle his way out of this, but the Russian would find it glaringly apparent who had orchestrated the theft of his bank money.

Anatoly scooted out of his seat, his corpulent stomach

spilling over his belt. He carried a smaller gun but had no need of it, given his well-armed henchmen.

He took a wide stance and shouted. "Jim Chrisman! You are a—" Harshly punctuated Russian words spewed forth. Anatoly's men understood them and snickered.

Ace stood between the powerful men, not budging. Let the titans clash this one out.

Jim gave his ingratiating smile. "Anatoly. Let's work something out, like men."

The large Russian cackled. "You are no man. You are a coward who hid behind his partner. So scared you had to play dead." He took a step closer. "Today I will show you what you had to fear."

Jim held up his hands. "Now hold up, big fella. Let's see what my stooge has brought me. Oh wait, I haven't made introductions." He pointed. "Ace, this is Anatoly. Anatoly, this is the clueless sap I landed in jail, then pulled out of there so he could find my money. A real ladies' man."

Blood rushed into Ace's ears, making his head pound. He had been such a fool. The invisible lowlife who had framed him years ago was the exact same man who had released him. Jim Chrisman had no intention of letting him go, even if he did have the money. He would send him right back to prison.

If only Anatoly would take the first shot.

Closing his eyes, he prayed silently. Peace washed over him and he knew he still shared Katie's faith in a loving God —a Father who watched out for His children. He promised to go back to Katie and make things right if he survived this encounter. But if not, she would eventually know what he had done to protect her family.

Jim repeated himself, obviously antsy. "I said it's time to show us the money, Ace. You do it or my men will do it for you."

Ace wheeled his piece of luggage closer, leaning down as if he would unzip it. Taking a deep breath, he gripped the sides, hurling the suitcase to the ground directly in front of Anatoly.

Anatoly jolted back but quickly recovered his composure as he realized Ace had given him the loot. He smiled like a doting parent. "You did well, my boy." He spoke one Russian word and reached for the suitcase.

As he did so, a single shot rang out. Ace dropped to the ground, a burning sensation spreading across his head. Pain blinded him. He rolled in the general direction of the SUV, hoping to slide under the oversized vehicle as a volley of shots unleashed.

Something warm and sticky dribbled into his eyes. He swiped at it, then realized it was blood.

He'd been shot in the head.

As the world grew fuzzy, he took comfort in one thing: Katie was safe.

12

"Oh, Lord, please no. Please don't take him, Lord." Katie squeezed Ace's limp hand in hers, staring at the blood still spackling his hastily-cleaned face.

Two FBI medics spoke rapidly to one another. She could only catch blips of the conversation.

"Another unit of blood."

"That's right."

"Is he responsive?"

Ace's hand shifted slightly under hers. "He's alive!" she shouted.

The dark-haired medic smiled her way. "Yes, he is. He got lucky. That bullet only grazed his head and ear. It'll take a little stitching, but he'll survive. He was exceptionally brave, going up against two powerful criminals."

She hugged Ace's hand to her face, kissing it. "Yes, he is. The most devoted bodyguard ever."

When Ace opened his eyes, a bearded man with wild red hair was peering at his face. Where was he?

But the moment Brandon spoke, he recognized him.

"Dude! You're awake!"

Lowering his gaze from the faded hospital ceiling, Ace smiled as the three McClure women rushed his way.

"Thank the Lord!" Mrs. McClure said.

"You scoundrel." Molly winked. "I knew if anyone could pull it off, you could."

Katie leaned over and brushed his forehead with a kiss. "When you're all better, you're going to explain why you told my sister about your meeting of imminent doom, but not me. And then I'll tell you about this really *interesting* car ride I had..."

Much as he struggled to stay alert, his eyes fluttered closed. "Love...you," he mumbled.

Suddenly, Katie's strong voice was right next to his ear. "I love you too," she said.

Two days later, Katie explained the events of that day to Ace one more time, even as she lightly traced his stitches. They were healing fast.

"From what the agents said, Jim shot at Anatoly and the bullet grazed you. It killed Anatoly on the spot. Then you dropped and the men blasted into a shooting free-for-all, which came to an abrupt halt when the FBI agents showed up. Jim didn't get hit, because he hid in the car—the loser. Now he's heading straight for prison." Her voice dropped. "He still swears he had nothing to do with Dad's death."

He gripped her hand and she felt renewed encouragement.

She edged closer to his leg from her perch on the side of

the couch. "They investigated your record and said it's officially expunged. It was obvious Jim set you up so he could get to us."

He adjusted his legs to make more room for her, then took a slow sip of unsweetened iced tea, thankful he was around to enjoy it. "But I don't understand what happened to that 1.5 million. Jim swears he hid it on your dad's boat."

"I know, it's so weird. There's no way Dad could've spent all that. Mom would have known. And by the way, Mom came clean and said you'd told her about Jim before your clandestine meeting with him. Did everyone know but me?"

Catching the last of their conversation, Brandon strode over, dropping his overstuffed rucksack to the floor. "I knew nothing, sis—promise. I just wanted to get the FBI in on things. Little did I know your bodyguard would suggest another plan to them." He gave Ace a high-five before his look turned serious. "You're a real hero, man. I have mad respect for you. I hate to fly out now, but I need to get back. Hey— maybe I'll see you around sometime? I'm thinking I might come back in October. To tell the truth, I miss fall in these mountains."

Katie beamed, thankful that her brother seemed to be feeling more connected to his family. "I hope you do. We don't see you enough."

Brandon shoved his aviator sunglasses on. "I was pretty wrong about Dad. I mean, he probably only wanted me to play baseball so we could do something together. And I pushed him away. Meanwhile, there he was, serving with an utterly corrupt partner who wound up ripping off a mob boss and staging his own death."

Ace reached for the coffee table, retrieving the bag of baseball cards. "That reminds me. I haven't even looked over these yet, but you should keep them. They were never meant for me."

Brandon hesitated, then silently nodded. As he took the partially-opened bag, the contents spilled out on the floor.

Katie bent over to shuffle the cards back into a pile. One caught her eye. "Hey—how cool is this? This card says it's from 1951."

"Could I see that?" Ace asked. He examined it as she began to sort cards by year.

"There are several with the older dates," she said.

Brandon took off his sunglasses, plopping down on the floor nearby. "You're right, sis."

Ace looked incredulous, barely holding the card between thumb and forefinger as if it were on fire. "This one is a Joe Jackson card of the Chicago White Sox."

She nodded politely, handing him another old one.

"And this is a Willie Mays," he said.

Shooting his sister a blank look, Brandon spoke up. "We really have no idea who they are, man. So you ought to keep these. They'll mean more to someone who appreciates baseball."

Ace propped himself up and grabbed at the pile of old cards. As he shuffled through, mumbling names, Katie shrugged. She began packing the rest away in the bag.

Finally, he beamed. "Brandon, Katie—your dad was no fool. He knew about Jim and he knew about the heist money."

"What makes you say that?" She was bewildered.

He dropped the pile of cards in her lap. "Because he took it and he bought baseball cards. *Extremely valuable* baseball cards. It probably took months to get hold of all these. Just one of these could be worth up to a hundred thousand dollars or more. To avoid suspicion, he mixed them with modern cards, then packed away the bag in the attic. No one would even think to look for cards instead of cash."

Brandon sighed. "So, Dad was crooked after all?"

"No. He was smart. He was aware if the cash was found on his boat, he'd be an instant suspect in the theft. He'd look like a crooked FBI agent, and he could lose his job or even get sent to jail. So he pretended to be oblivious to Jim, meanwhile disguising the money for later."

"Still doesn't seem legit," Brandon muttered.

"I think he was probably worried about us," Katie said. "If he lost his job because of suspected theft, I'm sure the FBI would have made it hard for him to get hired anywhere."

Brandon laughed. "Come to think of it, I think he'd finally be proud of me. Suddenly I find myself very interested in baseball."

She lightly punched his arm, shaking her head. "You aren't keeping these now, bro. We have to hand them over to the FBI so they can close this case." She looked to Ace for affirmation.

He nodded, touching his stitches as if they still pained him. "It's the right thing to do. But first we should probably let your mom know."

"And Molly—she'll want to be in the loop."

He grinned. "That's for sure."

One week later, when Ace's head was finally starting to feel normal, the FBI pulled up to the McClures' home.

The agents spontaneously broke into a round of applause as he walked out to meet them, carrying the bag of baseball cards. Katie squeezed his arm. He had never felt so respected in all his life.

The lead agent stepped up and shook his hand. "We can't tell you how much we appreciate your bravery, not to mention your discovery of the cards. Otherwise that money would've been lost forever. As a reward, the bank has agreed to let you keep your choice of two cards."

He gasped, then paused to think. "Let's see, I'll pick one for Brandon first. How about the Joe Jackson—the first card that tipped me off to what happened?"

Katie grinned. "Thanks for thinking of him."

As for himself, he knew just the one he wanted. Digging around in the bag, he found it and handed it to Katie.

"Joe DiMaggio. He didn't agree with his dad concerning his career, and he married a beautiful woman that was out of his league. I can relate."

She frowned. "What are you saying? Did you fail to tell me that you're married?"

Wrapping an arm around her slim waist, he kissed her cheek. "No, but I'll get married someday. And I have this particularly beautiful redhead in mind."

As Ace drove off in the somewhat-battered Lexus, Molly whistled. "Good gracious, I hate to see that boy go. He was really good for you, sis."

"I know." Katie tried to hide a smile. "He's not gone forever, you know."

Molly bumped hips with her. "I hope he comes to visit. And Mom told me he's going to the police academy? I guess he's racked up some experience fighting bad guys. We all knew he was great with weapons."

"That's for sure. And strangely enough, he wants to work for a small police station—just like the one here in Hemlock Creek."

Molly quirked an eyebrow. "Wait—you mean you're not following him up to New York City? I thought you were going to bust outta this town the first chance you got."

Relishing her new zeal for life, Katie shook her head. "The dreams I was chasing weren't the right dreams for me in the first place. It hit me when I was crouching in Ace's car, praying and fearing for our lives. I'm not meant to be on the front lines like that—like Dad was."

Molly's smile widened. "I think we always knew that was the case. But we couldn't convince you of that. You just had to find yourself."

"I have—the self God made me to be. When I'm honest, I have to admit I enjoy being a librarian, I love our small town, and I like living near family. Reba will want to retire someday, and I'm already thinking of ways to modernize the library. I feel like I finally have a mission."

Molly winked. "And does that mission include a certain Ace Calhoun?"

"He just took out a Hemlock Creek library card, so I expect him to be a regular patron."

"Stop hedging! Are you two an item or what?" Molly crossed her arms, feigning anger.

Katie thought of Ace's goodbye kiss. He hadn't spoken a word, but had pulled her into his arms and gazed at her until, as if magnetized, she tipped her lips to meet his. "My future is with you," he'd murmured. "You're my hero, Katie McClure."

"And you're my champion—my ace," she'd said.

And now she was ready to face the future, unafraid. To stand tall on the feet God gave her, tipsy as those feet might be. Ace would be there to support her.

"We're more than an item." She hugged her sister. "We're engaged."

Dear Reader,

I'm so glad to introduce you to the McClure siblings of West Virginia—my home state. Katie, Molly, and Brandon are such vivid characters in my mind, maybe because I married into a family with redheaded siblings (disclaimer: the McClures' personalities are purely fictional). As I wrote this story, Ace Calhoun kind of wriggled his way into my heart and went from being a semi-scoundrel to a hero—and I realized why his unusual name (he insisted on it!) fit him so well.

Thank you again for sharing this Appalachian adventure—there's almost nothing I enjoy more than bringing a taste of modern "wild and wonderful West Virginia" to my readers. If you want more fast-paced West Virginia reads featuring the Greenbrier Resort and other southern West Virginia locales, I'd recommend you check out my *Barks & Beans Cafe* cozy mystery series, which features sibling sleuths Bo and Macy Hatfield, Macy's rescue Great Dane, Coal, and a cafe where folks can pet shelter dogs. Teens and adults alike are enjoying this clean mystery series.

If you enjoyed this book, please take a moment to share a review at the online retailers of your choice. Reviews are a great way to get the word out about fantastic books...as well as word of mouth!

Be sure to sign up for my newsletter at **heatherdaygilbert.com** for my latest book updates, giveaways, and bargain news!

-*Heather*

UNDERCUT

Dedicated to Sky, our lifelong blessing from the flood

1

Zane Boone had carried the weight of his guilt longer than he cared to admit.

As his psychologist repeated himself, Zane rubbed a sweaty hand over his cargo pants. His blood pressure was probably sky-high. He was in fight or flight mode, and he couldn't flee.

"I said it's obvious that you still have issues you need to deal with, Isaiah."

Why did the man persist in calling him *Isaiah*? He'd told him he went by *Zane*. And why did he always seem so condescending? Had he spent hours camped on rooftops in Afghanistan? Had he ever killed someone for his country?

Zane wished he hadn't let his ex-wife choose his psychologist, but he'd been so blindsided when Krista had cleared the house out and filed for divorce. Reeling from her sudden enmity, he was willing to agree to anything to ensure he could have regular visits with his five-year-old daughter—even if it meant signing a release that his smug new psychologist could contact his ex at any time if he deemed Zane unfit for visitation.

He tried to give a winning smile. "I'm sure I do, but don't we all?"

Doctor Christianson leaned forward, adjusting his clear glasses frames. Early in their sessions, Zane had asked the man a few questions of his own and had determined they had absolutely nothing in common.

"There is no need to be so cavalier," the doctor said. "Your recent persecution complex is very real, and we must get to the bottom of it."

Zane sank into the plush chair, wishing the floor would swallow him up. He couldn't seem to explain that it was no complex. He really *was* being followed. The terrifying thing was that he couldn't prove it.

As he drove to The Greenbrier Resort, his cell phone rang. He hit the speaker button.

"Zane, where are you?" His ex-wife's voice, with its melodic alto tones, always disarmed him—even though he knew anger simmered just beneath.

"I'm on the road, heading to a job. Gotta check on my crew."

"Well, Doctor Christianson contacted me. He thinks I should come to the next session."

Zane punched his truck's dashboard.

Krista must have heard it because her reaction was swift. "What was that? You didn't break something again, did you?"

Of course, she'd have to bring up the *one* time he'd knocked a glass lamp from the nightstand when he'd roused from a nightmare. Now she was convinced he was cracking up.

But the truth was, he was in a much better place now than he'd been in two years ago, just back from his second tour of duty. Back then, he'd suffered from insomnia for four straight months. It was all he could do to sit in his chair and play video games, much less try to be a husband and dad.

He knew his inability to cope had played a large role in the destruction of his marriage, but the divorce had changed everything so swiftly and so irreversibly. Now he mostly saw Lola on weekends, no longer waking to her daily "I love you, Daddy," as she face-planted into his chest for a hug.

He tried to sound carefree. "I'm fine. No worries."

He glanced in his rear-view mirror at a black sedan that was following too close on the curving mountain road. He eased off the gas and tapped the brake. By slowing, he would protect both himself and the death-defying driver behind him. The driver was probably not from West Virginia and had no concept of the switchbacks to come.

The car continued driving so close, it nearly clipped his bumper.

"Shoot! Knock it off!" He sped up a bit.

"What's going on? Who are you talking to?" Krista's voice held an accusatory edge.

"Just some joker following too close on the mountain. Listen, I'll call you back tonight so we can talk about Lola's schedule for next month. I want to help out more. And we can talk about my next session."

Krista sighed, and he could picture her sitting at her desk, twirling her pen between her narrow fingers. "Okay, sure. Just don't forget."

As if he ever had.

Hanging up, Zane rounded a curve and stole another glance into the mirror. Sure enough, the car was practically glued to him. He wasn't even going that slowly anymore—he was exceeding the speed limit. If they were determined to push it to 65 on the mountain, they could pass him on a double line and risk their own necks.

Then the driver did something unthinkable. He sped up and bashed into Zane's bumper.

He knew then. It was the same people who'd been following him the past few days. There had been different cars, different people, but they had one thing in common—they were closing in on him.

He knew this road like the back of his hand. There was an abrupt turnoff coming up. He would dodge onto a winding side road, slick as a bullet through an oiled gun barrel.

If his tail followed him, he'd be ready. He might be an honorably discharged Marine, but he was still always ready. He patted the Colt he kept snug in his belt holster.

Seeing the dirt road to his right, he made the turn at the last moment. The sedan nearly plowed into him, but had to keep going. He knew there wasn't another turnaround for at least five more minutes. He'd be nearly to The Greenbrier by then, parked in an area reserved for workers where his truck wouldn't easily be seen.

He slowed the car along with his breath. He didn't want his men to think he looked half-crazed. When he finally parked, he glanced down and noticed a slight tremor in his hand—his shooting hand.

He pushed his dark blond bangs out of his eyes. He really needed a haircut, but who had time for that, between running a business, trying to be there for his daughter, and dealing with stalkers who seemed to be invisible to everyone else?

If only Krista could've been in the car with him instead of on the phone, she would've seen he wasn't making this up. But why did he still care what Krista thought?

He pictured Lola's heart-shaped face, an exact replica of her mother's. Her dark eyes and hair that made her Krista's Mini-Me.

He didn't want his daughter to wind up thinking her

daddy was crazy. And he wanted to show Krista that he wasn't still trapped in that wordless, helpless zone he'd been in a couple of years ago. He needed to prove he was more than capable of being a great dad.

A difficult thing to do when he was always looking over his shoulder to see if someone was following him.

Outside The Greenbrier, Zane picked his way toward the creek bank where his men were still chopping and loading logs uprooted by last year's horrific June flood. His foreman, Brett, hailed him with a loose salute. It was a gesture that indicated his respect for his military service.

Dad had said the men worked harder for Zane than they'd ever worked under him. "Don't downplay their loyalty, Zane," Dad said. "Those men can't even put into words how much they appreciate the tours of duty you did for this country." The way Dad's eyes crinkled and welled with tears had told Zane he felt the same way.

Zane surveyed the area and slapped Brett on the shoulder. "You've made a lot of progress this week. Probably finish the job tomorrow?"

"Sure thing, boss. Wanna join us?"

His grin slid into a grimace. "Actually, I have to head inside to square away some billing details in person. Not as fun as chopping, but somebody has to do it."

Brett scanned Zane's attire and rubbed at his beard. "You figure they'll let you in, dressed like that?"

It was an honest question. The Greenbrier was a high-class resort, and he was wearing his usual plaid flannel shirt, cargo pants, and heavy boots. Not to mention a three-week-old beard he hadn't gotten around to shaving.

He tucked his shirt in, which was no easy feat with his gun holster. He didn't carry a small gun.

"I'll only be in there a few minutes, hopefully. I'll check in with you before I leave."

Brett nodded, pulling on work gloves before returning to his job.

Zane took a shortcut toward the main building, striding across the immaculate golf course. Just last year, the grounds had been strewn with debris from the heavy flooding. It hadn't taken long for locals and volunteers to clean up most of the damage, but the haunting imprint of lost homes and tragic deaths had scarred everyone in the affected counties.

Maybe that's what had happened to him. The imprints of those whose lives he had taken—those he had sniped in the line of duty—would always haunt him, even though he didn't consciously dwell on them.

Maybe he was being chased by their ghosts. Maybe he *was* losing it.

Deep in thought, he nearly careened into a woman in tall heels as he stepped onto the green-and-red carpeting inside the front door. "Excuse me, ma'am," he mumbled, allowing his eyes to travel from the unique springhouse design in the center of the carpet to her face.

He startled. Molly McClure. He'd recognize that curling auburn mane and those gold-hazel eyes anywhere. Molly was a hard woman to miss. But why was she still working here? Last time he'd seen her, she'd said she was looking for another job.

Struggling to come up with something to say to fill the awkward silence, he felt relief when she spoke first. But her words weren't what he expected.

"Well, look what the mountain lion dragged in...a real, live lumberjack." She slowly eyed him up and down, and her eyes snapped with something that belied the dazzling smile on her peachy lips. "Where in the blazes have you been, Zane Boone? Do you know I actually waited for you to call me back after that last date? I mean we've known each other since what...sixth grade? You could've at least let me know you weren't interested." She lifted one shoulder, as if shrugging off any offense she might have taken.

2

Despite her affected indifference, Molly felt a wound had just been reopened. Zane Boone was the one man who'd ever dared to disappear from her life with nary a by-your-leave. As she took in his appearance, made even more rugged with his beard, she tried to hold onto some shred of pride.

She'd had a crush on this man since sixth grade, truth be told. And when he'd asked her out last year—post-divorce— she'd jumped at the chance. But he'd been distant, different from the carefree leader she'd known in high school. Still, it came as a total surprise when he'd never even asked her on a third date, and he'd never contacted her to explain why.

He held her gaze, his gray eyes smiling, but she caught that shadow of sadness he seemed to carry everywhere now. "Nice to see you, too."

She couldn't tell if he was mocking her. That was the infuriating thing—Zane was often unreadable. Or maybe she just hadn't learned to read him yet? Her sister Katie would say she was only attracted to him because he was hard to get and didn't throw himself at her like her other suitors.

She rallied. "Did you come back to apologize? You're only...seven months late?"

He took her verbal lashing and didn't rise to her bait. Instead, his eyes traveled over her smoke blue suit and carefully-twisted updo. "You still working the front desk?"

"No. I'm the wedding coordinator now."

He whistled. "The weddings here...Krista always said they were out of a fairy tale."

Molly tried to hide her frown. Why did he always bring his ex-wife into the conversation, after what the thankless woman had done to him? From what she could piece together, his ex had left him high and dry when he got back from Afghanistan, just because he had some difficulty adjusting to civilian life again. Molly could never forgive her for that. A woman should stand by her man, plain and simple, for better or for worse.

Zane suddenly stepped toward her, taking her arm and forcefully shifting her to the side.

"What on—"

He moved in front of her, as if bodily guarding her against the darker-skinned man who'd just walked in. The man— probably Middle Eastern—shot them an irritated look, but he kept up his fast pace toward the sunken casino area.

Unsure of the intense look in Zane's eyes, Molly placed a calming hand on his shoulder. "You okay?" she whispered.

He nodded slowly. "Sorry about that. He was walking too fast and his hand was in his jacket. I notice things like that."

"Of course you do." She took a deep breath. "Listen, I have to get back to the bride-to-be. Did you really come here to see me again?"

"Sorry I didn't explain. I came to see the accounts manager about a logging job we're working."

Her smile didn't budge. She was a Southern girl, after all,

capable of swallowing disappointments like sweet tea on a hot day. "Sure."

Muted piano music filtered through the open area, giving visitors their cue to head up for the afternoon tea. She stepped out of the way and continued, "Alex can give you directions down at the concierge desk. I really should get going."

Zane nodded, but followed her toward the stairs. His hand shot out and rested on her arm, setting off a ripple of unexpected pleasure. His smooth baritone voice sounded near her ear. "Molly, what would you say to another date? Maybe this Friday night?"

She turned and tried to read his look. Did guilt over their last date drive him to ask her out now, or did he still harbor some interest in her?

His eyes softened, and so did her resistance. She really didn't care why he had asked her out again. "Sure. You can pick me up at Mom's—I know she'll want to see you again."

Molly could hardly concentrate on what the overly-tanned bride-to-be and her wedding planner were saying, although it certainly sounded as if this would be another unforgettable Greenbrier wedding. Hot pink peonies and green hydrangea. Steak and seafood. A Hollywood Glamour theme. Every detail was already nailed down, thanks to Heidi, the wedding planner she'd worked with numerous times before.

Heidi nudged her out of her stupor. "Did you hear what I said? I need one of your people on the lights in the ballroom at least twenty minutes before the end of the meal, just to be sure." She shook her head, short dark hair covering one of her warm brown eyes. "You're unusually quiet. You aren't even taking notes today. What's up?"

"Don't worry—I heard everything you said." Molly parroted her list of responsibilities back to Heidi. "I'll write it down as soon as I pick up my bag. I just got waylaid on my way to meet you."

"Oh. Okay." Heidi gave her a probing look. Finally she gave a short nod of satisfaction, as if she'd decided to take her word for it. "I know you're in high demand around here."

Molly offered an enigmatic smile. Sometimes she was in higher demand than she wished, especially with the male clientele. It wasn't unusual for her to be asked out on a weekly basis.

She took Heidi's arm. "Let's go to the ballroom so you can show me what you're looking for there."

When she trudged downstairs over two and a half hours later, Molly wanted nothing more than to take off her heels and collapse onto one of the blue overstuffed couches outside the wedding planning room. Instead, she walked by them into her office, grabbed her bag, and locked up. Then she meandered down the sloped hallway of shops, not even glancing at the latest displays of designer shoes and fashions. It seemed to take all her effort to push open the glass paned door to exit the building. Fumes from an idling green shuttle bus assailed her, so she hurried along a landscaped pathway toward her car. She was sure Zane had left long ago, but she found herself wishing for his company.

A lone man slouched against a tree not far from her Honda. He stood as she came closer. She fumbled in her roomy purse for her keys, hearing her sister's lecturing voice in her head. *Always be prepared*, Katie would say. *Have your keys ready and your finger on the car alarm. Make sure you constantly scan your environment.*

The large man walked toward her, causing her to search more frantically through her leather tote. Her hand skimmed past cough drops, lipsticks, and tissue packets. She had to find her keys.

Just as the man stopped short in front of her, her fingers closed around her Greenbrier keychain. She withdrew the keys, gripping one between her fingers like a weapon, just the way Katie had shown her.

"Excuse me, ma'am?" He was wearing a baseball cap pulled low over his eyes. His brown leather jacket looked well-worn. And his hand was in his pocket.

The urge to respond politely was so deeply ingrained, she nearly answered him. But Katie's voice rang even more loudly in her thoughts. *Run and scream! Get as far away as you can!*

Kicking off her heels, Molly turned and did just that. And when one of the groundskeepers hurried to her aid, she pointed toward her car and dropped into a heap on the grass, all her remaining energy spent.

He went to investigate, but came back shrugging. "No one's there, and I don't see anyone around," he said. "Maybe you'd better report it."

The man stood by as she shakily pulled out her cell phone and called Katie. Oh, she'd report it, all right—to her sister's fiancé Ace Calhoun, who happened to be a police officer.

Molly could tell Katie was upset when she walked into the lobby. Although her face reflected her normal librarian calm, Katie's long red hair had been tossed into a crooked ponytail and she wore a pair of oversized leather flip flops that probably belonged to their brother.

Ace, on the other hand, looked like a superhero with his

dark, short hair and blue police uniform. He ran his icy gaze over the lobby, flexing his jaw occasionally. Molly didn't care for guns, but she was relieved to see that Ace carried his, and she knew Katie always had a concealed gun somewhere on her person. Her sister didn't like to be caught unawares.

As she herself had been.

She stood and hugged Katie. "I'm so sorry to bother—"

"Don't you dare say that. Who was that creep? What did he do? Ace didn't tell me much."

Molly met Ace's serious blue gaze, then focused on Katie again. "Honestly, not much to tell. Just some guy in a baseball hat who approached me and started talking. I got worried because his hand was in his pocket and he was blocking my way to my car. I couldn't really make out his face."

Katie squeezed her hand. "Go on."

"Well, I heard your voice in my head, sis. So I started screaming and I hightailed it out of there."

"Good job! Nice to know all my self-defense lectures weren't in vain."

Ace's deep voice piped in. "The fact that he ran when you screamed means he was probably planning something. Anything unusual happen today? See anyone strange lurking around?"

"Just a regular day." Molly twirled one of her curls as she mentally rehashed the events of the day. "Well, just one unusual thing." She stopped abruptly.

"And that was?" Katie probed.

Molly didn't want to tell Katie about Zane. In fact, she'd never even mentioned that they'd dated last year. Katie would find endless ways to tease her about her lumberjack obsession, then she would tell their brother Brandon, and he would be even worse.

She turned to Ace. "Could I talk to you alone for a minute?"

Katie placed her hands on her hips. "Oh no, you don't. You know perfectly well that Ace tells me everything. We'll be married before you know it. No secrets, sis."

Molly's deep sigh drew even more attention their way than Ace's uniform had. "Okay. You remember Zane Boone from school? Went into the Marines right after graduation?" She rambled on before Katie could guess there was more to the story. "Anyway, I ran into him today—he's doing some kind of contract work at The Greenbrier. While we were talking in the lobby, he saw this man who was acting strange, so he sort of shoved me out of the way in case the guy was a threat. He really seemed to get his hackles up."

"And you think this strange man was the same guy you saw outside?" Ace asked.

She pondered a moment, then shook her head. "No, not really. That guy was all dressed up and thinner than the man by my car. But it was the only out-of-the-ordinary thing that happened today."

Katie scrunched her nose, a sure sign she was thinking hard. "Zane Boone, you say? Wasn't he that guy who played nearly every sport—you know, the one who looked like Heath Ledger? It seems like you had this huge crush on him..."

Actually, now he better resembled Captain America with a beard, but she wouldn't elaborate. "I'm trying to explain about the guy in the parking lot."

Her forbidding tone must've been clear, because Ace gave her a long look. "I'll go check around your car." He paced toward the front door. He'd been around the McClure family long enough to sense when a sisterly tiff was brewing.

"We'll be right behind you," Katie shouted toward his back. She took Molly's arm and lowered her voice. "Come on. Tell me everything, because you know I'll find out anyway."

By the time they reached Molly's apartment, Molly was having the visual aura that usually preceded her migraines. She was glad she'd let Katie drive for her, because the flashing lights and temporary loss of vision always forced her to pull over. Of course, this meant she'd been trapped with her younger sister, who had easily deduced that her high school infatuation with Zane was still in full swing. Luckily, she was too tired and out of it to care.

She hugged Katie and gave Ace's arm a friendly pat before they left. "Thank you so much for coming to help. Just tell Mom it was nothing, okay?"

Ace muttered something noncommittal and Katie shrugged. "We'll tell her the truth. Mom can handle more than you think."

Molly closed the door firmly, turning her deadbolt. She was ready for some pain relievers, a candlelit hot bath, and cozying into her favorite silk pajamas, even though it was hardly dark outside yet. Had she overreacted? Ace hadn't thought so. But sometimes she wished she didn't have to look out for herself quite so much. She worked hard to make her own money. Yes, she could buy all the upscale clothing and take-out she wanted. But at the end of the day, her heart was lonely because she had no one to share things with. Katie was engrossed in wedding plans, and Brandon lived in Arizona. Mom had always been a willing confidante when it came to romantic struggles, but now she was preoccupied with Katie's wedding, too.

The intoxicating thing about Zane was that even if she could hardly get beyond that impenetrable exterior, he was the kind of listener who seemed to genuinely care what she said. He wasn't playing an angle to get close to her, like most of the men she'd dated. He was one of the few men she'd ever met who would dare to contradict her.

As she sat by the tub and drew her bath, she wished she could call Zane to tell him about her mysterious run-in today. But she tamped down the urge to pick up her phone. She had to admit that Zane had the air of a taken man. Was it possible he still carried a torch for his lame ex-wife?

What Molly wouldn't give to have a chat with that woman.

As she slid into the hot, jasmine-scented water, her skin pinked up. She closed her eyes and let her thoughts drift, but they returned time and time again to Zane's thoughtful gray gaze. Friday night couldn't come soon enough.

3

Zane's dad pushed the salad bowl across the farmhouse-style table, his forehead wrinkling when Zane didn't take any. "Not hungry, son?"

Zane forced a smile that probably looked as fake as it felt. "I caught a late lunch with the guys."

In reality, he couldn't stop rehashing his run-in with Molly, wondering what he could have said differently. While it was true he'd cut things off abruptly after that last date, it wasn't out of callousness. It was because he wasn't ready to have his heart trampled again so soon after the divorce, and he knew a rejection by Molly would do him in. Molly was like those mythical women he'd read about as a kid—maybe Calypso or Helen of Troy—and he was certain that when she turned her full attention on you, it would be so intoxicating you could never return to your old life.

He redirected the conversation to safer ground—the logging business. "I figure I'll take that job over on Ellison Mountain."

Dad took a sip of iced tea. "You sure? Might be dangerous. Some tall trees up that way."

"We've got the equipment and our guys are experienced. Only one I'd worry about is Trevor because he's so young, and Brett keeps a close eye on him."

Mom returned to the table with a basket of rolls. "Fresh from the oven. Sorry it took a little longer to get those done inside."

Zane broke a roll open and applied a liberal pat of butter, his mom's home cooking whetting his appetite. "They look great. How's Basil?"

He'd never been close with his brother, who was ten years his elder. Basil had lived in Maine for seven years, and in that time, Zane had only seen his brother's wife twice.

Mom frowned. "He's afraid they're going to downsize at work, so he's job-hunting. Your father is trying to talk him into coming home and partnering with you in the business."

"Oh, really? Sure, that would be an option." Zane tried to feign excitement. Basil knew next to nothing about logging, and he was the type who didn't negotiate. It was his way or the highway.

Dad stole a glance at Mom, then fixed Zane with a serious look. "I should tell you that Krista called. She's worried that you might be under too much stress. I started thinking maybe Basil could handle some of your load. Besides, you always said you didn't want an office job. You could be out in the woods, chopping with your men."

Zane pushed his empty plate back, irritated that Krista went behind his back. "I'm out enough to suit me."

Mom leaned closer and covered his hand with hers. "You'd tell us if you were having problems, wouldn't you?"

His lips twisted. It was clear that Krista had given his parents an earful, but he didn't feel like chitchatting about his personal life. He began to gather dirty plates. "Lola might stay over Friday night, if that's okay?"

"Of course." Mom's concerned look was replaced with a

smile of excitement. "You know she's the joy of our lives. What's going on Friday?"

He turned from the dishwasher. He might as well be candid, since his parents would find out sooner or later. "I'm going out with Molly McClure again."

"That beautiful redhead?" Dad asked. "I wondered why you dropped her last year."

"John!" Mom nudged Dad's elbow.

"Well, I felt bad for her. The McClures are a good solid family. I had a lot of respect for Sean McClure."

"Sad he died so young." Mom's voice was subdued.

Zane nodded, but was forced to stifle an inconvenient yawn.

"You're not getting enough sleep," Mom scolded.

It was the truth. Ever since he'd realized someone was following him, he'd been on edge. His emotions were like a grenade, and one real or perceived threat was all it would take to pull the pin.

"I'm not," he acknowledged. "I'm going to head back now. Thanks for the meal, Mom."

Zane's rental cottage sat on the outskirts of the tiny town of Hemlock Creek. Although he didn't have a view of his neighbor's house, the fact he had a neighbor at all made him antsy. As he shoved his key in the door, he realized he hadn't stopped scanning the perimeter of his house for anything amiss.

And something was amiss.

He straightened, hand instinctively resting on his Colt 1911. The twilight was falling fast, but he could tell his front window was barely cracked. He was sure he'd locked it in the morning—it was one of his rituals, securing everything before he walked out the door.

Striding around the small front porch, he checked the gravel turnaround behind the house for another vehicle, but there was none.

Wiping sweat that beaded his brow, he looked at the window again. It was flush to the sill—closed.

He was seeing things.

He was losing it.

He forced himself to focus on something trivial. The pale blue paint chipping off the wooden steps. He needed to repaint. Maybe he'd pick some up tomorrow.

Resisting the uncalled-for urge to pull his gun, he stepped to the door and unlocked it.

He entered the living room and flipped on a light. After searching the open area, he did a quick sweep of the kitchen. Once he was satisfied the front rooms were empty, he turned to check the window. It was down completely.

But it wasn't locked.

He slid his Colt out, on full alert. And not without reason, because a metal shower curtain hook shifted in his bathroom.

Noiselessly edging toward the bathroom door, he used the toe of his boot to push it open. The camouflage curtain hung partially open, even though he'd pulled it closed after his last shower.

At the sound of a movement nearby, he spun to face the intruder who must have hidden in the laundry basket cubbyhole under the bathroom shelves. The masked man loomed toward him and Zane caught sight of a long, serrated knife. He fired the same moment the man lunged for his gun hand, so his shot went wide.

The edge of the knife caught the top of Zane's hand and drew blood, but the stranger's weapon hand had lost strength. Zane could see blood pooling near the man's shoulder, so his bullet hadn't been totally ineffective.

Seeing his opportunity, Zane grabbed the stranger's wrist and yanked him toward him, then brought his own elbow down into the crook of the man's arm. The man screeched and his knife clattered to the floor. He tried to squirm away, but Zane had no intention of letting him escape. Here was proof positive that he wasn't crazy, that someone had targeted him.

Wrapping an arm around the man's neck, Zane dragged him toward the bathroom door. Too late, he noticed the stranger pulling something from his belt with his left hand. He felt a sharp blade sliding across his stomach, and his grip loosened.

Taking the split-second opportunity, the stranger broke free and staggered toward the front door. Clasping his shirt to his seeping stomach wound, Zane tried to catch up with him, but the man picked up speed and hurtled down the steps toward a silver car that had raced up the driveway. Weakening, Zane made it to the porch, but the car was already throwing gravel as it tore back toward the main road.

He stumbled inside and managed to grab his phone before sinking into his faded couch. He dialed 9-1-1 and shakily explained his situation.

He didn't want to look directly at the bleeding gash for fear he might pass out. Grabbing the soft quilt his grandma had made, he whispered an apology to her before shoving it up against his stomach. At least his hand seemed to have stopped bleeding so he only had to focus on one injury.

Adrenaline kept him wired until he heard the ambulance wailing up his driveway, then his eyelids flickered closed. Voices surrounded him and he felt himself being lifted onto a stretcher, but the only thought in his head was that he hadn't called Lola today.

Zane drifted in and out as his wounds were cleaned and stitched, rousing only when they moved him to a hospital bed. Mom's face swam into focus, and she rushed to cover his bandaged hand with hers.

"Oh, my dear, dear boy. Who did this to you? They said just a tiny bit deeper and that cut would've gone right into your stomach muscle."

Dad stepped closer, placing a hand on Mom's shoulder. "Now, let's not drown him with questions just yet." Although Dad's tone was teasing, Zane saw the relief in his gaze.

"Break-in," Zane croaked. One of the last things he'd noticed was his video game system, lying on the floor. His big-screen TV had also been unplugged, as if they'd planned on taking those before he'd shown up and thwarted their plans.

A burglary attempt seemed the most likely explanation. It probably had nothing to do with him personally, as he'd initially suspected. Yet who would be willing to kill for such mediocre plunder?

"Did you see him?" Dad asked.

Before he could answer, a uniformed police officer stepped into the room. "He's talking?"

Mom nodded.

The cop held up a hand, as if to halt Zane from saying anything else. He looked at Zane's parents. "I'll need to ask him some questions. I'm sure you understand."

Mom's brow crinkled and worry edged her tone. She gripped Zane's hand protectively. "Are you up for that, sweetie?"

Zane took in the tall cop's serious blue gaze. The man was quiet but intimidating and built like he worked out daily.

"Mom, I'm a grown man and a police interrogation isn't going to hurt me. Thanks, but I'm okay."

The cop strode closer, flashing his badge. "Deputy Ace Calhoun, city police. Tell me what happened."

Zane liked the man's easy manner and straightforward approach. He recounted the events of his evening, finishing with an apology that he never managed to tear the intruder's mask off or get a license number. When he finished speaking, Deputy Calhoun rubbed his chin.

"Just to clarify—you said someone tried to run you off the road this morning, but instead of reporting this event, you went straight to The Greenbrier to handle business for your logging company?"

An uncomfortable silence fell over the room. Zane adjusted his thin sheet and blanket. Finally, he met the deputy's scrutinizing gaze.

"Yes, that's what I'm saying."

The deputy didn't smile. "You thought you could handle it."

"I guess so."

Mom interrupted, her cheeks pinked with pride. "Zane was a Marine, so he can handle most anything."

New respect flooded the deputy's features. "Sorry to be so pointed, but we had an incident at The Greenbrier today. I'm just trying to see if these events are linked somehow."

"An incident?" Now Zane's face mirrored the deputy's previous concern. "Was anyone hurt?"

Deputy Calhoun shook his head. "No, but a woman felt threatened by a man lurking near her car. When she went for help, the man bolted."

Zane's throat tightened. "Could you tell me who the woman was?"

"You know, it's strange, because she mentioned she'd

spoken to you earlier today. Said you'd been nervous about some fellow going into the casino?"

Zane pressed his palms into the bed. "You mean the woman was Molly? Is she okay? Was it the man I saw?"

The deputy crossed his arms. "First, I need you to explain your relationship with Molly to me."

"Of course. I dated her. I mean I'm dating her. We grew up together."

Deputy Calhoun's tightened lips slid into an understanding smile. "Well, nice to make your acquaintance. I'm engaged to Molly's sister."

4
_____

The last thing Molly expected to hear at 11:10 p.m. was Ace's deep, serious voice on the other end of her cell phone.

He explained that Zane had been attacked in his home and was in the hospital for knife wounds. By the time she finished talking to him, she'd changed clothes and twisted her bed-wild curls into a loose bun. Thank goodness her headache was nearly gone.

Trying not to think about the possibility of a stalker outside her apartment, she locked up and rushed down to her car. By the time Ace met her in the hospital parking lot and filled her in, she was as alert as if she'd drunk three cups of coffee.

Ace led her through Zane's hospital room door, then excused himself to call the sheriff. Molly glanced around, quickly taking in the scene. Mrs. Boone sat in an oversized chair, stroking the dark hair of a sleepy girl in her lap. Mr. Boone stood just inside the doorway, talking to a petite brunette. The woman shot a questioning look toward Molly as she walked past.

Zane welcomed her with a smile. "You came. Not the best day for either of us, was it?"

She was pulled in by his unexpected warmth and hesitantly stepped to the side of his bed. "You okay?"

"I lost some blood and I might scar, but it's nothing that will kill me."

"Thank goodness you survived. What happened?"

"You tell me your story and I'll tell you mine."

"My story seems tame compared to yours. Maybe it was all just in my head."

Zane's smile flicked into a frown. Under the fluorescent lights, his eyes looked more blue than gray, and they swept her face as if searching for hints of irony.

She tried to offer a reassuring smile before continuing. "It was just some stranger in the parking lot, blocking my way. I tend to freak out easily—just ask my sister. Not something I'm proud of."

Behind her, the brunette gave a slight cough. She had left off chatting with Mr. Boone and now stood at the foot of Zane's bed. She was slowly edging into Molly's personal space.

The woman piped in. "Yes, Zane, I'd like to hear your story in your words. Your Dad told me some of it."

Before Zane could speak, Molly turned and extended her hand to the woman. She suspected she was Zane's ex, since the small girl was probably their child, but she wanted to make sure.

"I'm Molly McClure—sorry I didn't introduce myself sooner. I was just worried about Zane and wanted to see him for myself."

"Didn't we all," the woman murmured. She accepted her hand and gave it a firm shake. "I'm Krista, Zane's ex-wife." She motioned to the girl, who had drifted to sleep. "That's our daughter, Lola."

"Very nice to meet you," Molly said. Her curiosity satisfied, she turned back to Zane. "Yes, please tell us what on earth happened."

By the time Zane finished his story, his eyes had taken on a slight glaze and it was obvious he could hardly stay awake. Molly realized with a start that the doctors had put him on some kind of pain medicine. She suspected he felt more miserable than he let on.

A strong man, and a proud one. He reminded her of her dad. It had taken her years to understand that Dad's unwillingness to show emotion wasn't because he *lacked* emotion, but because he kept a tight rein on it. Molly wasn't wired the same way. She figured if an emotion wanted to take her over for a while, she might as well let it. Bottling things up was unhealthy.

"Could I talk to you a minute?" Krista asked quietly.

Molly nodded and murmured a goodbye to Zane, hoping he wouldn't mention their date on Friday. She would contact him later to see if he even felt like going.

Krista took her elbow with a surprisingly firm grip, steering her past the Boones and Lola and into the hallway. She launched into her concerns, bypassing any niceties of small talk.

"What do you think—is he telling the truth?"

Molly blinked, hoping she'd misheard. "I'm not sure what you mean."

Krista pointed at her with a manicured burgundy nail. "I mean, is this some cockamamie story about a masked man breaking into his house with a knife?"

Molly held up her hands, as if she could stop this strange

line of questioning. "That's impossible. His stomach was sliced and he was cut on his hand."

Krista tapped a frenzied beat on the floor with her ankle boot. The nervous energy emanating from the birdlike woman was impressive. But Molly didn't like the mental trail Zane's ex was following.

Molly adjusted her stance, looming over Krista. "He wouldn't have hurt himself."

Krista narrowed her dark eyes. "You might think that. But you don't know him like I do. You didn't have to live with him after his last tour."

Anger edged into Molly's voice. "I'm sure active duty has changed him, but I've known Isaiah Boone half my life. One thing I'm dead-sure of is that he's *not* a liar. Now, I hope you'll excuse me. I know we've both had a long night."

She wheeled around and strode toward the elevator. Glancing at Krista when she pushed the button, she fought the urge to stick her tongue out as the doors slid closed.

When the morning alarm dinged on her phone, Molly wanted nothing more than to turn it off and stay tucked under her fluffy white duvet. But she had to go in and oversee a breakfast tea for a large bridal party.

Rummaging through her walk-in closet, she found her favorite black 50's style skirt with latticework detail on the hem, then chose a white and black blouse to match. Setting out her red heels and a red leather purse, she felt somewhat prepared for her day. She prayed the man who'd been lurking had fled The Greenbrier for good.

She was putting the finishing touches on her makeup when Katie's ring sounded on her phone. She pushed the speaker button.

"Sis, I'm getting ready to go." She brushed a couple of strokes of mascara on her lashes.

"I know. Ace told me about last night and wanted me to tell you he'll stop by when you get off work, just to see you to your car. What time are you cutting out of there today?"

Katie always made it sound like she didn't have a real job, which would have struck Molly as funny if she hadn't wondered the same thing herself. She would be thirty this year, and while she knew her dreams of being a top model or an actress were unrealistic, she wished she'd had other dreams to fall back on. It stung that her younger sister's goals of getting married and taking over the library would come to fruition long before Molly even figured out what her goals were.

"I'll probably leave around four, maybe five. I can call Ace beforehand." She teased her loose curls out with her fingers.

"You're coming over for *Gilmore Girls* and supper at Mom's, right? I think she's making peach pie, your favorite. Brandon's going to Skype in, too."

Molly stifled her sigh. She didn't feel like talking tonight, but Mom wouldn't be happy if she bummed out on family time, especially if she'd made peach pie.

"I'll be there." She gave a wobbly laugh. "As long as some psycho doesn't grab me first in the parking lot."

Katie's voice was calm but unyielding. "Trust me, that psycho would get a whole lot more than he bargained for if he tried something with Ace around."

Molly smiled, but it quickly faded. What if the psycho got to her when Ace wasn't around?

5

Zane refused to wear his ridiculous, gaping hospital gown one second longer than he had to. The moment the doctors gave the all-clear, he pulled on the clean clothes Mom had brought over and walked down the hall to check out.

Ignoring the flirtatious glances of the young woman at the nurse's station, he took his paperwork, went downstairs, and wandered into the parking lot. As he scanned the parking spaces, he realized he didn't even know if someone had dropped his truck off here. He should've called his parents first.

Did he even have his keys? He rummaged through the small bag Mom had dropped off, relief flooding him as he touched his keychain. Pulling out his cell phone, he called her.

"Mom, I'm on my way home. Is my truck here?"

"Hey, honey! I take it you're feeling better? That was fast."

He grunted what he hoped sounded like an affirmation. In reality, he probably should've taken the stronger pain medication they'd offered him. But he'd seen too many friends get addicted to the stuff in order to wipe out their nightmares, only to fall prey to the creeping oblivion of addiction. He refused to further torpedo his relationships with the people he cared for the most.

She continued. "Your dad parked the truck over around the left side of the building. Sorry it's so far from the entrance. You want me to pick you up?"

He walked that direction. "I'm fine. Thanks, Mom."

"Now listen, I just made a fresh batch of biscuits and gravy. I'll run those over for your lunch, okay? You sure you're okay to get back to your house?" Her voice faltered.

She hated it when Zane was in any kind of danger, although in reality he was better equipped to handle deadly situations than she was. *Once a mom, always a mom*, she'd said before he went to boot camp. *That means you always call me first, to let me know you're okay.*

But there were some things you didn't even tell your mom.

Rounding the side of the building, he caught sight of his truck. "I'm sure. I'll need a hot shower when I get back, but feel free to stop by around one. Love you."

"Love you, son."

Once he'd adjusted the driver's seat—Dad always moved it up because his legs were shorter—Zane slowly backed out of his space.

Two cars down, another car slid out of its space and inched up near his bumper.

Tailing him?

He paused, unwilling to push the gas. Surely his attackers hadn't followed him to the hospital? Ace would have been monitoring new admissions, watching for someone with a gunshot wound to the shoulder, but he'd mentioned nothing.

Zane checked his rearview mirror—the car wasn't one he'd seen before. The driver tooted the horn. Probably some worn-out family member, going home after spending all night at the hospital. He obligingly drove toward the exit. As he pulled into traffic, he spared a quick backward glance.

The car was nowhere in sight.

Unsure whether he should feel alarmed or relieved, Zane steadied his thoughts and focused on the road. When a tight pain squeezed at the stitches in his stomach, he clenched his jaw. His lips turned up in a grim smile. His injuries had been a high price to pay, but maybe now his shrink would take him seriously if someone started tailing him again.

⁓⁓⁓⁓⁓

At home, Zane jammed the blinking play button on his answering machine. Krista's voice filled the room—her message short, but nowhere near sweet:

"If you're listening, I guess you're back. Of course, Lola is worried half to death and wanted to stay home from school so she could visit the hospital again, but I made her go. Could you stop in tonight so she can see you're doing okay?"

He closed his eyes. Had there really been a time when Krista loved him? It seemed impossible. She hadn't taken long to get back into the dating scene after their divorce, occasionally begging off from picking up Lola when she and her dates stayed out too late.

Striding into the kitchen, he turned on his coffee maker, ready for a cup of stronger brew than what the hospital offered. He poured in enough hazelnut creamer to give him a serious sugar rush, then called Molly to see if they were still on for Friday night.

As her phone beeped and went to voicemail, he left an awkward message and hung up. He pictured Molly when she'd walked into his hospital room in the middle of the night —a gesture that had spoken volumes. He'd noticed how Krista had covertly studied Molly, like she was sizing her up.

And maybe she had good reason to do so. Molly had never been one to hedge around, and her actions showed she had a genuine concern for him.

Unlike his ex-wife.

After taking a long shower, Zane dug into Mom's biscuits and gravy. Once he downed a couple more cups of coffee, he felt refreshed enough to return to work.

First, he stopped in at the office, where his matronly office manager, Mrs. Gransky, filled him in on details of their upcoming logging jobs. True to form, she made a fuss over his injuries, saying she didn't know what this world was coming to when someone broke into a good man's house and tried to kill him.

Finally extricating himself from her sympathies, he drove the winding road up Ellison Mountain to meet his crew. The trees had lost their leaves, and he slowed to take in the gentle, blue-gray lines of the Appalachian ridges.

"Montani Semper Liberi," he whispered. He'd learned the West Virginia state motto as a teen, and it still spoke to him today. *Mountaineers are always free.*

He located his men easily enough by following the line of felled trees that carved a road to the primary cut site. He parked and hiked up a low hill, following the heavy sound of a tree thud.

As he approached, Trevor turned to greet him. "Did you see that? Brett hit a good shot."

Zane glanced at the tall, thick pine that now lay on the ground. "Sad to say, I missed it."

The young man's eyes were bright. "Fell right where he wanted to drop it, as usual. When are you going to let me be the high climber, Zane?"

"When you're older than twenty—a good bit older."

"Such a stick-in-the-mud." Trevor got serious. "You okay? We heard someone broke in and attacked you? Did it have something to do with that foreigner who showed up this morning?"

Zane's smile faded. "Foreigner?"

Brett made his way over in his steel-spiked boots, dusting wood chips off his reinforced pants. "You telling him about that guy this morning?"

Trevor nodded, stepping back as Brett shook hands with Zane and took up the tale.

"Foreign fella came all the way up here this morning— darker skinned and had an accent so thick, I could hardly understand him. From what I could make out, he'd been to the office. Mrs. G must've told him where to find us. Seemed like he wanted us to work a job all the way over in Logan County as soon as next week, but I told him we were booked. He said something about talking to my boss, but I said you weren't here. Got really nosy about when you'd be joining us on the mountain."

Trevor butted in. "Brett told him to get lost."

Brett shook his head. "Not in so many words, but I told him I wasn't sure and he should call first."

Zane rubbed at the bandage on his hand. Was it possible the same man who'd attacked him was now hunting him down? A few of his loggers carried guns to work and they could easily overpower one man, but what if several showed up?

He needed to talk with Ace and see if the cops had turned up anything. But first, he needed some good old-fashioned manual labor to clear his head.

"Thanks, Brett. I'll check on that. But I came to help out some." Before Brett could protest, Zane pulled on his gloves, took the chainsaw from Trevor, and walked over to the next small oak in their path. He made a top notch, ignoring the twinge in his stitches. After shouting a warning, he gave the final undercut that would fell the tree.

If only he could deal with the problems in his own life so easily.

Molly returned his call around 4:30, surprising him by expressing a desire to swing by his work site. "I'm tired of being cooped up inside and I'd like to see what lumberjacks do," she said.

"No strange men lurking around your car today?" Zane asked.

"Ace walked me out, and there were no weirdos in sight." She lowered her voice. "What about you? Are you doing okay? I can't believe they let you go back to work so soon."

Truth be told, he hadn't listened to the doctor's instructions or read the paperwork they sent home with him.

As his stomach growled, an idea struck him. "I'm doing okay, but I'm pretty hungry. Do you want to go out to eat from here? Just someplace casual?" He wouldn't mind company tonight, and if they had an early meal, he'd still have time to swing by and hang out with Lola.

There was a pause that lasted longer than he'd expected. He spoke into the silence. "I guess I'm putting you on the spot."

Molly cleared her throat. "Not really, and I'd love to, but my mom was fixing a family meal for us tonight. You want to come over and join us? Ace and Katie will be there, too."

He remembered Mrs. McClure from high school—she was the mom who sent cupcakes in for her kids' birthdays, who cheered loudest at ballgames, and who could always spare a minute for an encouraging pep talk. It would be a treat to see her again.

He agreed to the meal, then texted Krista to let her know he'd drop by around eight to see Lola. As he tucked the phone into his pocket, he couldn't help but reflect on how flexible Molly was. Krista never liked impromptu dates. Nor would she ever visit his work site, since she despised the outdoors.

He had to admit his shrink was probably right about one thing—to stop focusing on his failed marriage, he needed to start looking to the future. And Molly McClure, with her numerous charms, represented a future he hardly dared dream of.

6

After hastily calling Mom to let her know there'd be one more for supper, Molly pulled off her black jacket, untucked her blouse, and drove off toward Ellison Mountain. It wasn't a long trip, but it had the kind of unpredictable curves that kept her eyes glued to the road.

Why had she boldly offered to go to Zane's work site? Yes, it was true that she'd always been curious about the lumberjack profession, but only *mildly* curious. Maybe the real pull for her was seeing Zane in his natural habitat.

Which was the complete opposite of hers.

Growing up, Katie had been the one who camped out with Dad on their small boat, *The Vixen*, and Brandon had always enjoyed risky things like whitewater rafting. Both Brandon and Katie had gone shooting with Dad at the range. But Molly had spent most of her time at the mall, hanging out with friends and figuring out new ways to style her hair. She hadn't been bookish, like Katie, or witty, like Brandon. She'd just been pretty, so she'd learned to capitalize on her looks. Boyfriends came and went, just like her dates did now, but no lasting connections were made.

She supposed she had one talent—getting what she wanted. She nearly always did, when she knew it was something she had to have. More than once, her boldness and refusal to back down had pushed her on to success where others had failed.

She knew she was getting close when she saw several bands of felled trees. Catching sight of Zane's red truck, she pulled in behind it. A young man sauntered over to her door.

"You looking for the boss?"

The kid looked all of eighteen, a cocky grin on his dirt-smudged face.

"I sure am. He's expecting me."

"Molly, right?" He opened her door with a flourish. "I'm Trevor. Most of us are heading home now, but Zane will show you around. He's just over that hill." His gaze trailed down to her skirt and heels.

Sensing he would offer to walk her to Zane, she smiled. "I'll be fine. Thanks."

Trevor gave a brief tip of his hat and strode toward a small car parked nearby.

Picking her way through brush and logs, Molly made her way up the hill. At least her calves would get a thorough workout in her heels. Topping the small rise, she paused to take a breath. When she looked up, a logger dipped his head at her, and Zane turned from his conversation with the man. His intense look melted into a quirked smile.

She gave a quick intake of breath.

Standing there in dirty logger boots, wearing bright orange suspenders over two Henley shirts, his sleeves rolled up to expose the blond hairs on his forearms, Zane Boone looked for all the world like what a man *should* look like.

She returned his smile, trying to recover her poise. Zane ambled to her side as his logger friend left to gather up equipment.

"What do you think?" Zane gestured around them.

She propped one of her tired feet on a low tree stump, taking in the gaping spaces between the other stumps. The loggers had carved a passable dirt road for their larger machines, taking out bands of trees in the process. It looked stark and unnaturally empty.

"Well, to be honest, it looks kind of strange. I hate seeing that many trees down."

He looked thoughtful. "I used to think that, too. I'd visit my dad's sites and think how it looked apocalyptic, with trees strewn around and nothing but stumps all over the place. But thinning actually makes the forests healthier, taking out the smaller trees so the big ones can get stronger. Not to mention, it leaves less fuel for forest fires, if one should break out."

She nodded. "Makes sense, I guess."

He cupped a rough palm under her elbow, sending a little shiver through her. "Let's head back. It's getting dark and I don't want to keep your mom waiting. Plus, I promised Lola I'd stop in tonight."

For one candid moment, his smoke-colored eyes met her own and revealed an undercurrent of worry. Although he hid it well, he was still thinking about the break-in at his house. And why shouldn't he? If someone had attacked *her* in her own apartment, she would've broken her contract and moved out on the spot.

She decided against asking how he was doing, because a man like Zane wouldn't admit he was struggling. Instead, she simply started walking toward the car and said, "Sounds good."

The silence that fell between them seemed pregnant with unspoken words. Did Zane Boone ever open up to anyone?

She was willing to hang around and find out.

Molly rapped on the front door and Ace opened it, his short bangs standing on end. Apparently, Katie had been running her fingers through his hair again. After nodding at Molly, he clapped a brotherly hand on Zane's shoulder. "Made a break for it, did you?"

The two fell into easy conversation and Molly kicked off her heels before making her way to the couch. Her sister lounged in book-patterned leggings and an oversized oxford shirt that seemed to drown her. Probably Ace's. She'd tucked a couple of chopsticks into her loose bun.

Katie gave her a once-over. "Want to borrow a pair of jeans? That outfit can't be comfortable."

"Just because I'm wearing a skirt doesn't mean it's uncomfortable," Molly said.

"Well, aren't we snappy today?" Katie mumbled, turning back to the TV.

Mom emerged from the kitchen, wearing her favorite yellow apron that said *Make Me a Sunbeam*. She gave Zane a big hug. "Lawsie, the way Molly described your injuries, we were afraid you wouldn't get out of the hospital for a while. Thank the Lord you weren't hurt worse. Little Lola needs her daddy."

Molly's cheeks flushed. How was she to know that Zane would bounce back so quickly? Or had he? The way he'd winced when Mom hugged him showed he surely wasn't fully healed yet.

He grinned. "Thanks, Mrs. McClure. My parents were pretty worried, too."

"I'll bet. You tell your momma and daddy hello from me. Now y'all come on in for some hot stew and pie. Then we'll give Brandon a call."

The meal was uneventful, except for Katie and Ace's undisguised looks of longing. Molly wished they'd just get married already.

Mom stood to make the coffee, and Molly joined her to dish up the pie. The men started talking about weapons. Both Ace and Zane unsheathed and unloaded their guns and swapped. When Katie joined the conversation, Molly noticed the pleasant surprise on Zane's face.

Was that what he wanted? A woman who could handle a gun?

"My ex wouldn't even touch guns," Zane lamented as Katie dry fired his gun.

Molly sauntered up to his side, placing a dish of warm pie in front of him. The smell of cinnamon and peach seemed to loosen her lips.

"Our dad used to take us shooting." The moment she said it, Katie stared, and Molly could feel Mom's gaze on her back. She had just opened the door for her sister to expose her as a blustering idiot. Her whole family knew she wasn't the one who'd *shot* the guns at the range with Dad.

Ace raised an eyebrow, a twinkle in his eye. Molly gave him a death glare, and he discreetly tucked into his pie.

"I have an idea." Zane focused on Molly. "I've been meaning to get away to my cabin, and what better time than this weekend? I have a shooting range up there and we could hike around, or I could take you out on my pond in my boat. It's very relaxing."

Molly started shaking her head. She couldn't think of anything *less* relaxing than spending hours shooting or hiking. Katie was shaking her head, too.

Zane continued, as if musing to himself. "I've needed to take a break, you know? And after the break-in—"

Ace interrupted. "Which we're trying to get to the bottom of."

Zane nodded. "I know you are. But I don't want Lola staying with me until you find these guys. I've heard that sometimes burglars return to the same house."

"Sometimes, but I don't think you need to worry," Ace said.

Molly cleared her throat. She hated to shoot down Zane's invitation. "I don't think..."

Zane's lips twisted downward and he dropped his gaze to the table as if waiting for a blow. He really did want her to come along.

Inexplicable fresh hope infused her, one that laughed in the face of her sporty shortfalls. "I don't think I could pass up such a fun opportunity. Count me in."

Three pairs of eyes shot dubious looks her way, but Zane seemed oblivious. "It's a plan! Let's do that Friday night instead of a date."

She ate a bite of pie and tried to look thrilled, but her mind was whirring. There wasn't time for Katie or Ace to take her to the range to practice. She wished she'd paid more attention when Dad had shared shooting advice.

But she was going to make this work. It was worth it to have Zane's undivided attention at the cabin—at least for an hour or two, before he realized she was a total phony.

Brandon Skyped in, and Molly relaxed as she saw her brother's smile. He looked like he was sitting in his car, given the taupe upholstered headrest behind him.

"Hey, guys. Who's that?" Brandon jabbed a finger at the camera to point at Zane.

Zane spoke up. "Hey, Brandon. I was a little behind you in school. Isaiah Boone."

"Dude! You've grown up! What're you doing at Mom's?"

Zane glanced at Molly. "Um—"

"Wait—you dating my sister, man?"

"Chill, Brandon," Molly said. She turned to Zane. "Big brother gets a little protective."

Ace nodded, as if he'd been there, experienced that.

"Someone has to." Brandon blew a kiss at the camera. "Hey Mom, love you."

Mom leaned in as if she wanted to give her son a hug. "I miss you, honey. When are you getting a break?"

"I don't know. Hey, could you pan out the front window so I can see the weather there? I miss having a proper winter out here in Arizona."

Molly obliged, walking toward the window and turning the laptop around. "You know it looks pretty bleak this time of year."

"Who has that sweet hybrid there in the driveway?"

"Hybrid?" Molly lowered the computer and stared at the pale orange car that had parked directly behind hers. Zane only took a split second to move to her side. She could sense the tension radiating from him.

The car door opened. Zane pushed her down in one swift move before dropping into a shooter stance, hand on his reloaded gun.

Brandon's voice screeched from the computer. "Whoa, hold up! I see you there in the window, dude. It's *me* in the car! Surprise—I'm already home! Hey Ma, I hope you're stocked up on Dr. Pepper!"

7

Zane drove toward Krista's, musing over Brandon's unexpected visit. Zane had never met someone with a personality so opposite his own. Where he was disciplined, Brandon seemed to have no boundaries. Where he kept his emotions tightly hidden, Brandon blurted out whatever he thought.

It was refreshing, really.

Krista had always been passive-aggressive, hiding her true thoughts behind half-smiles and rueful sighs.

Funny how he was starting to see Krista in a whole new light. Molly was like a world unto herself, and she cast a very long shadow, whether she realized it or not. He reflected a moment, strangely unable to put his finger on what she had that so moved him. Obviously, she was gorgeous, but that hadn't even played strongly into his attraction to her. Maybe it was her unaffected nature, her up-front truthfulness he admired. The way she gave him her undivided attention, as if she really believed he had something worthwhile to say.

By the time he rang Krista's doorbell, he was so absorbed

in his contemplations of Molly, his "hello" came out stilted. Krista's dark eyes flashed in irritation, but Lola provided a welcome distraction as she danced down the carpeted steps toward him. She wore mesh angel wings and a fluffy purple skirt over her pajamas.

She fell into his open arms. "Ooh, Daddy. I was scared."

He wiped the warm tears from her cheeks. "I'm fine, baby girl."

As Lola launched into a detailed retelling of her "tough" day at kindergarten, in which her friend accidentally kicked her nose while dancing and her teacher made her write her name over because her L's were backward, Zane felt a burst of fatherly pride. Lola was everything that was right in the world—carefree, imaginative, and confident of her parents' love.

When her energy finally lagged, Zane gave her a hug and Krista shooed her off to bed.

"You seem happy tonight," Krista observed.

He knew she was probing, but he didn't feel like explaining. It didn't matter, because she rolled on without a pause.

"Dr. Christianson and I have talked about your recent injuries. We both feel it's safer if Lola doesn't have visitation with you this month."

He leaned against the wall. "Of course. I was going to suggest that myself. I'm hoping the police—"

She waved her hand as if his words were annoying pests. "Zane, you still aren't where you need to be in terms of recovery."

"Recovery? I'm not an alcoholic or an addict, Krista."

She crossed her arms. "No, but you have PTSD."

"That doesn't mean I'm not making progress."

Krista's lips formed a tight line.

Sudden weariness claimed him and he realized he'd overdone it today. He didn't want to argue. "My parents will be glad to have Lola stay with them this month."

Her dark eyes glinted. "Only this month? Then back to your house?"

He tried to read what she was thinking, but her displeasure repelled him like a force field.

"Or until the police find the burglars," he added.

She nodded. "Mm-hm. Okay. I'll work things out with your parents. Good night, Zane."

All the way home, he tried to understand how he had failed Krista, how he had turned her ardent love into the disapproval he felt every time he was around her.

Trudging up the steps to his front door, he hardly had the energy to check things, but he turned on his phone flashlight and made a quick scan of the lock and windows. Everything seemed untouched.

His spirits deflated, he dropped his clothes to the floor and tumbled into bed. As he dozed off, a vivid memory rose up and toyed with his mind yet again:

He lay on the gritty rooftop in Afghanistan, the windowless compound in his sights. Through his scope, he watched his Infantry unit use a water charge to blow the mud wall that surrounded the buildings. Before the dust could settle, they breached the main building, moving inside in a quick, practiced line.

The Marines were pushing through the area, hoping to funnel their primary target, terrorist leader Walid Habib, toward a kill zone at the town border, where the Abrams tanks and Bradley armored personnel carriers were in position.

All too soon, a loud explosion tore into the air. His men rushed out, a smoke cloud trailing behind them. He honed his sight on the door, but it couldn't penetrate the thick gray vapor huffing out.

He counted helmeted heads...one, two, three and four, five, six, seven. The eighth man must be trapped inside.

His spotter groaned as he followed the action with his binoculars.

"Did they pop one of those Russian grenades, you think?"

"Looks like it, with all that dust."

"Any chance of sniping one of them?"

"Not unless they run outside where they're exposed."

The ground unit had reconnoitered. Two Marines jogged toward the back courtyard and two pushed into the front door while the others held positions outside.

A sole man stumbled out the back door, his hands held high. With his loose pants and tunic, he looked to be a native...until Zane looked closer at his exposed arm, which bore a henna marking of a snake entwined with crossed swords—Habib's personal calling card.

He was looking at Habib himself. The Marines quickly pinned him to the ground, but they seemed to be more focused on whoever remained inside.

They didn't recognize the threat right in front of them.

As most of the men pushed back into the building, one carrying a metal detector to find IEDs and weapons, Habib rolled over. The Marine who guarded him stepped closer, but he couldn't possibly see the grenade Habib had rolled out of a fold in his tunic.

Zane took the shot before the terrorist could pull the pin. The Marine stepped back, realizing what had happened.

Pines, Zane's spotter, rushed to his side. "What's going on?"

But Zane had no time to explain. The Marine had alerted his unit, and three Marines raced from the back door to join him. In his peripheral vision, Zane caught a slight movement by the front of the building.

Scoping that area, he was confused to find no one standing

near the front door or gate. All he saw was a small group of women and children who stood gaping at the ragged hole the Marines had blown in the wall. He scanned over the onlookers, but saw nothing that resembled a weapon.

Suddenly, another grenade exploded outside the front door, causing the women and children to scatter. Zane couldn't see what was going on as the Marines swiftly secured the front of the compound.

The ground leader radioed him as the cloud dissipated. "Building is clear. We think two escaped and took one of ours hostage."

"Who's missing?" How had they escaped his sights? He had seen no one running away.

"Sitko."

Staying focused on the Marines and the compound, Zane flexed and relaxed first one foot, then the other. It was the only way he could dispel extreme distress without altering his position.

Sitko was only twenty-two and was one of the cheeriest soldiers Zane had ever met. He was constantly joking and brought smiles into the most stressful situations. Zane had met Sitko's mother before they shipped out and she had clung to her son like a lifeline.

Sitko.

He had lost Sitko.

Zane jolted awake from his living nightmare. This time, he'd envisioned what had really happened, but usually, his imagination filled in gory details. Once he'd dreamed of Sitko, a bloody gash across his stomach, screaming for Zane as terrorists dragged him by the arms up that dirty street. Another time, he'd seen Sitko, his white-blond hair bloody, his pale face blue and purple with beatings, opening a cavernous, toothless mouth before terrorists cut off his head.

He could tell himself a million times that there was no way he could've stopped them. He'd had no line of sight after that explosion.

But it didn't matter. Sitko's blood would always be on his hands.

8
_____

As Friday afternoon rolled around, Molly slipped into one of the elegant Greenbrier bathrooms to change, hoping she'd brought the right clothing for Zane's outdoor expedition. Katie had let her borrow a lined, cargo-style jacket, which was probably two sizes too big and certainly did nothing for her figure. Nevertheless, it was supposed to get cold tonight, and they would likely be outside the entire time. Zane had mentioned something about cooking food on a grill. Even if he made hot dogs, which she didn't really care for, she'd gladly eat them just to spend a little more time with him.

Pushing the white wooden bathroom stall door open, she stepped into the sitting area, where she had more room to pull on the wool socks and sturdy knee-high boots her mom had loaned her. They were far too dated to be stylish, and she cringed as a couple of well-dressed guests eyeballed her unusual garb.

She wished she'd had time to buy new boots, but this was such a last-minute plan. Grabbing her tote, she shoved her work clothing and heels inside, then pulled out her makeup bag. If nothing else, her face would look nice.

She chose her favorite lipstick, Blushing Ginger. It was the perfect peachy-nude shade that brought out the gold in her eyes. She re-applied mascara and eyeshadow, tousled her hair so the curls lay better, and determined to rock her adventure-girl look.

As she walked out into the shop-lined hallway, a woman who was sitting nearby glanced away quickly, almost as if she'd been watching the bathroom door. It was hardly standing room only inside, so her expectant interest didn't make sense. Molly paid more attention to the woman, who was now trying hard to ignore her. A sweeping curtain of black hair. Medium-tan skin with gold bracelets jingling at her slim wrists. Her fitted pants and tailored shirt spoke of wealth. Molly couldn't get a good look at her side-turned face, but her profile was striking, almost like that famous bust of Nefertiti. Probably just a bored guest, embarrassed to be caught gaping at nothing.

But as Molly walked toward the door, her heavy lug soles squeaking, she could feel the woman's gaze burning into her back.

She stepped into a courtyard that was edged with boxwoods and smaller magnolias and immediately caught sight of Zane, who had somehow managed to make a turtleneck sweater, jeans, and boots look upscale. With his beard and slicked-back hair, he could pass for a hipster, but his personality was quite the opposite.

He stood and waved, giving her a thorough once-over as she drew closer.

She smiled. "I know—not my normal attire."

He returned her smile. "It is...different. Not really you,

somehow. But it's appropriate for tonight." He pointed toward the side parking lot. "I'm over there."

She hoped her visit to his cabin would convince him that this outfit wasn't so far off from who she was...or at least who she *could* be. She strode to the passenger door of his oversized truck, opened it, and launched herself up onto the leather seat as if she rode in trucks every day.

What she didn't count on was that whoever previously sat in the seat must have had really short legs. Her knees bashed into the dashboard with a loud thud, and she had to pinch her lips together to stifle a squeal. She waited until Zane shut her door to try to massage the pain away.

He walked around and climbed into the driver's seat. Before he turned the key, he gave her a long look. "You brought gloves? A hat? They're saying it could snow some."

Wishing those concerned, luminous eyes had lit on her for a more poignant reason, she gave a light reply. "Sure did, thanks."

As they wound around the familiar mountain curves, she felt some of the tension of her strange week release. "Your stitches healing well?"

"They are." He gave a short laugh. "Poor Lola. She didn't like seeing her daddy hurt. Good thing I'm not on active duty anymore."

"Well, it must seem like you are—I mean you did just survive a knife attack in your own home," Molly said, examining his face.

His gaze stayed on the road ahead, and she knew she'd sent him deep into his own thoughts. Sunlight flickered over his honey-colored hair and eyelashes. She followed the line of his Roman nose that tapered to slightly flared nostrils. His angled jaw was tightly clenched.

His focus was so extraordinary, in fact, she wondered if he'd forgotten she was sitting next to him.

She turned to look at the rolling valley stretching below them. They had climbed at least halfway up a mountain.

Zane's thoughtful voice broke the silence. "I'm not convinced my attack was just a bungled robbery attempt, but my psychologist and my wife—sorry, *ex*-wife—would claim I was being paranoid if I made a big deal of it. So I haven't mentioned my theory to the cops."

"I'm listening." She tried to cross her legs but they were folded tight under the dashboard. She really needed to figure out how to adjust the seat, but didn't want to distract him.

"I'm starting to wonder if I've been put on a watch list— kind of like a terrorist watch list, only in reverse. The terrorists might be looking for *me*."

"I don't understand. Why?"

"I was a sniper in the Marines."

"I know, but what does that have to do with it?"

"I was a very *good* sniper."

She chilled as she realized what he was saying. "You took out someone big."

"More than one."

Zane fell silent. He wasn't going to elaborate, that was for sure. While she appreciated the humility that was at the core of his personality, she wondered if that humility had made him downplay the danger he could be in. If he'd been placed on a hit list, how long would it take the terrorists to get to him here in the United States? Was this a common occurrence, terrorists bumping off ex-snipers?

He glanced in his rearview mirror before quickly pulling off onto an unmarked dirt road. The rutted lane meandered downward. Molly remained quiet, following Zane's lead.

The forest they drove through finally opened up to a clearing, where a large pond sparkled in the sunlight. Behind the pond, a cedar-shingled cabin was tucked into the trees at the foot of a small mountain. Two rough-built storage shacks sat on a slight incline to the right of the cabin.

He nodded toward the storage buildings. "My boat's in that one. Just a little square johnboat, but sturdy for fishing. I cleaned the other building recently to make an extra sleeping space, in case, by some fluke, my family ever plans a getaway here."

"Oh, that's right. You have an older brother, don't you? I never knew him in school."

"That's because he's ten years older than us. Kind of a whole different generation, really."

"Married? Kids?"

"Just married. He didn't want to have kids and she agreed, I guess."

"Too bad. You'd make a great uncle."

He flashed a brilliant smile and she returned it. Their gazes lingered a moment before he opened his door, then came around to open hers.

"I'll give you a tour." He offered his arm with a flourish. She jumped down to take it, and he led her toward the cabin. She relished the feel of his taut muscles, clinging to his forearm as they made their way across the bumpy grass terrain.

He stopped and gestured toward the woods at the edge of the pond. "My shooting range is near a tire bunker I built over there. I thought we could get some shots in while it's light, then eat before I have to get you home. I'll have to take my guns out of the safe first, though. It's too late in the day to fish, but if you wanted to take a spin in my boat, we could do that, too."

She smiled in the face of his uninhibited eagerness. It was nice to see him so enthusiastic about something, even if she couldn't share his excitement. Although she couldn't hide from Zane's date plan forever, maybe she could stall him a little.

"So tell me about Lola," she said, slowing her walk.

"Well, now." He gave her a thoughtful glance. "She's obsessed with ballerinas and mermaids and possibly T-Rexes, although I think deep down they terrify her. Her hair shines like silk after it's been washed. She has a knack for reading people, like she can see into their souls."

She wished he would keep talking, but they had reached the green cabin door. She released her grip on his arm so he could put the key in the lock.

"Sounds like an interesting little girl. Do you think she likes redheads?"

Zane chuckled. "I don't know how anyone *couldn't* like you, Molly McClure."

It seemed he circled around compliments but never gave her one directly. Did he find her attractive or not? Did he have any interest in dating her beyond this or did everything hinge on her gun savvy this evening?

When he pushed the door open, a waft of stale air escaped. He strode inside, opening windows. He motioned to a well-worn leather couch. "Please, have a seat. This might take a few minutes."

As he busied himself removing guns and ammo from the safe, she observed his skilled movements. There were a couple of longer guns and then some kind of handgun—maybe a revolver?

One thing was clear: Zane Boone knew how to handle a firearm.

She glanced around the one-room cabin, impressed with its worn-in style. Red plaid curtains hung on the windows, and the plaid theme was repeated on the throw pillows and kitchen towels. A cozy wood stove occupied one corner of the sitting area, with a good-sized stockpile of wood sitting in a large tote nearby. Maybe he would eventually light a fire to ward off the evening's chill, which seemed to be deepening.

Worn books lined a wooden ledge that seemed to have been built for that purpose. She stood, skimming over classic titles like *War and Peace* and *The Jungle Book*.

She glanced into the bathroom, which had a shower and sink. The galley kitchen not only had a sink, but an oven, too.

"Do you have electricity out here?" she asked.

He looked up from the zip-up carrier bag he'd placed the guns in. "I have a generator, so I use that for the water pump, lights, and stove. But there's no hot water."

"Gotcha." She strode to his side. "Can I help?"

"No, but thanks. I have it all loaded up. We'll just drive the truck to the range to save time, since the sun will be setting in the next hour or so."

It seemed to take no time at all until they were standing in front of Zane's targets. He had one that looked like a mannequin torso on a pole, as well as several metal gong-style targets.

"Let's start out with something you're probably more familiar with, since your dad was an FBI agent," he said, pulling his light brown handgun from his belt holster. "This is a Colt 1911—a close quarters battle pistol. It's already loaded, so be careful."

He turned the gun around and extended it to her, the barrel pointing toward the ground.

Her fingers trembled, and she couldn't bring herself to take it. "It looks bigger than my dad's pistol."

"Not sure what he had, but you're right, this is a larger-sized handgun. Would you rather start with a rifle? I have a nice .50 caliber I built myself."

Was that even safe? Besides, rifles were probably more complicated. "Do you have anything smaller?"

"Hm. I have a revolver, but it's a .45. Still, it might be a little easier to hold than my Colt. Your fingers are long, so I don't think you'd have any problems."

Wishing for a natural catastrophe to divert Zane's attention, she feigned confidence. "No problem, I'll start with this 1911 and then work my way up to that .45."

He gave a short laugh. "Actually, the 1911 is a .45, too."

What genius had come up with ten different ways to say the name of the same type of gun? She shrugged, trying to give nothing away. "I thought so."

He pushed the gun closer and she realized she still hadn't accepted it yet. Wrapping her hands around the barrel, she pulled it closer, still aiming at the ground.

He shot her a quizzical look. "You'll want to put your shooting hand on the grip."

She nodded. The *grip*? Must be the textured section. She turned toward the targets, propping the gun on the palm of her left hand as she loosely held onto what she hoped was the grip.

"Okay." She looked at him, hoping her desperation wasn't evident.

"Okay," he slowly repeated, his gaze trailing from her hands to her face. "Molly." He looked like he was wrestling with what to say. "It must've been a while since you went shooting with your dad, right? Why don't I give you a little refresher demonstration first?"

She turned toward him, startling as he dodged close to her side. She realized too late she had pointed the gun right at him. He wrapped his fingers over hers, then retrieved his Colt.

"Let's just begin at the beginning." His breath tickled her ear.

She exhaled a silent breath, but hurried to disguise her relief. "You certainly are a thorough instructor, aren't you?"

9

It had been obvious Molly didn't know how to shoot, from the moment she took his Colt. But the fact that she'd tried to hide it—that she'd led him to believe she knew exactly what she was doing—somehow made her charade all the more endearing.

Once he'd gone over basic gun safety with her, demonstrated shooting techniques, and let her dry fire, she'd grown more comfortable handling his Colt. In fact, she seemed to enjoy it, since the gun fit her hand nicely.

He watched as she squeezed the trigger. Once again, she shut her eyes just as the shot discharged.

"Eject your magazine and dry fire a bit more," he said. "Then reload and shoot in rapid succession. That's what some shooters do to minimize their tendency to blink."

She looked dubious, her hazel eyes tinged with the same gold of the sunset.

"Believe it or not, even seasoned shooters sometimes blink," he continued.

"Do you?"

He had to be honest. "No, but I've been shooting all my life. It's my job. Well—it *was*."

She did as he'd asked and began to dry fire, but she was leaning backward. He moved closer to adjust her stance, placing his hand on her back and pushing gently. "Lean forward from the waist and don't forget to bend your knees a bit."

The moment his hand touched her, she turned and caught his gaze. And she held it a moment too long.

He couldn't look away. If eyes were the windows to the soul, Molly's soul was full of hopefulness and some kind of dauntless charisma.

It was an irresistible blend.

Drawn to her warmth like a heat-seeking missile, he leaned in, catching her lips with his own. Slipping a hand beneath her bulky jacket, he pressed her closer. But instead of reciprocating the kiss, she abruptly pulled her head back.

"Um...I still have your gun."

She had wisely pointed it at the ground, but it was loaded. What foolishness had possessed him to ignore basic gun safety, to throw his cautions to the wind? He had sworn he would never get involved with a woman again. He had given Krista all he had to give, and it hadn't been enough.

He took the Colt and unloaded it. Darkness was falling fast. "I guess that's it."

She looked like he'd smacked her. "That's *it*?"

"I need to get these weapons packed up, then cook you up some supper." He noticed her shiver. "Also, the weather's changing fast. Smells like snow, don't you think?"

Molly wasn't so easily distracted. As he tucked his rifles into the bag, she touched his forearm. "Zane, we had a moment there. I didn't mean to ruin it, but I also didn't want to shoot your foot off."

"I know. No problem."

"But I wanted you to keep kissing me."

"I know." He set the bag in the back of the truck and opened her door.

Still, she persisted. "You didn't. Why?"

Molly was like a dog with a bone, and he knew she wouldn't give up until he gave her some reason, conflicted as his thoughts were.

"I'm probably not the best person for you to get involved with right now, given my recent near-deadly encounter."

She stared at him expectantly, as if she knew he wasn't telling her everything. But how could he explain that he still struggled with the nightmares that had turned him into a reclusive husband and inattentive father?

He finally gave in and added, "To be honest, I'm not in the best place right now."

Molly's eyes took on a sheen, but she simply nodded. He appreciated that about her—she was never at a loss for words, but she knew when he needed silence.

"That said, I really enjoyed that kiss," he added. "You're quite a handful, Molly McClure, but I like that about you."

Molly smiled, but he saw the flicker of disappointment in her eyes. He wished he hadn't been so brusque, but he had done it out of respect for Molly. She was an all-or-nothing woman, just like he was an all-or-nothing man.

Zane rolled up the truck windows when he noticed Molly pulling her jacket tighter. She gazed out the window, seemingly captivated by the lemony yellow sunset that faded into a deep lavender. Snowflakes had started falling and were building up on his windshield. If he was going to use the grill, he needed to move quickly.

Molly helped him unload the truck, then he stashed the

guns in the safe before heading out to the deck to fire up the grill. When it was hot, he arranged the marinated chicken, potatoes, and asparagus on the grill racks. Snowflakes hit the briquettes and sizzled.

Molly's eyes widened. "I thought you'd do hot dogs."

"There's more to grilling than hot dogs. Trust me, I'm a real 'grill daddy'—lots of time in the field."

At her laugh, relief flowed through him—maybe he hadn't totally ruined things between them. Then again, she might not show it if he'd hurt her by refusing a second kiss.

"Would you mind starting a fire in the wood stove?" he asked. "The lighter's in that left-hand drawer, and there's kindling in that basket near the wood."

She blinked, but responded quickly. "Sure."

As he focused on adjusting the temperature of the grill, he heard her shuffling around with her task. By the time he grabbed a sturdy paper plate and piled the chicken on it, he peeked inside. She was kneeling next to the stove's door, flicking the lighter repeatedly.

"Having trouble?"

"A little."

He removed the crispy potatoes, shook a little parmesan on top, and wrapped them in tin foil. Then he walked inside and peered into the stove.

She had been far too sparing with the kindling and had set it in a wide circle around the bigger logs. The pine cones didn't touch each other or the wood itself.

There was no way she could start a fire that way, much less keep one going.

She'd never made a fire before.

Apparently, Sean McClure hadn't taught his children basic survival skills, which Zane would've expected from a highly-trained government operative.

Once again, though, Molly was acting as if this were the

most normal fire-starting setup in the world. A short laugh burst from his lips, but he covered it quickly with a cough when Molly shot him a questioning look.

"Let me check that lighter," he said.

When she handed it to him, he began to scrutinize it as if that were the problem. "Would you mind pouring us some of that sweet tea? That's another thing I'm good at, by the way— I'm a great sweet tea brewer."

"A Grill Daddy and a Sweet Tea Brewer. I'm in luck tonight." She walked out toward the food on the deck table.

He hastily rearranged the kindling, lit it, and slammed the heavy iron door. Just in time.

Molly swept back in, toting two large plastic cups. "You know, I thought I heard something over in one of those sheds."

He washed his hands at the sink. "What did it sound like? Raccoons come around sometimes, and skunks tend to get active this time of night."

"It sounded like something fell. Maybe an animal knocked something over?"

"Probably. Luckily, bears aren't really interested in my cabins because I don't store food here. I'll check it out, but let's eat first."

Molly filled her plate and followed Zane to the small table inside. Before digging in, she pulled her phone from one of her jacket pockets. She punched at the screen. "You don't have any cell service at all? What if there's an emergency?"

"You still worrying about that raccoon?" He grinned. "Seriously, just up that hill to the back of us, there's wireless reception. So I'm not totally stranded. Just really secluded."

"I'll say. I hope you learned medical skills in the Marines."

He popped a small red potato in his mouth. "Are you planning on getting injured?"

She dabbed her mouth with a napkin. "Of course not. But you should always bring someone up here with you."

Was she angling for another invitation? He certainly hoped so.

Before he could formulate a response, she spoke again. "Did you ever think you were going to die when you were out there? Was it Afghanistan?"

He nodded. "But I knew I was ready to go, even though I'm not a real churchgoer."

"Why aren't you?"

Mom and Dad were always asking him the same question. "I guess when you see people die—good people—you ask yourself how a good god could let that happen." He blinked back embarrassing tears as he thought of Sitko's joking antics, his carefree love of life. Gone.

Molly leaned in. "But wouldn't that be putting yourself in the place of God? I mean, you're coming at it like your reasoning could possibly equal His, like you could understand the big picture of what's good and what's not."

"I...hadn't thought of it that way, actually."

"I just figure if we really believe God *is* God, we have to believe the Bible 100 percent, you know? So we have to believe what God says about Himself."

"You're a deep girl, Molly."

Her mellow laugh broke the tension. "No way. I just have a great pastor who talks about this stuff a lot. How to give an answer for our faith." She speared a piece of asparagus. "Hey, you should visit church with me sometime."

Some strange part of him stirred, a part he'd buried during his first tour of duty. "Maybe I will."

A loud rap sounded at the door, startling them both. Zane felt for his Colt, forgetting if he'd returned it to his holster. He hadn't. That meant he'd left everything in the bag he'd shoved in the safe.

He jumped up and rummaged through the kitchen drawer for the sharpest knife he could find. When Molly stood, he placed a finger on his lips so she would stay quiet. He was probably being overly cautious. Maybe someone had made a wrong turn, or maybe a distant neighbor had seen their vehicle and decided to pay a call. Or maybe his parents had decided to show up.

He strode over and opened the door just a sliver, and his heart shot into overdrive once he saw the familiar figure standing outside.

He'd recognize that white-blond hair anywhere, because he'd seen it hundreds of times in his nightmares. Maybe he actually *had* lost his mind, because he was staring at a ghost.

Sitko.

10

"You're a hard man to find, Isaiah Boone." Sitko spat tobacco juice into the fast-thickening layer of snow on the doorstep. He brushed past Zane, deliberately banging into his arm in the process. This was no ghost.

Zane couldn't hide his surprise. "Wha—what happened?"

Sitko laughed, but there was no mirth in it. Hatred tinged his words as he wheeled around. "Bet you asked yourself that a lot, didn't you, Boone? It was a riddle I pondered every time they strung me up and beat me like a piñata. I just kept thinking, what happened to make Boone miss that open shot when those *hajjis* hauled me out the front door? Why didn't he take them out before the grenade distracted everyone?"

"But I didn't see you. I looked. There was no one."

"I'm sure you tell yourself that." Sitko sauntered over to Molly in his heavy black boots. Though her eyes were wide with fear, Molly stood straighter as he approached.

"And what have we here?" He turned back to Zane. "A buddy of mine said he saw your lady friend and spoke to her, but she wasn't inclined to chat."

Zane processed what Sitko was saying. Sitko's "buddy" was Molly's parking lot stalker.

He felt blood rushing through his veins as his anger boiled up. This wasn't the Sitko he'd known in Afghanistan. This was a new, cruel Sitko who was looking at Molly like a wolf looked at a rabbit.

Zane took four long strides and shoved himself between Sitko and Molly.

He jabbed a finger at Sitko. "You need to back off."

"But why, when I've come this far? Like I said, you're a hard one to pin down. Who would've guessed you'd go into the lumber business up in hillbilly country?"

When Zane maintained silence, Sitko pulled an exaggerated frown. "I thought we'd have a great reunion and catch up on old times. Like, say, that time you shot me in the shoulder."

"I didn't—"

"It was just the other day, in your house, remember? You've set yourself up pretty well, but that house could use a little work. Or did you really think I came for the TV?"

"That was you."

Sitko sank into the couch, stretching an arm out as if he owned the place. "I'll admit my knife skills aren't what they once were, before...well, before they took me."

From the newer scar on Sitko's forehead, Zane guessed the terrorists had done terrible things to him. But he knew better than to open that door. The man was out for revenge and was probably unhinged enough without rehashing his torture. Yet...how had he escaped?

Sitko watched him closely, then nodded ever so slightly. "Putting the pieces together, are you?"

"They turned you?"

"Not really. Someone in power just took pity on me, that's all. Now I hate to cut the small talk, but seriously, you know

I'm going to kill you both. I'd like to have a bit of fun with the redhead first. I wouldn't advise you to interfere—after all, you *owe* me." Sitko stood, pulling his own gun from a belt holster. He motioned toward the bathroom. "Drop your knife and head in there, *brother*."

It was a mockery of their Marine code. *Semper Fi* meant nothing to Sitko anymore. They were no longer brothers.

Zane dropped his knife and took a couple of steps toward the bathroom. Abruptly, he whirled around to face the gun. Slamming his open palm into the wrist of Sitko's trigger hand, he flipped the firearm out of it with his other hand in a move he'd learned in a Krav Maga class. Sitko brought his knee up, but Zane dodged and jabbed him in the shoulder he'd shot.

Sitko gave a shout of pain, glaring as he spat out a threat. "You're not getting out alive, Boone. I've got people outside."

"Where?"

"Wouldn't you like to know?"

Molly shifted her gaze toward the back of the building, reminding Zane she'd heard a noise in the storage shed. The others were likely holed up there.

He refocused on his old friend. "Why? Because you think I let you down?"

Unnatural elation twisted Sitko's mouth into a grin. "Because you never lived there—with the people. Once I did, I realized that Habib wanted to help them."

Wood heat had made the cabin toasty. Zane swiped sweat from his forehead, keeping the gun poised on Sitko. "You don't believe that. He would've killed his own people."

"No, he wouldn't have."

"How do you know what his plans were? He's dead now."

"We were lied to. We were fighting the wrong war."

Zane had no time for this. He had to disable Sitko so he could eliminate any other threats on his property.

He shoved Sitko's gun into the back of his waistband, then turned to Molly. "Could you bring me some of that black paracord in the drawer next to the sink?"

Molly's steps were a bit unsteady, but she managed to retrieve it for him. She avoided his eyes as she handed it over, and he realized she was on the verge of tears. Refocusing on the task at hand, he knotted the thick cord around Sitko's wrists and led him toward the bathroom.

"Lock the door and stay low," he instructed over his shoulder.

⁂

Molly was shaking so badly she could hardly put one foot in front of the other. How ridiculous, how minuscule her plans to impress Zane seemed now. When it came to a real survival situation, she was completely helpless. A pretty face, waiting to die.

No. She wouldn't let her thoughts go there.

She fumbled at the locks and had nearly turned the bottom one when shoes crunched toward the door. Even as she registered that it must have snowed considerably in the brief time they'd been indoors, she hurried to slide the chain lock into place.

Behind her, she heard a dull thud in the bathroom. She only hoped that meant things were under control. Zane hadn't seemed as terrified as she was, but she knew he was trained to hide his fear and to act in the face of it, just like her dad had been. Zane had disarmed the rogue gunman with his bare hands, but he'd made it look like something he did every day, like brewing up a cup of morning coffee. Still, if the man had been a fellow Marine, which is what it sounded like, she was sure he was a formidable enemy.

With both locks secure, she stepped back and scanned

the room, trying to ignore the rattling noises outside the front door. She needed a place to hide, but there was none. She hurried toward the back door and inched it open, accidentally allowing a layer of snow to push into the room.

She peered out, and although it was dark, she could make out at least four inches on the ground. Thick flakes covered her face in seconds. This was no light snow—it looked like a blizzard.

Gunshots ripped through the night, and she slammed the door shut before racing toward the bathroom.

"Someone's shooting from the shed, and someone's outside the front door!" As she turned the corner into the bathroom, she ran smack into Zane. He caught her in his powerful arms, pulling her into him for a brief, comforting hug that spoke more than words. As she peered over his shoulder, she saw the intruder slumped against the wall as if he'd been knocked out. There was also the possibility that he was dead.

Right now, she didn't really care which.

A volley of shots fired again, into the side of the cabin. Zane unlocked the gun safe and retrieved two rifles and his handgun.

"I'm going to get the shooter and whoever's out there," he said, his voice steady. "What I want you to do is go out the back door and climb that hill. At the top, there should be a cell signal. Call Ace or whoever you can get a hold of."

"And then what?"

"Then you wait for me."

She remembered the thick blanket of snow outside. "You'll have to put on your coat and hat. It's snowed a lot."

"Will do." He shoved a longer magazine into his Colt, racked the slide, and handed it to her. "It's loaded. Do you remember how to use this?"

"I think so." Stupid tears welled in her eyes. "I have to now, don't I?"

He took off his belt and holster and threaded both through the belt loops on her jeans, finally inserting the loaded gun into the holster's hard casing. Although the belt drooped considerably, there was no time to fix it. He cupped her cheeks in his large hands, his eyes intense. It was the last straw. She choked back a sob and her tears began to flow freely.

He brushed her cheekbones with his thumbs, his voice deepening. "Molly, listen to me. I have a snowmobile in that other shed. I'll come get you as soon as I can. You hear me?"

She drew strength from his resolute gaze, managing a slight nod. "I know you will."

And she did trust him to come for her—if only he could manage to stay alive.

11

A sense of determination propelled Molly as she pulled on her gloves and shoved the back door open again. It would be a freezing, exhausting hike up that steep hillside, but Zane had given her marching orders, and she wouldn't slack off when he needed her most.

She felt her way along the darkened deck, trying not to trip over anything. When she reached the railing, she planted her hands in the snow and clambered over it. There was a steep incline behind the deck; she had no choice but to make her way up it. She didn't want to think about how long her climb might take.

Blindly, she grabbed at the snow-laden surface, hoping for trees or roots to cling to. Each time she latched onto something to pull herself up, her foothold gave way and she slid down even more. All it would take was for someone to turn on a porch light or shine a flashlight in her direction, and she would be a sitting duck.

Shots boomed behind her. One of her feet slid from its tenuous perch, and she nearly toppled backward. Frantic, she flattened against the hill and reached above her, praying she'd hit on something solid. This time, her wet, gloved fingers curled around a jutting rock ledge.

She used all her upper body strength to crawl up to the ledge, kicking snow loose in the process. She was able to scramble into a standing position by holding onto a slim tree trunk. She shuddered to think what would happen if she fell from this height, but at least she could no longer be spotted from below. Feeling around, she found more rocks above her. Perhaps this was a cave area.

The cabin was dark. She wondered how Zane had gotten out, with someone outside the front door and someone shooting from the shed. He wouldn't have gone out the back deck door because he wanted to deflect attention from her precarious mission.

Had he sniped the shooter already? Had he taken out the other person who was lurking around the cabin?

Knowing she was kicking snow down to the deck, she gritted her teeth and continued her ascent. She had no idea how far she was from the top of the incline, which was definitely more of a mountaintop than a hill.

With each heave upward, with each fresh cut the cold rocks gave her stomach and hands, she reminded herself that Lola needed her daddy and this was the only way to save him.

Suddenly, the lights came on inside the cabin. Was it a sign Zane was okay? Had he already managed to take out both intruders? There was no way of being sure until the snowmobile came for her, so she had to keep going. They would need backup, one way or another, and it was solely her job to call for help.

She swept her hand into the dark space above her and found a tree branch. After testing its strength, she slowly heaved herself upward again. Her boots slid onto a flat, snowy surface.

She had reached the top of the hill.

Zane managed to launch himself through the narrow window opening, landing with a quiet thud on the snow. He was glad he'd grown up hunting deer in the snowy mountains, so it couldn't be much different to hunt down the shooter. Except that now it was pitch-black. Hopefully, the darkness would cloak him so he could stay unnoticed.

It was possible the shooter had a flashlight, but given the way he'd been shooting, if he did have one, he wasn't using it to aim. The regular sprays of bullets seemed more of a fear technique than an attempt to take out a specific target.

Or maybe they were trying to flush him out of the cabin, in which case, he'd obliged them.

As he crept toward the shed, he couldn't stop thinking about Molly. She'd probably had no experience with camping or hiking in the dark. She had kept her head when Sitko came in and threatened them, but if she wasn't able to handle the snow and panicked in her climb, she could give away her position and lead the terrorists right to her. Given her limited shooting skills, she probably wouldn't have much chance of hitting someone in the dark, if she was brave enough to shoot at all.

He took a deep breath and continued to creep forward, despite another burst of gunfire that went over his head, as if the shooter were pummeling the roof of the cabin.

He would take out this guy first and eliminate one threat to Molly. Then he'd swing around and check for other terrorists, since Sitko had said he had *people* outside.

Zane couldn't lose one more person on his watch.

12

Feet planted in the deep snow, Molly pulled out her phone. She was relieved to see three bars show up, even if it was down to five percent battery power. She stripped her gloves off, stared at her home screen, and groaned as her mind seemed to blank out from the pressure.

Something rustled nearby—probably an animal, but it was enough to snap her into action. Fingers stiffened with cold, she finally managed to pull up her contacts list and find Ace's number. That would be faster than explaining things to 9-1-1.

She pushed call and waited as it rang and rang. "Pick up, pick up!"

Finally, the voicemail beep sounded, and she started talking as fast as she could.

"We're at Zane's cabin, and there are terrorists. They're shooting at us. I'm on the hill. Come *now!*"

For good measure, she scrolled down to Katie's contact information. Before she could push the call button, two shots rang out, and a shelf of snow slid off the rocks below her.

She peered over the edge.

The porch light was suddenly on. Was Zane giving her an all-clear signal?

She had half a mind to skitter down the hillside, back into the warm cabin. But Zane had told her to stay put until he came for her on the snowmobile. She was sure Katie would tell her that was the best plan, too. In the meantime, she needed to find a safe place to hide.

She decided to go a little farther to make sure she wasn't visible to people down below. Although if she kept walking along this unfamiliar terrain, it was possible that she could fall right over a cliff or crack her head into a tree trunk.

Still, it seemed safest to move forward instead of backtrack. She cautiously trekked away from the cabin.

Zane had a clear shot into the shed—the terrorist was standing close enough to the window and he had some kind of light source behind him. It was almost too easy.

Zane shot twice just to make certain, then went to check the result. Sure enough, the larger, swarthy-skinned man lay rasping for breath on the floor. Zane kicked the man's rifle out of arm's reach and scanned the rest of the shed, but it was empty.

He gave the man another glance—he was already dead. Silently, Zane stepped out into the snow. As loud as a shout, light splayed from the front door of the cabin. Who had turned on the porch light?

Walking more quickly, he moved toward the cabin's back door, which he'd left unlocked. Had Molly returned even though he'd told her to stay put, or would he find the second terrorist inside?

One thing was certain—Sitko wouldn't be a problem. Because Sitko was dead.

It had been inevitable, of course. There was no way an ex-Marine so bent on destroying both Molly and him could have been stopped otherwise. And in the bathroom, Sitko had made it clear that he knew all about Lola—where she went to school, when she had visitation, and more. Zane hadn't wanted to take his life, but when Sitko had tried to trip him and grab for his gun, Zane had put him in a choke hold. He hadn't watched as the light went out of his old friend's eyes.

Slipping into the back door with Sitko's handgun in position, he swept it back and forth over the kitchen and living room. He saw no one.

Stepping cautiously toward the bathroom, he thought he heard a movement. He had a brief moment of irrational fear that Sitko had risen from the dead to haunt him, then he shoved it aside and stepped into the bathroom doorframe.

Sitko still lay in a heap against the wall. The room was otherwise empty.

A heavily accented, venomous voice cut into the air behind him. "Put your hands up, pig."

He turned to find a striking, dark-haired woman pointing a gun at him.

Zane slowly placed his gun and rifles on the floor. His mind whirred. The woman's accent sounded Syrian.

She spoke again. "I am Kamar *Habib*. I was there in the crowd, the day you murdered my father."

Realization set in. She was the brains behind this operation—the one who had instigated this revenge mission.

She widened her stance, her finger dangerously close to the trigger. "I made sure my father's men took a hostage, and it happened to be Bradley."

Bradley Sitko.

"He was lonely, you see. So when I stopped his beatings and started feeding him from my table, he told me all I needed to know about the sniper who'd killed my father."

"And he helped you hunt me down," Zane said.

"Of course. A man will do anything for love." She smiled wickedly, her dark eyes glinting. "And I see you must have killed him, which makes things easier for me. I don't need his deadweight when I fly home. My father's empire won't run itself."

Her gaze sharpened, and she spat at him. Below her collar, he could make out a twisting henna snake.

"No more talking," she said. "Get down on your knees."

He hoped she would move closer because she would be easier to disarm that way. He began to move into a crouch, but even as he did so, she shot.

The bullet slammed into his coat. He felt a searing sensation, like a white-cold cut tearing through his chest.

Kamar's laughter echoed in the cabin.

He grabbed the handgun from the floor and pulled the trigger twice. She fell before she knew what hit her.

He knew he was losing blood and his vision was growing bleary, but all he could think was that Molly would be watching for him in the cold. She might get frostbite or even die as she waited for him to show up on the snowmobile. She might not have reached anyone on her phone.

Staggering to the front door, he pulled the shed key from his pocket. He blinked the front porch light three times, hoping Molly might see it. Then he lurched out into the night.

13

When three more muffled shots sounded from the general direction of the cabin, Molly backed up under low-lying spruce branches that draped the snowy ground. She'd decided she would be unnoticed here if anyone chased her, and the tight green branches broke the swirling winds that had picked up.

Who had shot down there? Was Zane alive? Had Ace received her voice message yet? The signal came and went on top of this mountain, and now she was too far out of range to receive any return texts or calls.

Her stomach clenched; she felt parched. The snow under the tree was relatively clean, so she scooped a handful and ate it, but it only served to make her feel colder. It was getting difficult to feel her toes. How long was it safe to stay outside before frostbite was possible? It probably wasn't below zero at this point, but the temperature had fallen so dramatically since the time they'd gone shooting.

Shooting. She felt the weight of Zane's Colt where it drooped on the belt. Could she even slide it out of the holster if the terrorists followed her here? Would she be able to pull the trigger with her stiff fingers?

What a fine kettle of fish she'd landed herself in, trying to impress a man who would doubtless be far from impressed with her measly attempts to save them.

Her wet, frosted hair blew into her face again, stinging as it did so. She grabbed a handful and shoved it into the coat collar. Katie's coat.

She fought back tears. What if she never had a chance to return Katie's ugly, oversized coat? What if she never got to hug Mom again? What if Zane didn't make it back to Lola?

This whole situation seemed so far-fetched, but on some level it made sense. This remote cabin was the ideal place for Zane's stalkers to corner him.

A noise ripped into the darkness—it sounded like the whir of a chainsaw. That didn't make sense. Was Zane chopping up a tree that had fallen? Were the terrorists coming for her with a chainsaw?

She felt for the thick tree trunk behind her and pressed into it, trying not to entertain the worst-case scenarios floating through her mind. This was like a horror movie.

The whirring moved closer, and suddenly, lights topped the hill. It took her a moment to realize they were moving in tandem. It was a snowmobile! Zane had come.

She crawled toward the edge of the branches, shoving them aside before struggling to her feet. She couldn't let him pass her by. Waving her arms wildly, she screamed his name, but the word seemed to be swallowed by the engine's roar.

The vehicle went right past her and she nearly despaired, but then it slowed. It kicked up snow, turning in a tight circle to return to her side.

The driver geared down and dismounted. She stepped closer, but hesitated when she noticed a ski mask hid his face.

As he stood to full height and loomed before her, she froze. He was taller than Zane, certainly—and larger built.

This wasn't Zane.

Unable to recall how to extricate the Colt from its holster, she turned and bolted for the woods.

The man grabbed for her arms, causing her to trip and face-plant in the snow. He fell on top of her, his weight pinning her down.

If Zane were still alive, he wouldn't have let someone make off with his snowmobile.

Maybe he was already with Jesus. If so, she'd probably see him soon.

Zane stirred. Wind whipped around his head and he felt like he was floating.

He tried to focus on the older woman who hovered above him. She seemed to be doing something with his shirt.

She glanced at him and shouted over the wind. "You're awake. Hang on tight. We're going to get you fixed up."

He felt pressure in his chest. His vision started to fade, but not before he saw a flock of crows flying right alongside him.

A strong hand yanked at Molly's collar and pulled her up. She spat snow from her mouth, stumbling back from her attacker.

As he started to pull off his mask, the black muzzle of a large gun protruded beneath his coat.

She immediately fumbled for her Colt, but a familiar deep voice stopped her. "I don't think you want to do that, Molly."

It was Ace Calhoun.

She gave a thankful yip, then rushed toward him and slammed into his chest. "It's you!"

He wrapped her in a brotherly hug. "Sorry I grabbed you. Didn't mean to knock you down, but you seemed panicked."

"Wh—where's Zane? Why didn't he—he come?" She was shaking so hard she could hardly push her words out. "What's going on?"

He tucked an arm under hers, leading her to the idling snowmobile. "I'll tell you when we get to the cabin, but you need to get warmed up. Hop on."

Awkwardly, she positioned herself behind him, hunching low to avoid the frigid wind. He revved the engine and exhaustion drove her to press her face into the thickness of his coat. He followed a cleared trail down another side of the hill, then looped around to head for the cabin.

All the while, she had the sinking suspicion that he hadn't answered her question because Zane was already dead.

Ace carried Molly to the cabin's door, where he knocked five times. A police officer met them, pointing to the couch as he shouted at someone in the bedroom. "Cal!"

Using her teeth, Molly removed her wet gloves. But a relentless tingling had claimed her fingers, and she couldn't even grip the top of her boot.

Ace stepped in and began to pull the heavy boots off. The man called Cal strode into the room, taking in the pinched look on her face. He held out a hand to Ace. "Gentle there. She might have some frostbite." He gave Molly a reassuring look. "I'm a paramedic."

Pain kept her from speaking as the men worked to

remove her coat, hat, and socks. Cal examined her ears and face first and gave a brief nod. Next, he took a towel that had been warming near the fire and began to dry her mottled fingers and toes.

"You're lucky you had such heavy boots and your head and hands were covered," he said. "It's just frostnip—the stage before frostbite. We'll get you warmed up."

Easier said than done, since her extremities had gone from tingling to burning. She turned to Ace and managed to ask the question that was torturing her. "Is Zane in the bedroom? Is he okay?"

Ace gingerly covered both her hands with his large ones. He looked directly into her eyes. "We don't know yet. He had to be shuttled down the mountain and airlifted out because he'd lost a lot of blood—he took a bullet, Molly. They couldn't say how extensive his injuries were. By the time we got here, Zane had collapsed outside the cabin door. I saw he was gripping something and I took the snowmobile keys from his hand. He managed to rouse and say something about the hill top. I figured he was going for you, so I had Cal wait here while I went out to search."

The lights in the cabin seemed unnaturally bright, and part of Ace's face blinked out. Perfect. A migraine was coming soon. She quickly asked her next question. "But the terrorists? Where are they?"

Ace glanced toward the bedroom the police officer had disappeared into. "They're dead."

"Both of them?"

Cal continued his warming ministrations, but Molly caught him raising his eyebrows at Ace.

Ace shook his head. "Three of them."

"What?"

"Two men and a woman."

A woman? What would a woman have to do with this?

Zane had said this was a terrorist hit...why would a woman be involved?

"Is she here?"

Ace gave a brief nod. "In the bedroom, lying where she fell. From what we can tell, she's the one who shot Zane."

"Can I see her?"

"No—"

Despite the flashing lights, she managed to pin Ace with her gaze. "I need to know the full picture, don't I, if I'm going to give a statement about what happened here? I'm pretty sure I can tell you some things about one of the men you found."

Ace hesitated, then picked her up without a word, carrying her to the bedroom doorway. He flipped on a light.

A beautiful woman lay on the floor. Her black hair spilled around her face, which was stiffened in a grimace. Darkened blood stained her shirt.

Molly would recognize that Nefertiti profile anywhere. It was the woman who'd sat outside the bathroom at The Greenbrier.

She *had* been stalking her.

"I've seen her before, at The Greenbrier," Molly said.

Ace nodded, then turned abruptly and walked into the bathroom. The blond stalker lay slumped in the same position as before, only now it was obvious he was dead.

"I think he was a Marine—a POW," she said. "He came back for revenge because he thought Zane hadn't protected him from the terrorists over there." She pressed fingers into the back of her head. "Would Cal have pain relievers? I'm getting a migraine."

"Of course." Ace carried her back to the couch. She accepted a mug of hot tea from Cal and swallowed the pills he handed her, hoping they would also dull the throbbing pain in her fingers and toes.

"Lie back," Ace said. "We'll get you home soon. Katie was frantic to come along, but we didn't know what we were walking into, given that message you left. She's back at your apartment. We didn't wake your mom, but we'll let her know what happened in the morning."

Molly tried to relax, which seemed nearly impossible. Finally, the medicine seemed to kick in, and she dropped into a restless sleep.

14

Zane woke to the regular beeps of a heart monitor. An oxygen mask covered his face and tubes extended from his chest and hands into bags hanging nearby. His chest felt like it was on fire.

Mom sat beside him, clutching his hand in hers.

He pulled his mask up a bit, but couldn't seem to force words out.

Mom gasped and pressed several kisses to his forehead. "Don't even try to talk. We were so worried. Your father's just down the hall, getting some crackers." She took a deep breath. "The nurse said she's never seen someone get so lucky with a gunshot wound. Apparently, you were shot with a bullet that wasn't a hollow point—I forget what they call it—"

Full metal jacket. Kamar must've gone cheap with her ammo.

Mom continued. "And it tore straight through you, but managed to miss your arteries. It nicked your lung, but they're draining any blood from it and they've got you on the oxygen, so it should be okay. It also broke a couple of ribs."

He tried to trace the letter "M" to ask about Molly. It took Mom a couple of guesses, but she finally realized his concern.

"That nice police officer called about an hour ago. He said Molly just had mild frostbite—no serious damage. She's at home with her sister."

Thankfulness washed over him. He sank back into his pillow, unable to stay upright.

Mom noticed. "Now you just lie back and get some sleep. Let that lung heal. Don't worry—Krista said she'll bring Lola by as soon as the doctors give the go-ahead."

Before he drifted off, he decided it was time to give thanks to the very same God he'd been questioning for so long. It was undeniable that God had been watching out for him, Molly, and even Lola. Turns out He was a Protector, which was something Zane understood very well.

Katie had hot chocolate ready when Ace brought Molly back to her apartment. After fussing over Molly a bit, Katie seemed to accept that her sister was in no mood to talk. She pulled warm socks onto Molly's feet and hands, tucked her in, and curled up next to her on the bed for the night.

Around six-thirty in the morning, Katie gave Mom and Brandon a call. Brandon was duly irate that he hadn't been first on the scene, but he grudgingly forgave Katie for not throwing Mom into a panic in the middle of the night when there was really nothing she could have done.

Mom arrived around nine with fresh cinnamon rolls, relieving Katie of her self-appointed nursing duties. Molly shared her story once, only to be asked to repeat it in more detail. Mom couldn't *quite* believe that her timid daughter had shot firearms, stared into the face of a murderer, climbed up a snow-covered hill in the dark, and carried a gun as she did so.

Finally, Mom shook her head, her blonde layers shifting to frame her petite face. "Molly Anne McClure, I would ask what's gotten into you, but I already know. That Isaiah Boone is more than a looker—he's the real deal. He's the kind of man who doesn't shy away from commitment—you can see how he looks after his daughter—and he seems to know the way you tick. I mean, who else could have managed to get you to shoot a gun? Not even your father could do that, and he was a hard man to say 'no' to. A little strong-headed, like you." She smiled.

Molly stretched, basking in the rich scents of the cinnamon rolls and freshly brewed coffee Mom had arranged on a tray. Life would calm down for Zane, now that his terrorist stalkers were out of the picture. Would Krista finally acknowledge how much danger her ex-husband had been in all along? Molly would like to see her eat crow on that one.

She looked around the familiar comforts of her room. Katie had once told her, "No matter where you live, it always feels so homey." It was true that she loved to be comfortable. Safe. She liked having extra money to pamper herself, and she liked to shop.

But now...she couldn't go back to that life. Someone had come along and upended everything. Even in the face of her silly bravado, Zane hadn't mocked her once. He had taken her seriously, unlocking a whole new level of strength she didn't know she had.

Mom swallowed a bite of roll and fixed Molly with a thoughtful look. "I think I know someone who could use some cinnamon rolls. I brought extra and I'm happy to drive you over to say hello. But you might want to change out of your PJs first."

Molly gulped the rest of her coffee, hoping it would give

her an extra boost to go through with this. It was entirely possible that Zane didn't want to see her face again. Although her SOS had managed to get through, she hadn't gotten it out in time to protect him from getting shot.

But she knew the man hated hospital food. The least she could do was to take him some cinnamon rolls.

Krista was nowhere in sight when Molly walked into Zane's room, but Lola sat on the wide chair with her grandma, coloring.

Molly peeked over her shoulder. "Is that Princess Jasmine? She was my favorite."

Lola looked up, her grin wide. "I have a Jasmine doll, too. You want to see it?"

"I'd love to."

The little girl rushed to grab her glittery backpack and extricated a doll with clumped-up black hair and rubbed-off eyes that only vaguely resembled her animated counterpart.

"I can tell you love her a lot," Molly said.

Lola beamed. "You're pretty."

"Thank you. So are you."

Mrs. Boone stood and stretched. "You missed the hubbub this morning."

Molly stiffened, hoping it wasn't bad news.

"Those lumberjacks can be a salty lot, but they have hearts of gold and they'd do anything for Zane. They showed up with enough peanuts, popcorn, and deer jerky to last him a month."

Molly let her breath out, relieved. "He must be a great boss."

"He learned from the best. John put his heart and soul into that business, and he was proud to pass it on to Zane.

Basil never showed much interest, but maybe things will change."

A weak voice trailed over their way, distracting Molly from her follow-up question. Lola immediately rushed over to Zane's bedside.

"Daddy! Grams said I couldn't talk to you, but I knew you'd want to talk to *me*!"

Molly hesitated, taking in Zane's appearance. His eyes had circles under them and his face was a bit discolored. He held a breathing mask in his hand, which he likely needed to put back on without delay. Monitors and tubes dominated the floor space near him, but Lola had squeezed in right next to the bedside.

Molly really didn't even want to see what had happened to his chest where the bullet had torn into him.

She silently backed up, hoping he hadn't seen her. Handing Mrs. Boone the glass dish of cinnamon rolls, she whispered, "I'm going to let him rest. Be sure to take some for yourself and Lola, too."

Mrs. Boone squeezed her hand. "We sure will. Thank you for coming by. I'll let him know you stopped in."

Molly stepped into the hallway and glanced around. Krista sat on a couch at the end of the corridor, texting furiously. Although she had acted like a dutiful mother, bringing her daughter to see her daddy each time he was injured, Molly suspected that was as far as her loyalty went. She still emanated irritation and distrust.

Molly's fingers throbbed, and she clenched and unclenched them. Krista wasn't someone she wanted to deal with right now.

She met Mom where she waited in the lobby and asked her to drive her home. It was a good thing work had called to let her know everything was under control. Her feet still tingled from the frostbite, and all she felt like doing was putting on fluffy socks, warm gloves, and climbing back under the covers.

As they walked to the car, she had to admit that her feet and fingers weren't the only parts of her feeling pained. It had been difficult to see Zane lying there so helpless, and hard to force herself to walk away. When he recovered, he would probably remember how inept she had been at doing everything he loved to do.

Much as she'd tried to pretend, it must've been obvious that she'd known nothing about logging, shooting, fishing, hiking, or all the outdoorsy things that made Zane who he was. He needed a woman who could share his interests, someone to have fun with and make his heart lighter after his divorce and the traumatic few weeks he'd had.

Tugging her hair around her face to hide a few stray tears from Mom, she determined she'd back off and let Zane find someone better suited to him. For once, she'd give up on something she really wanted.

Because Zane was worth it.

15

Three weeks had passed and Zane hadn't heard from Molly.

Maybe she'd been too traumatized by the series of events at the cabin to return his calls. Maybe the frostbite still bothered her.

He didn't want to think about the final option—maybe she wasn't interested and had moved on.

His recovery had been slow, but Basil had actually shown up and taken over some of the office work at the logging company. It turned out his brother had a knack for the paperwork Zane disliked. Basil wasn't ready to commit to a move, but Zane could finally see how a partnership with him might play out, and it wasn't nearly as bad as he'd feared.

Finally, Zane felt safe in his own home, and he'd talked Krista into letting Lola visit a couple of times. When his daughter was around, he found it easy to focus on her and not on his own problems.

He was still short of breath and his rib bones almost felt like they were rubbing together, but his doctor assured him that he was healing well. He had started walking around the house, but couldn't get very far before he had to sit down.

Brandon McClure stopped by with a meal from his mom, and they chatted for a long time. When Zane asked Brandon about Molly, Brandon hedged and said she had several weddings coming up. But Zane thought he saw pity in his eyes.

He couldn't stand to be an object of pity.

The next day, although it took him at least fifteen minutes, he changed from his loose shorts and shirt into a clean button-up and jeans. He couldn't wear T-shirts because he couldn't pull them on and off. Every move shot fresh pain through him, but he didn't care.

He had to see Molly. He had to know she was okay, not only physically, but mentally, after their ordeal. He carefully climbed into his truck, only to realize the tightened seatbelt would put too much pressure on his aching ribs. Grabbing a heavy jacket from his seat, he positioned it over his stomach and stretched the belt around it.

His drive to The Greenbrier took about twice as long as it should have, but he finally pulled up into the old train depot parking lot across from the resort. He caught the shuttle bus and made his way into the main doors, all too aware that he was once again underdressed.

He had to ask at the desk where Molly's office was, but it turned out it was in the wedding planning room, which wasn't far away. He stepped into the soothing turquoise-and-coral space, taking in the oversized wedding photos of famous couples and the fake, tiered cakes displayed on lavish table settings.

Movement from a side room caught his eye. He caught a glimpse of a red mane, then saw Molly lean back in her chair as she spoke on the phone. He stood in silence, watching her graceful movements.

As if she felt his stare, she glanced his way. Her eyes

widened and she paused, then held up a finger so he would wait as she finished her call.

When she walked out, he felt more breathless than before. She wore a straight, silky-looking navy dress that fit her perfectly. Her nude heels boosted her to match his height. Her auburn curls looked so smooth, he had to restrain himself from touching one.

He couldn't think of a thing to say.

Thankfully, her eyes brightened and a smile played on her lips. "And what are you doing out on the town, crip? Brandon told me you were supposed to lie low until your ribs heal."

So Brandon had reported back to Molly. Zane let his gaze play over the soft lines of her face. Did she still feel anything for him? When her eyes began to glisten, he realized she was holding back tears.

He took her hands in his. "What if I asked you to go out with me again? Would you run for the hills?"

She made a little choke-gasp noise and shook her head slowly. "I would never run from you. But I'm afraid I'm not what you need."

He released her hands to thumb away tears that spilled onto her cheeks, even though lifting his arm was enough to remind him of the beating his body had taken. "What are you talking about? You're just what I need, Molly. What I've always needed."

"But I'm not outdoorsy. I'm a girly-girl who likes clothes and makeup and weddings and—"

"I'm not going to ask you to give up your girly things. I like that. I like that you're so different and...*other*... from me. I can't get enough of you."

"But I'm scared of things. Spiders. And I don't like housework or cooking. And—"

He smiled. "I'm not bad in the kitchen." He cupped her face in his hands, relishing the softness of her skin against his work-roughened palms. He couldn't look away from the natural beauty of her flushed cheeks and her bright amber eyes.

When Molly started to protest again, his gaze drifted to her mouth.

"But—"

He slid a thumb over the full curve of her bottom lip, and her words stuttered to a halt under his caress. In a voice rough with emotion, he said, "Trust me, it'll work."

A tremor raced up his spine when he felt her sway toward him, her eyes growing soft, her lashes lowering slightly. "I trust you," she murmured, before she pressed her mouth to his in a kiss that made his breath catch.

He threaded his fingers through her silky hair, then he wrapped his arms around her and slowly drew her to him. As she melted into his embrace, he realized that he felt no pain. Not one bit.

Dear Reader,

I hope you've enjoyed spending time with Molly McClure and Zane Boone in this story. As I researched *Undercut*, I was blessed to be able to celebrate our twentieth anniversary with a one-night stay at The Greenbrier Resort. If you'd like to see pictures of The Greenbrier and the characters I envisioned for *Undercut*, please check out my Pinterest board under the same name.

A huge thanks to Jason and Josh for their input on military procedures and guns. Any mistakes along those lines are all mine!

The flood of 2016, referred to in the book, was a real event that took lives and affected many people across West Virginia. As mentioned, it did do damage to areas of The Greenbrier Resort's grounds. However, in true West Virginia fashion, residents banded together to do cleanup work and to donate cleaning items, clothing, and food for those affected. Others from out of state showed up to help in the crisis, such as God's Pit Crew, an organization that served meals to those who suddenly found themselves homeless.

Thank you again for sharing this Appalachian adventure— there's almost nothing I enjoy more than bringing a taste of modern "wild and wonderful West Virginia" to my readers. If you want more fast-paced West Virginia reads featuring the Greenbrier Resort and other southern West Virginia locales, I'd recommend you check out my *Barks & Beans Cafe* cozy mystery series, which features sibling sleuths Bo and Macy Hatfield, Macy's rescue Great Dane, Coal, and a cafe where folks can pet shelter dogs. Teens and adults alike are enjoying this clean mystery series.

And if you enjoyed *Undercut*, please be sure to tell your reader friends about it and to leave a **review** at your online retailers of choice. Reviews are a wonderful way to encourage authors and to let them know you want to read more of their books!

Finally, be sure to sign up for my newsletter at **heatherdaygilbert.com** for my latest book updates, giveaways, and bargain news!

-Heather

DEADLOCKED

Dedicated to my redheaded lawyer husband, David, who took the time to read over all my courtroom scenes to make sure I didn't botch them too badly. I'm so thankful you enjoy my books, and I can never thank you enough for all the hours you spend listening and talking me through this crazy writing career.

1

Brandon turned his alarm off, sat up in bed, and rubbed his beard. He really needed a haircut, but hadn't made time to get one since moving back to West Virginia a couple of months ago.

"You awake?" Ma sang out from the kitchen. Esther Sue McClure was nothing if not chipper in the morning. It was obvious she was thrilled to finally have her only boy back home from Arizona, although Brandon knew she doted on her two sons-in-law nearly as much. That was fine with him —he had to admit his sisters had chosen wisely when it came to their spouses. During the past year, both Molly and Katie had gotten married, and they'd both settled nearby.

"Yup," he shouted. Groaning, he stood and stretched. He scrounged in his drawer for a pair of jeans. He'd finally unpacked a couple of weeks ago.

When the supervisor at his old whitewater rafting and helicopter tour job in Sedona had turned unreasonably critical of his work, Brandon had determined to find a job where his skills would be appreciated. Although he'd moved to Arizona before his dad died, the West Virginia mountains had tugged at his heart for years, and when his childhood friend Sammy Jenkins asked him to go into business with him and lead whitewater tours on the Gauley River, he'd jumped at the opportunity. He'd only been working for a month and a half when he'd received his jury summons.

And today was jury selection day. Sammy didn't care if he missed a few days of work, but Brandon chafed at the possibility of being cooped up in a courtroom, listening to boring testimony in some small-town case. Hemlock Creek wasn't exactly a hotbed of crime.

Ma poked her head in the door, doing a quick once-over of his attire. "Brandon, honey, don't wear those beat-up jeans. Hang on—I've washed your church pants and a nice shirt."

"I'm most comfortable in a T-shirt, Ma," he grumbled to her retreating back. "They aren't going to care what I'm wearing."

"I don't care. You need to look nice." She returned quickly, bearing a fresh pair of khakis and a bright blue polo shirt. "You'll still be comfy in this. Now, why don't you come in and get you some breakfast."

Sometimes Brandon felt like a teenager again, with Ma fussing over him like he was in high school. Still, he had to admit it was nice having someone else wash his clothes and cook for him. He'd discovered years ago that housekeeping and organization were not among his strong suits.

After rubbing in a little beard oil and combing his thick, flyaway red hair, Brandon headed for the kitchen. Ma handed him a plate of bacon, scrambled eggs, and biscuits. He gave a quick prayer before he started to chow down.

"I hope your selection process won't go long, but if it does, maybe they'll give you a nice lunch break. Will you try to come home and eat?" Ma took plates from the dishwasher and stacked them in the cabinet.

Brandon spoke around a large bite of biscuit. "I don't

know." After taking a swig of orange juice to wash it down, he said, "I'm hoping I won't get chosen for the jury. Sammy was just saying how grateful he is I've been around, since Gauley season has been booked solid. Besides, I haven't been living here for years, so I don't know why they tapped me for this."

Ma's brow crinkled. "Now you know that's your own fault —you kept your West Virginia driver's license, so you're still technically a resident." She patted his hand, probably trying to soften her words. "Even if they do pick you, it'll likely be a short trial, like that one I sat in on where a Little League treasurer was embezzling."

Brandon glanced at the microwave clock and wiped his mouth with a napkin. "I hope so. I'd better get going. I noticed there's a skiff of snow on the ground today. It's getting cold early this year."

Ma nodded. She reached into the fridge and pulled out a couple of chilled bottles of Dr Pepper, his caffeinated beverage of choice. Pressing them into his hands, she said, "Come home for lunch if they let you."

"I'll text you once I find out." He stood and gave Ma a hug, pressing her blonde hair against his chest. It was funny that she was so petite when all three of her children had turned out exceptionally tall. In that way, they took after their dad.

If Brandon was honest with himself, that wasn't the only way he took after Sean McClure. Dad worked for years as an agent for the FBI, and he surely hadn't been averse to risk-taking. Brandon lived for adrenaline highs. That could be part of the reason he still wasn't married at thirty-three. Sure, he'd found plenty of women who shared his love of the outdoors, but they all seemed to be missing something. What that something *was*, he still hadn't figured out.

Grabbing a heavier jacket, he headed out to his light orange hybrid car. Someday he wanted to trade up for a more versatile, four-wheel drive truck like the one his brother-in-law Zane owned, but he'd have to save up for it.

The snow seemed to have melted on the mountain roads, so he drove as quickly as he could. Although the courthouse was only fifteen minutes away, he didn't want to show up late, like he usually did.

The courthouse was a three-story, flat-roofed brick building tucked into a clearing near a wooded hillside. After pulling into a parking spot in the relatively crowded lot, Brandon stepped out, taking a deep breath of the bracing morning air. He glanced along the ridgeline of the mountains, enjoying the look of the snow-frosted trees. He'd missed the way the plants and trees responded to the nudges of the seasons here. The Appalachian mountains had a rolling, gentle look about them that seemed to envelop their children in a protective hug. With a jolt, Brandon realized that his wanderlust might have been slaked for good—he didn't *want* to move away again.

Tucking the Dr Peppers under his arm, he took the courthouse steps two at a time and jogged into the lobby. After passing through the metal detector, he joined the other potential jury members in the courtroom as they waited for the judge and lawyers to arrive.

As the prosecutor, defense attorney, and the defendant showed up, a collective gasp escaped from the members of the jury pool near Brandon. Unsure why they'd reacted so strongly, Brandon took a closer look at the defendant. He was a graying man in his fifties who wore black-rimmed glasses. He looked comfortable in his fitted dress shirt and silk tie, which indicated he was a businessman of some kind. His dark eyes scanned the jury, but Brandon didn't recognize him at all.

Suppressing his inclination to ask the kind-looking elderly woman next to him who the defendant was, Brandon sat in silence until the judge began to explain what was going to happen.

Judge Stowers, a balding man in his sixties, explained there would be several questions to pick a jury that could be fair and impartial, and they were to raise their hands if they answered "yes" to any of the questions. This process was called *voir dire*.

But what he said next shed light on the gasps from the jury pool. This was no in-and-out trial of trivial importance. Instead, this was a murder trial.

And the defendant was none other than Harlan Wells, one of the wealthiest men in the county.

Brandon held his breath that the lawyers—and Harlan, who was actively consulting his lawyer as potential jurors were questioned—would decide he wasn't at all what they wanted. But as question after question was asked, he had no cause to raise his hand. One after the other, people around him were excused.

In the end, although the pool was still larger than twelve, Brandon was informed that he had been selected and that he and the other jurors needed to go into the jury box to be sworn in.

When Brandon took a seat to wait for the judge to finish talking with the lawyers, his leather swivel chair let out a tremendous squeak. Embarrassed, he sank lower, resting his face on his shielding hand. The chairs had likely been here since they'd built the courthouse. It was a wonder that in all those years, they hadn't replaced them with something a little less tenuous. Brandon sat stiffly to avoid distracting everyone with another loud creak.

The judge took a moment to explain their duties, then Brandon and the others were sworn in. He felt sick to think he was going to have to tell Sammy that, barring a miracle, he was probably going to miss the end of whitewater rafting season.

As the first day of trial unfolded, Brandon listened carefully as the prosecutor calmly laid out the case against Harlan Wells, who had been accused of shoving his wife down the stairs, causing her subsequent death in the hospital later that night. The prosecutor's arguments were convincing. In contrast, the defense attorney's opening statement didn't seem to poke any discernible holes in the murder theory. It was more of a bombastic tirade, and Brandon wasn't impressed.

When they dismissed for a lunch break, Brandon rushed home, happy to find that Ma was serving up a big portion of leftover chicken pot pie for him. She didn't expect him to tell her about the trial—after all, she knew the jury rules of keeping silence in regard to the case, even amongst fellow jurors. She probably also knew the news would report on it soon enough.

But after regarding Brandon in silence for several minutes, she finally blurted, "Do you have any idea how long this trial will last?"

He knew she was trying to figure out how high the stakes were. He tried to be a bit cagey. "I'm really not sure, but I'm guessing there will be at least a couple more days of testimony."

She nodded and gestured to his cooling pie. "Eat up, hon. It might run long today."

He bit into the buttery, flaky piecrust that gave way to a creamy blend of chicken and vegetables. Ma never used store-bought crusts, claiming it was more relaxing to make her own. His sisters Molly and Katie had been trying to replicate Ma's crusts, but, given the last two dried-out and over-floured pieces of pie they'd offered him, he figured they weren't getting there fast.

He finished off his lunch with a long sip of iced Dr Pepper. It seemed surreal that he was walking back into a trial for a local man who'd allegedly killed his wife. Hemlock Creek was such a small town, one where many people were related and where no one could even hope to act with complete anonymity. Yes, in the past few years, Brandon's sisters had experienced some run-ins with dangerous people, and yes, his dad had been FBI, so he certainly wasn't naive, but, still...how did one impartially render a verdict that would determine the entire course of another man's life?

It was a heavy responsibility. After giving Ma a big hug, Brandon stalked out to his car and dropped into the seat, taking a couple of moments to pray that the evidence would be presented clearly and lead jurors to the right verdict.

There was a knock on his car window, and he glanced up to see Zane, his brother-in-law, standing outside in his logging clothes and heavy boots. Zane ran his family logging business along with his brother Basil, and he was content to spend most of his time in the woods. Brandon found it amusing that such a brawny man—and a former Marine sniper, no less—had married his girly-girl sister Molly.

Brandon rolled down his window. "What's up, dude?"

"I was in the neighborhood and your mom invited me over for chicken pot pie. There's no way I could resist. What are you up to—off to work? How's Gauley season?"

Brandon shook his head. "It's winding up, but there's no Gauley for me right now, unfortunately. I got called in for jury duty. I just grabbed lunch, and now I'm heading back over to the courthouse."

Zane raised a dark blond eyebrow as his look turned

serious. "I have a reporter friend who mentioned a big trial he's sitting in on...do you happen to be on that jury?"

Brandon gave a brief nod, knowing Zane wouldn't push him for details. A quiet man, Zane always gave the impression that he'd be a steel trap for secrets. He wasn't the kind to go blabbing everything he heard...like Brandon's sister Molly. It seemed opposites did attract.

Zane gave the car roof a light smack. "I'll be praying for you, brother," he said.

Brandon could tell Zane was holding back from saying more. He got the distinct feeling that Zane might've had a run-in with Harlan Wells at one point or another—which would make sense, since the Boone Lumber Company served a wide variety of local clients.

"Thanks," he said. As Zane headed toward the house, Brandon rolled up his window and backed into the road. He turned on the music in his car, and one of his favorite songs by the country band Carolina Crush filled the air. He sang along loudly, wishing he could avoid the heaviness of the task set before him.

2

As the helicopter touched down on the helipad atop the courthouse, Nasha Patel breathed a sigh of relief. For the past eleven months, she'd been in the witness protection program, safely tucked away in a tiny town in Arizona. But three days ago, she'd flown back to West Virginia to prepare for the trial, and now she couldn't shake the feeling that one of Harlan Wells' goons would figure out where she was holed up and take a pop shot at her. It certainly wouldn't be the first time.

She'd experienced first-hand how Harlan's dirty-dealing tentacles had a stranglehold on Hemlock Creek. As soon as she'd made a police statement about what Wells' wife said with her dying breath—which conflicted with Harlan's story that Maureen took a swing at him in a fit of rage and fell headlong down the stairs—she'd become a target. She had narrowly escaped two attempts on her life, thus prompting her admission into the witness protection program. The U.S. marshal assigned to her, Bruce Stewart, said he didn't doubt it was Harlan's men who'd tried to run her off the road and take her at gunpoint. Since the Feds had long known that Harlan was involved in drug-running but had been unable to prove it, they'd been anxious to step in and make sure Nasha was safe until she could testify against him.

In both instances where Nasha had nearly been killed, it seemed a Divine hand had spared her. She didn't want to walk into the same room with Harlan Wells today, but God must've allowed her to make it this far for a reason. She had to trust He would protect her as she testified.

Making a brief stop in the chilly bathroom to adjust her blouse, Nasha wiped a sheen of sweat from her forehead. She was nervous, all right—too nervous. Hopefully her fear wouldn't paralyze her when it was her turn to speak up about what had happened. After all, she had a responsibility to Harlan's wife, didn't she? Poor Maureen had turned and spoken her dying words to Nasha and no one else.

And those words would likely put Maureen's cold, scheming husband behind bars for life.

Despite her measly attempt to bolster confidence by wearing the dusty rose shade that flattered her most, Nasha felt miserably unprepared. Although the prosecutor had come to her bed and breakfast last night and done a run-through with her, she felt less like the professional healthcare worker she was and more like a frightened young woman.

Glancing down at her heels, she wondered if they were too high to be taken seriously. They were her only dressy shoes, which she'd bought for a blind date a couple of years ago. She'd actually bolted on that one, since the guy had gotten drunk and turned way too frisky.

But perhaps the black leather heels would give her the illusion of height, since at 5'3, she wasn't the most imposing figure in a room. All her work shoes were thoroughly practical and not fit for the courtroom, and she hadn't made time to go shopping lately.

Truth be told, she hadn't gone out much the entire past year. Outside of doing her medical rotation and going to church, she rarely had a motivation to leave the safety of her Arizona apartment. She hadn't been in contact with her mom, but if she had, she was certain Mom would think she was getting agoraphobic.

Maybe she worried about that a little, too.

As she opened the door, Bruce abandoned his post at the top of the stairs and walked to her side. "You don't take the stand until after lunch, so we're going to wait in a side room until then."

She looked up at the imposing man who'd been with her both at the start and what was now hopefully the end of this ordeal. His crew cut, wide shoulders, and the pistol in his chest holster made it clear he wasn't the kind of man to be trifled with.

"Okay, that sounds good." She was aware that her flat voice lacked enthusiasm, but she guessed that was to be expected. She followed Bruce down the hallway, lost in her own thoughts.

How many witnesses had he been saddled with over the years? And how much longer would Nasha be in his charge?

If Harlan didn't get convicted, she had to face the possibility that she might not be able to return to her normal life for a good long while. Even though her family lived close to the courthouse, she'd been strictly forbidden from seeing or even contacting them for the duration of her witness protection stay. Her younger brother Tarek, who was only seven years old, couldn't comprehend why she had to pack and leave so abruptly. She knew he must feel her absence acutely.

Her parents weren't even aware she was in town. Most of the public didn't know that Harlan Wells' trial had started today, but she'd seen several reporters in the hallway, so soon it would be splashed all over the local news. Her parents might guess that she'd been brought in to testify, and how would they react? Would they try to visit the courtroom for a chance to see her? She hoped not. She was skittish enough as it was without looking down and having her repressed emotions flood over her.

After passing through the security check, Bruce ushered Nasha into an unmarked room to the right of the courtroom. A female marshal waited inside. Her dark hair was swept into a severe bun, but her blue eyes were compassionate as she slid a turkey sandwich and a bag of chips toward Nasha.

"Please, have something to eat," she said. "I'm sure you're hungry. We could be waiting awhile." As Nasha sat down, the woman continued. "My name is Leah. I'll be sticking close to you for the duration of the trial, while Bruce will be maintaining a perimeter. We don't anticipate trouble, but it's our job to be prepared for it."

After eating, Nasha felt a little more relaxed. Leah chatted away, sharing some of her gregarious stepson's capers, and Nasha warmed to the description of the boy, who was close to Tarek's age. Although her brother was far more bookish than Leah's daredevil son, Nasha craved the carefree life both boys led.

Bruce finally opened the door and popped his head in. "It's time," he said.

Nasha stood, dusting invisible crumbs from her pants. She wasn't ready for this. Although the prosecutor had advised her to focus on him or on the jury when answering, she knew that sooner or later, her gaze would fall on Harlan —the man who must have given the orders for his men to kill her, eleven months ago.

She took a final drink from her water bottle. "Okay," she said, hating the way her voice cracked.

Leah gave her a sympathetic look. Her distress was probably evident to everyone.

Nasha gave her blouse a final tuck, then thought better of

it. "I'd like to make one more trip to the bathroom first, please," she said.

Leah nodded at Bruce. "I'll take her," she said. "Meet you in a sec."

As she locked the bathroom door, Nasha mentally ran through some of the pep talks her parents had given her over the years. Knowing their daughter was an introvert, they'd tried to bolster her courage as she'd prepped for her med school interview. She had surprised herself by performing well. When she'd landed a plum rotation in the Lewisburg emergency room, she'd been ecstatic.

Then came that fateful night when Maureen Wells was brought into the ER. The poor woman's internal injuries were extensive, and her neck had been broken in her fall down the steep marble staircase in her home. As the anesthesiologist was called and the doctor prepared for exploratory surgery, Nasha was left alone with the groaning woman.

And Maureen chose that moment to croak out the words Nasha still heard in her nightmares.

She'd have to sit in the witness stand very soon and share the testimony that had put a target on her back, at least as far as Harlan Wells was concerned. She still hadn't processed the fact that he'd sent his henchmen after her not once, but twice, and that she'd narrowly escaped death both times. The prosecutor said he couldn't mention the events that had landed her in witness protection in court, since they had no proof Harlan had instructed his men to kill her. It seemed unfair to withhold all the facts from the jury, but then again, without solid proof, could they be considered facts at all?

There was a brief rap on the bathroom door. Leah was still waiting outside, letting her know she needed to speed it up.

Nasha smoothed her long, black hair one last time. She

hadn't worn mascara, just in case she broke down and started crying on the stand, but thankfully, her naturally thick lashes really didn't need it. All her lipstick had disappeared when she'd eaten, and she'd forgotten to pack a spare in her purse...

Another knock sounded, this time more urgent. "We need to get in there." Leah's voice was firm.

Nasha had developed a real skill for procrastination when she was staring down the barrel of an activity she had an aversion to. But there was nothing left but to suck it up and testify, letting the chips fall where they may.

She had to hold onto the hope that her testimony would result in Harlan Wells getting hauled off to prison. That was the only way she would ever get her own life back.

3

Brandon eased into his squeaky seat, thankful that it only let out a halfhearted groan under him. Glancing around, he noticed that the courtroom was even more packed than it had been before.

A dark-haired woman walked up, flanked by a woman who was open-carrying a pistol. As the female guard took a seat toward the front, the petite brunette stepped up to the witness stand. Brandon's gaze was drawn to another man standing at the rear of the courtroom who was also open-carrying. The man's watchful eyes never left the witness. It was safe to assume the brunette was some kind of a security risk who needed protection.

The witness was on the shorter side, with long black hair that glistened as it swayed, even under the harsh courtroom lights. As she placed her hand on the Bible and promised to tell the truth, Brandon admired her classic profile. The moment she settled into her seat, she turned to face the jury, and he felt an instant frisson of recognition as her eyes met his. She crinkled her brow for only the briefest of moments, and he felt it was possible she remembered him, too. But where had they met?

She was of Indian descent, and her liquid brown eyes were fringed with thick lashes as dark as coal. She looked terrified, like a rabbit caught in a snare. It was clear she had purposefully angled her body toward the jurors to avoid looking at Harlan Wells.

Had Brandon run into her in Hemlock Creek? He raked through his mind, trying to picture her at any of the places he frequented. Yet the only place that seemed to fit was on a raft. He was sure he hadn't run into her during the brief time he'd been working the Gauley, so where had it been?

When the prosecutor introduced her as Nasha Patel, he recalled that there was a Patel family living in town—the father was a doctor his mom had visited at some point—but he was quite certain he'd never personally met them.

The prosecutor asked Nasha if she recalled where she was on the evening of September eighth of last year—the night Maureen Wells was admitted to the emergency room—and Nasha stated she was on duty in the emergency room. The prosecutor then asked basic questions about where Nasha was positioned and what she was doing that night to help the severely injured woman. Following her brief answers, he segued into a more serious line of questioning.

"Miss Patel, you stated that you were briefly left alone with Mrs. Maureen Wells, who had been silent up to that point. Could you walk us through what happened next?"

Nasha nodded. As if unable to stop herself, her eyes darted ever-so-briefly toward Harlan Wells. She pulled her sweater tighter, although the courtroom was on the warm side.

"Yes, sir. I was prepping the patient for an emergency surgery when she whispered something. I leaned in closer, and her voice got stronger." Nasha hesitated.

"And what did she say?" the prosecutor prodded.

Nasha took a deep breath, no doubt to calm herself. "She said, 'Harlan pushed me.'"

Several audible gasps sounded in the courtroom.

The prosecutor nodded. "And how did you respond, Miss Patel?"

Nasha focused on the prosecutor, who had stepped closer to the stand. "I didn't know who Harlan was, but I decided not to ask her about that, because I knew the anesthesiologist was on the way. Instead, I held her hand because she was clearly in pain, and I asked her *why* he would've pushed her."

The prosecutor leaned on the railing of the witness stand and turned to face the jury. "A good question. And what was Mrs. Wells' answer?"

Nasha's pink lips seemed to pale, as did her face. Brandon hoped she wasn't about to pass out. Every eye in the courtroom was focused on the reticent woman on the stand.

"Uh...she said she was going to the FBI."

The prosecutor shook his head. "Did she elaborate on that statement?"

"No—by that time the anesthesiologist had arrived. Mrs. Wells moaned and then closed her eyes."

The prosecutor strode toward the jury box. "The anesthesiologist has made a sworn statement that the only thing he heard from Mrs. Wells was that groan." He turned back toward Nasha. "Miss Patel, were you aware that Mrs. Wells had indeed been in contact with an FBI agent a week before her accident on the stairs, and that she was preparing to turn state's evidence on her husband, linking him to numerous money laundering and drug operations?"

Nasha raised her eyebrows.

The defense jumped in. "Objection, your honor. No one has testified to that in the record."

"Sustained," the judge replied.

The prosecutor nodded and rerouted his questions. "Not long into that exploratory surgery, Maureen Wells died on the operating table, is that correct, Miss Patel?"

Nasha dipped her head respectfully. "She did, yes."

"No further questions, your honor."

As the prosecutor stepped down to open the floor for cross-examination, the defense attorney stood. He proceeded to try to cast aspersions on Nasha's recollection of events, given that she'd worked two back-to-back shifts the night Maureen Wells was brought to the ER. But Nasha firmly maintained she'd been fully alert at that time of night, thanks to an energy drink and several slices of pizza.

Brandon found himself mentally cheering the petite witness on. He could see why she'd needed extra security. Her testimony was practically unassailable, and it couldn't be written off as inadmissible hearsay because, as the prosecutor had stated, it was a dying declaration, made by someone who claimed her death was intentional. Although the defense attorney had objected to the "dying declaration" statement, it was clear he couldn't really fight it.

Nasha was finally relieved of her station, and as she stood, she grasped the railing as if her life depended on it. She shot a frantic glance at the female guard, who was already hurrying to her side. As the woman escorted Nasha past the defense table, Brandon watched Harlan Wells' face. Although he'd seemed cool and somewhat smug during Nasha's testimony, now he didn't restrain himself from pinning her with a look that could only be described as downright menacing.

Brandon felt a surge of anger, and he wondered if the other jurors had been watching, too.

More than anything, he was convinced that Nasha was telling the truth, obviously at great expense to her emotional well-being. And the threat to her well-being was sitting at the defense table like he was the untouchable king of Hemlock Creek.

4

Leah clamped a strong hand around Nasha's elbow and steered her directly from the courtroom. Bruce pulled up the rear, firmly closing the door behind them. The sound reverberated along the empty hallway. Nasha slowed, taking a moment to gather her wits. Although she'd pretended to ignore it, Harlan Wells' unabashed death glare had served as a fitting wrap-up to a day she'd dreaded for months on end.

Thank goodness she wasn't expected to stick around and watch the other witnesses testify, although she had to admit that the lanky, bearded redhead in the jury box had captured her attention. She was sure she'd seen him before, but couldn't place where they would've met. He'd looked so understanding and compassionate that she'd found herself talking directly to him as she testified.

Now that her energy was completely depleted, Nasha couldn't wait to get back to the bed and breakfast and try to unwind. Maybe if her mind were clear, she could figure out where she'd seen the redhead before.

The marshals had checked her into the bed and breakfast

using her witness protection alias—*Ruby Burns*. The name irked her every time she had to say it, stripped as it were of her Punjabi heritage. Her grandfather had come to America and established himself as an allergist, and even as a child, Nasha had determined to follow his and her father's physician footsteps.

If only Maureen Wells hadn't dropped into her life and derailed her plans.

But the poor woman's face...those desperate blue eyes...and the way she'd gasped for each word she'd managed to eke out...Nasha couldn't let it all be in vain. No matter how hard it was uprooting from her family and taking on a new clinical rotation in Arizona, it was her duty to tell the dead woman's story.

"You okay?" Bruce asked, his dark eyes concerned. "You did well in there."

Leah nodded in agreement, punching a keycode in the door that would lead them to the courthouse roof. "The pilot's ready for us."

Nasha knew the drill, having experienced it this morning. A helicopter pilot would be waiting on the roof to fly them to the private estate of a man who'd allowed them to touch down there. Then Bruce and Leah would accompany her by car to the bed and breakfast, which was in a neighboring county so it wouldn't be easily discovered. Either Bruce or Leah would be with her at all times after that, taking turns staying in the room next door to her.

The marshals had decided a bed and breakfast was the best way to go, since the owner was an ex-military man they trusted to keep mum about his guests. However, his wife—a perky, pink-cheeked lady who reminded Nasha of Mrs. Claus —couldn't be more unlike her solemn husband. Nasha hoped Mr. Ellicott had told her about the seriousness of keeping her visit a secret. The friendly woman seemed eager to spill stories about the area and the folks who'd visited their place.

After getting situated in her seat and putting on her headset so she could talk to the marshals, Nasha held her breath as the chopper whirred to life. Although the mountains below were covered in the beautiful rusts and golds of late fall, she couldn't relax until her feet safely hit the ground again.

Once they landed in the field, Leah and Bruce shuttled Nasha into the waiting car. When they drove past the turnoff that could've taken them to her parents' house, Nasha blinked back tears and forced herself to look away. The loneliness of being in witness protection was staggering. Although she was a natural introvert, it had been so long since she'd been wrapped in one of her dad's big hugs or received a loving kiss on the forehead by her mom. And she couldn't even bear to think of Tarek, who was growing up without her.

They approached the metal gated drive of the bed and breakfast and Leah buzzed them in. The drive meandered through the woods, and Nasha took a moment to enjoy the tree-lined view. It seemed that fall had peaked early this October, and she hated that she'd missed it, because it was one of her favorite seasons.

She took a deep breath as they pulled into the circular drive in front of the bed and breakfast. The multi-turreted house was painted a blinding royal blue with hot pink accents. From its rocking chair-strewn porch to its cluttered entryway and rooms, the place resembled an antique hoarder's paradise. Nasha, who appreciated anything streamlined and jettisoned anything that didn't serve a purpose, felt claustrophobic every time she walked inside.

Reluctantly pulling up the rear behind Leah, she trudged up the front steps. Thankfully, Mr. Ellicott was the one to greet them, and he and Bruce fell into a friendly conversation. Nasha headed directly up to her room, put the key in the lock, and waved goodbye to Leah. They hadn't even discussed supper plans, but she knew Leah would text her later with suggestions for takeout. There was no way they'd allow Nasha to enter a restaurant where she might be recognized.

She kicked off her heels and collapsed onto the canopied bed, her face sinking into the plush pink bedspread. Although she didn't want to think about what was going on in the courtroom, she knew Wells' attorney would put experts on the stand to say his wife had died from a fall.

And the truth would further be obscured because the two attempts on Nasha's life had to be kept silent.

She rolled over, staring at the patched plaster ceiling. A cold sweat broke out as she once again tasted the despair she'd felt the evening she'd been attacked as she drove home across the mountain. A black SUV had zoomed up to the rear of her vehicle before abruptly swerving and speeding into the oncoming lane. The vehicle then began pushing Nasha's small car toward the steep edge of the cliff. Her right front tire had skidded off the pavement and she struggled not to hit the guardrail when another car fortuitously approached in the oncoming lane. The SUV was forced to drop back, allowing Nasha the opportunity to straighten her car. Catching sight of a turnaround on the opposite side of the road, she took her chances and made a U-turn into it before speeding off in the opposite direction. The unwieldy SUV was unable to maneuver so easily.

Nasha had driven straight to the police station, where she'd given a shaky account of the incident. By the time her dad had arrived on the scene, she was shivering uncontrollably and couldn't string three words together.

After that, she'd fervently hoped and prayed no one

would come after her again. But the next homicidal attempt on her life had been even worse. They'd targeted her at the hospital when she was working.

Unwilling to relive that harrowing day, Nasha sat up and smoothed out the bedspread. It was time to pull herself together. She pulled the shades down and headed into the bathroom, where she started pouring a hot bath in the claw-foot tub. The tub was one of the best perks of staying here, and she was determined to enjoy it. She dumped an entire mini-bottle of shower gel in the bath and watched as the white foam began to spread across the surface of the water.

Yet her mind was determined to replay the second time one of Harlan's men had tried to kill her. He had invaded a space where she'd previously felt safe, violating the very halls of the emergency room by grabbing her and pressing his gun into her back.

Nasha sank into the tub in the steamy, eucalyptus-scented bathroom. Memories fluttered to the surface of her mind, demanding that she sift through them.

The feel of that cold gun barrel against her thin scrubs had released a kind of primal fear in Nasha. She'd hyperventilated as the man had pushed her forward...and then she'd passed out cold in the hallway.

ER personnel raced to help her, forcing her would-be attacker to flee out the back entrance. Police were called to the scene, but the man had already managed to escape. Although Nasha was allowed to return home, it was the very next day that the FBI placed her in witness protection and moved her to Arizona.

Not only had she lost nearly a year of her life to that murderer, but she'd also lost the ability to sleep soundly for any extended period of time. Insomnia had ruled her life since the attack in the ER.

She set her jaw. It was time for Harlan Wells to get what was coming to him. She prayed the jury would see the truth —even without the benefit of her entire story—and give that murderer life without parole.

5

Brandon yawned. The past two days had been exhausting as jurors listened to testimonies from doctors, police, and any other expert the lawyers could dredge up. Despite conflicting information, Brandon still found it difficult to believe the defense's story that Maureen Wells had gotten enraged when Harlan had asked for a divorce, took a swing at him, then lost her balance and fell headlong down the marble staircase.

Yet Harlan's mistress, Courtney Bianchi, had come forward and confirmed that she and Harlan were involved in an affair and that she'd been badgering Harlan to divorce Maureen. The afternoon of his wife's death, Harlan texted Courtney, saying he was finally going to tell Maureen about their affair and ask for a divorce.

On the other hand, the prosecutor shared that in the Wells' prenuptial agreement, Maureen had restricted how much she would keep in a divorce *unless* it was discovered her husband was cheating. On top of that, disclosed bank records showed that Harlan went behind Maureen's back and tapped into some of her substantial family money to fund his own business. It seemed Harlan had strong motives to kill his wife before it was brought to light that he was having an affair.

Yet he *claimed* he had been the one to bring up the affair. Brandon found that hard to believe. Harlan didn't strike him as the kind of man who would own up to his faults. He was more like a proud, strutting peacock.

Brandon sat up straighter as another woman took the stand, and his chair let out an obnoxious squeak. The old lady next to him gave him an amused look as Maureen's best friend Emily Younts was introduced as the next witness.

As the questioning began, the tailored blonde swore that Harlan had never lifted a finger to his wife. She claimed he simply wasn't the violent type.

"He was always the perfect gentleman, bringing Maureen flowers and even installing a pool when she mentioned she'd like one," Emily said. She batted her long—and probably fake —eyelashes toward Harlan. "I was always telling her how lucky she was, landing a sensitive guy like that." Her voice was breathy, and it was clear to Brandon that the woman found Harlan attractive.

He shot a look at the defendant, uncertain why he was such a magnet for women. Sure, Harlan was a snappy dresser and carried himself with confidence, but there was a slipperiness to his half-smile that rubbed Brandon the wrong way. Maybe he was the kind of dude that men could see through, but women couldn't. Brandon had run into that type before—in fact, some of them had dated his sister Molly— and he wished more guys would step up and expose them as the jerks and users they were.

Still, he was trying to keep an open mind. Especially now, as Emily stepped down and Harlan Wells stood, ready to take the witness stand.

Once he was sworn in, Harlan offered a humble smile to the jury. The defense attorney instructed him to recount what happened on the evening of September eighth of last year.

Harlan nodded. "I'd had a crazy day at work dealing with a lot of shipment delays, so I came home a little earlier than usual—around six PM. To be honest, I was distracted and anxious about Courtney. As she told you, we'd been seeing each other for several months and she said she was sick of hiding our relationship. I told her I was going to tell Maureen about the divorce that night."

"And did you actually plan to divorce your wife, Mr. Wells?" the defense attorney asked. "Despite the prenuptial agreement that would restrict your access to your wife's extensive family funds if you were discovered to be having an affair?"

Brandon found it interesting that Wells' lawyer threw his possible murder motive right out on the table, but there must be a reason for taking that approach.

Harlan's gaze shifted downward. "It was a foolish move, and I knew it. But Maureen deserved the truth, and I'd promised Courtney our wait would be over." He looked up again, his eyes beseeching. "When love is involved, I guess the heart wants what it wants."

Brandon nearly gagged. Seriously? The man was sitting there spouting shallow catch phrases?

His lawyer nodded thoughtfully, as if Harlan had said the pithiest thing in the world. "And when did you inform your wife of your affair?"

"Well, I went upstairs to see her since she was in her room, so it must've been around five after six. I made some casual conversation, because I hadn't worked up the courage to tell her. But then she said she needed to go downstairs and check on the pot roast." His eyes turned glassy with tears. "My wife always liked to cook for us and wouldn't hear of hiring a personal chef, although we could've afforded one. She was a good woman," he choked out.

Darting glances at the jurors seated near him, Brandon felt pretty certain no one was buying Harlan's sorrowful story.

"And what happened next?" the lawyer prodded.

"I walked ahead of her and stopped her, just before we went downstairs," Harlan said. "I couldn't keep up the charade anymore. I told her everything—about Courtney, about wanting a divorce—everything. She got mad, like I knew she would. She said I wouldn't get a dime from her if I divorced her."

"And what did you say in response?"

"I told her I had my business and I'd be okay. I said she could keep the house." His face twisted. "And then she tried to punch me."

"Was this normal behavior for your wife, Mr. Wells?"

Harlan gave a vehement shake of his head. "Not at all, but she was very worked up. I believe she would've given me a black eye if I hadn't ducked."

"And what happened when you did so?"

Harlan's eyes widened as if he were watching the fatal events unfold before him. "When she missed hitting me, she teetered off-balance and started falling down the steps. I tried to stop her, but she was lightweight and rolling so fast..." His voice trailed off, and the courtroom fell silent.

The defense attorney cleared his throat. "But weren't you blocking the stairway when she went off-balance?"

Harlan had his answer ready. "When I ducked down, I shifted to the left. Unfortunately, when Maureen fell, it was to the right, into the open space where I'd been standing."

The attorney nodded. "I have no further questions for this witness, your honor."

The final witness was a young man named Dean Casteel. Dean was a nurse on duty the night Maureen Wells died. The poor guy had circles under his eyes and looked like he'd worked one too many night shifts.

But after telling the court that he'd come on duty at six PM the night of September the eighth, Dean went on to say that Nasha Patel had never, not for one moment, been alone with Maureen. "The only one who was at that woman's side from admittance to the surgery was me," the man swore. "And she didn't croak out one word."

The prosecutor didn't visibly flinch at Dean's statement, but Brandon could tell he'd been taken by surprise from the way his jaw tightened. When the judge asked if the prosecutor had any rebuttal witnesses, he asked to have until the next day to bring them in since it was already getting late.

As the jury was finally dismissed, Brandon found himself hoping the prosecutor could prove Dean wrong. Otherwise, it meant that Brandon had misjudged Nasha's honesty. He hated to think he'd merely been swayed by a pretty face.

Back at home, Brandon's youngest sister Katie was helping Ma set the table. A librarian and a total tomboy, Katie wasn't wearing a speck of makeup, and she sported her husband Ace's oversized sweater. Her flaming red hair was tossed into a loose knot and held in place by chopsticks.

"Is Ace coming over tonight?" Brandon asked. Katie's husband had been promoted to police sergeant, and from what Katie said, he was keeping busy.

His sister gave a light sigh. "Nope, he's staying late to review his men's performance evaluations with his supervisor." She slid into her seat and focused on him, curiosity written on her freckled face. "How's the trial going?"

Ma deposited the last dish on the table and sat down next to him. It was chicken and dumplings, one of his favorite meals. Placing her hand on his, she asked, "Yes, hon, how was your day? Do you have to go back tomorrow?"

He kept things vague. "There was a little curveball today, so it didn't wind up like it was supposed to. I'm hoping tomorrow will be the end of it." As he inhaled the steamy scent of dumplings, his stomach growled. "Let's pray, and then we can talk."

Katie and Ma nodded and bowed their heads. He said a brief prayer and passed the dishes quickly, ready to eat.

Katie grinned. "I can see your appetite hasn't been affected despite your grueling jury duty, bro."

He returned her grin and took a huge bite of dumpling, his mind wandering back to the courtroom. He still hadn't been able to place where he'd met Nasha before. He had the feeling Ma would be able to fill him in on the Patel family, but he couldn't discuss anything with her now.

Ma looked at him closely. "You look like you're thinking deep thoughts."

Katie laughed, nudging his elbow. "Don't hurt yourself."

He reached over and rubbed his sister's head, leaving her bangs sticking out in different directions. "Very funny, Oh Bookish One."

As she tried to smooth her hair again, Katie got serious. "It looks like maybe you'll make the last day of Gauley season, then? I'm sure Sammy will be glad to hear that. Are you itching to get out on the water?"

As he pictured himself rafting, a memory popped into his head. That group of teens he had to corral in Arizona...they were whitewater rafting with their youth leader and another woman. The other woman had apologized profusely about the kids' rambunctious behavior, and he'd gotten the feeling she wasn't used to hanging around teens. She'd seemed mortified and completely out of her element. As she'd struggled with her helmet, he had to get close to help her secure it.

That's where he'd seen those long lashes before, that hesitant smile.

Nasha Patel had been in Arizona, just a few months ago. But now he recalled that she'd introduced herself as Ruby.

What was going on?

6

Nasha wandered into the dead garden area behind the bed and breakfast. She shivered in the early morning air, wishing she'd packed a coat. Her morning meal had left much to be desired, with weak coffee, burned toast, and runny eggs. She needed to walk her breakfast off before they took her over to the courthouse. Just last night, the prosecutor had called, giving her the awful news that she'd have to return to court today to give a rebuttal testimony.

A rebuttal of *what*, she'd asked.

The prosecutor explained that Dean, a nurse she'd worked with, had testified that Nasha was never alone with Maureen Wells. It was a total lie, of course.

Nasha had tossed and turned all night, wondering how Harlan managed to get to Dean. She recalled a couple of times when she'd suspected that Dean might be using opioids, but she'd never had proof enough to report him. Assuming that Dean was involved in drugs, Harlan Wells would've known exactly what buttons to push to get the overworked nurse to give false testimony against her.

She supposed it was his word against hers. None of her

coworkers, as far as she knew, had noticed her brief moments alone at Maureen's side.

She hated to testify again, especially with no proof that Maureen had spoken to her. By the time the anesthesiologist had arrived on the scene, the room was bustling. No one had paid any attention to what she was doing.

Kicking a rock from the brick pathway, she wished for the umpteenth time she'd thought to hit record on her phone the second Maureen croaked out that first word. There had been a patient in the curtained bed next to Maureen's, but that patient had since died. It seemed pointless for her to do a rebuttal—hadn't she already been put in the spotlight enough already?

But she recalled what one of the FBI agents had told her before she got taken into witness protection. He'd stressed how important her testimony was to helping them finally close the vise on Harlan Wells, once and for all. He'd gone too far this time, and they finally had a chance to bring him in and destroy his drug-running operations, even without the evidence Maureen had been prepared to hand over to them.

Nasha rounded the corner and stepped onto the porch, where a tall redheaded woman was deep in conversation with the B&B owner's wife. She was gesturing to the windows, saying they'd need to place a wreath on each one for a wedding.

Mrs. Ellicott nodded her approval, then shot a glance at Nasha. She motioned for her to join them. "Come on over, Ruby."

Nasha reluctantly agreed, mentally kicking herself for not taking the back door since she needed to get ready for court. She didn't have time for small talk.

Undeterred by Nasha's reticence, Mrs. Ellicott grinned, placing a plump hand on the redhead's pale arm as she introduced her. "This is our local wedding planner, Molly

Boone. She's the absolute *best*." The woman launched into a list of reasons as to why her bed and breakfast was one of the premier places around for a wedding reception.

Molly was model-intimidating, with a long mane of auburn curls and designer clothing and heels. She towered over Nasha, who felt small in more ways than one next to the Amazon. But Molly's gold-hazel eyes were sparkling with unspoken amusement, and when she politely but definitively cut Mrs. Ellicott off mid-sentence, Nasha knew they were on the same page.

"Mrs. Ellicott, thank you so much for your time and for introducing me to your guest. Ruby, is it?" Molly's eyes locked on Nasha's.

For some reason, Nasha choked up. She didn't *feel* like maintaining the lie. Of course, she had to for her own safety, but Molly seemed like such an earnest and kind person. In fact, she was the second redhead she'd run into lately who seemed kind, counting that bearded juror.

"Yes," she practically whispered. "Ruby Burns."

Another guest walked up on the porch, so Mrs. Ellicott thankfully turned her attention to him. Molly took a step closer, her face etched with concern. "I know it's none of my business, but are you okay?" she asked. "I work with a lot of women, and pardon me for saying, but I recognize fear when I see it." Molly slipped a card from her leather tote and handed it to Nasha. "Listen, if you ever need anything—even just to talk—please call me."

Her eyes now brimming with tears, Nasha gave a mute nod. Molly couldn't know how on-target her observation was, except that it wasn't a boyfriend or husband Nasha was afraid of—it was a drug dealer who'd already tried to kill her twice.

How she wished she could get to the place where she could go through her days without a cloak of fear weighing her down! If only she *could* call Molly up for coffee and tell her everything she'd gone through.

"Thank you," she finally managed.

Molly leaned in and gave her a tight hug. "I'm serious," she whispered, then she turned to say goodbye to Mrs. Ellicott, who was once again drifting their way.

Nasha escaped into the house, pounding upstairs to her room. She unlocked the door, threw herself across the bed, and began to sob. All she'd ever wanted was to pursue her dream of becoming a doctor...to enjoy a normal life with her loving family. Why would God allow such a life-changing detour in her plans? She'd always been careful to follow the rules, to do the right things—and wasn't testifying the right thing, even though it could prove fatal?

⌁⌁⌁

Leah was early when she knocked on Nasha's door. "You ready to go?" she called out.

"Just a minute, please," Nasha responded.

Wearing her dark jeans and a sweater, Nasha felt too casual, but she'd already worn the only dressy outfit she'd packed. She decided to polish her look with the leather heels, although she cringed, knowing her feet would feel it at the end of the day.

Sunlight filtered through the blinds and she opened them. The sky was a cloudless, deep cornflower blue, promising better days to come.

She wished she could believe that. Taking the Gideon Bible from the drawer by her bed, she tried to steady her nerves by reading over one of the Psalms that had kept her going throughout this ordeal. She particularly liked the verse that said God would withhold nothing good from those who walked uprightly. It took faith to believe it was true.

Hadn't her grandfather had faith to make the journey to America and been blessed for it? And faith in the one true and all-powerful God should be even more rewarding than relocating for a better life. Nasha smiled, recalling how her grandfather had come to Christ in America, then devoted the rest of his life to teaching his family the truth. He had walked uprightly, and God had used him to change the lives of his children and grandchildren.

Nasha took a deep breath. She could do this. She might not even have to say much. Last night, the prosecutor told her that she'd basically just needed to confirm her initial testimony. There shouldn't be any further surprises.

She opened the door and followed Leah downstairs. As they climbed into the car that would shuttle them to the helicopter, she offered Leah a weak smile. "It's almost done, huh? I'll bet you'll be glad to get home to your son."

Leah gave a brief, distracted nod. It seemed she was far away today.

"Where's Bruce?" Nasha asked, suddenly concerned that the older marshal wasn't with them.

"Already at the courthouse, talking with an agent," Leah said.

"Do you mean an FBI agent?" Nasha asked, curious as to why the Feds would be getting more involved toward the end of the trial.

"Yes." Apparently, Leah was keeping her answers brief today. Maybe she, too, was hoping this trial didn't get dragged out any longer.

Nasha bit her tongue, determined not to badger Leah even though she had plenty of questions. For instance, would they fly her back to the bed and breakfast after the trial to retrieve her things? And then where would she go? She couldn't work up the courage to ask if she'd finally be allowed to see her family, and she suspected Leah had no definitive answer either.

Her future hinged on which way the trial went. If Harlan was sent to jail, she could breathe easy because the FBI would get busy looking into things, getting what they needed to bust up his drug ring. But if he walked away scot-free, then what? Back to Arizona as Ruby Burns?

She closed her eyes and saw Tarek's face...only it would've changed in the year she'd been gone. He would've gotten taller, and he'd be into new things she didn't even know about.

Her family was the one good thing she prayed the Lord would not withhold from her. Her medical career seemed to fade into the background. More than anything else, she wanted to be there for Tarek and her parents.

7

Brandon had wrestled with the Nasha/Ruby mystery for an hour the night before, then he'd finally given up and texted Ace at work. Without telling him any details of the trial, he asked why someone might show up in another state using a different name.

Of course, Ace's first suggestion was that the person was a criminal. That had been Brandon's first guess, too, but it didn't fit with Nasha's med student persona. Brandon also wondered if she were hiding from a violent ex or something like that.

But in the end, Ace offered a theory that actually fit. "Maybe the person is in witness protection," he'd texted.

The idea resonated. Those guards in the courtroom— they could've been marshals. And the fact that they'd accompanied Nasha into the courtroom at all indicated that she was in danger—a target for someone.

And the only someone who would have reason to target her would be Harlan Wells. Just a couple of people had stepped forward to testify against Harlan during the trial, and they had insinuated that the man was involved in underhanded operations. However, when questioned, they were forced to admit that they had no proof of their assertions, just hunches based on things they'd seen and heard.

Brandon stayed up too late wondering if Harlan had tried to hurt Nasha in some way, thus necessitating the witness protection. He suspected that was the case, and for some reason, Nasha couldn't mention it in court.

He felt the unfairness deeply. The poor woman had gone through a lot—probably much more than he knew—and she was unable to share it. He recalled how unsure she had been in Arizona, how hesitant to get into the raft. He had assured her that he'd led expeditions many times before and that their whitewater trip would only be a Class One, which would keep them on the calmest waters. She'd finally been convinced, climbing into the middle of the raft to join the impatient teens and the youth group leader.

Maybe he'd bring up his theory when the jurors hashed things out at the end of the trial. It couldn't hurt to float the idea past them, especially since he'd sensed they had a warmer response to Nasha's testimony than to Harlan's. He strongly suspected the jurors saw through the man like he did, but he wouldn't know for sure until they convened in the jury room.

Dean wasn't recalled to the stand, but the defense attorney brought in the anesthesiologist, who said that when he arrived on the scene, there were plenty of other people around and that Maureen wasn't talking. The prosecutor made quick work of that argument by asking a few pointed questions, forcing the anesthesiologist to admit that Maureen was indeed moaning when he got there, right before falling silent. That fact seemed to back up Nasha's story that the woman had exhausted her voice by talking beforehand.

Brandon was surprised to see the prosecutor call Nasha back into the courtroom. She was not-so-subtly accompanied by the two guards he was now certain were U.S. marshals. She had circles under her eyes and her long bangs kept falling over her face. As she shoved them behind her ears, gold hoops were revealed in her double piercings. Brandon couldn't help but notice that her ears were delicate and small, like her petite frame. She brought to mind an exotic flower...maybe an orchid. He gave a brief shake of his head, trying to regain some semblance of an attention span.

After asking Nasha to give another rundown of her brief interactions with Maureen, the prosecutor brought up how Dean had sworn under oath that Nasha hadn't been alone with Maureen during the dying woman's ER visit. The prosecutor asked, "Could you explain to the court how Dean might form this impression?"

Nasha turned her large, dark eyes to the jury. "I can't explain it," she said simply.

"Did Dean perhaps dislike you, or have any reason to lie about such a thing?" the prosecutor pressed. Brandon wasn't sure where he was going with this line of questioning, outside trying to prove Dean was a liar.

"We got along well enough," she said. "I wasn't close to any of my coworkers, although they were all friendly. We certainly hadn't argued, if you're talking about something like that."

The prosecutor nodded. "What was your impression of Dean at work? Was he efficient?"

Nasha glanced at Dean, who was sitting on the right side of the courtroom. "He often seemed tired and could occasionally get snippy. He did miss quite a lot of work." She took a deep breath. "And I did notice his eyes were often bloodshot, which made me wonder a little bit."

The prosecutor pounced on this. "Wonder about what, Miss Patel?"

"Drug use," she said.

Several quiet gasps sounded in the courtroom and Dean shifted in his seat.

Brandon admired the way Nasha didn't hedge around with her answers, trying to sugarcoat things. She had a medical mind, he suspected, and was probably able to distance herself from her emotions to a certain degree.

"Objection, your honor," the defense attorney said.

The judge called him to the stand. After a couple moments' heated discussion, the defense attorney strode back to his chair and the judge turned to the jury box. "The jury will disregard that last remark," he said. "Counselor Keaton, please move on."

The prosecutor nodded. After a thoughtful pause, he asked, "Did you notice anything else unusual or amiss in the emergency room on the evening of September eighth of last year, Miss Patel?"

It was evident to Brandon that the lawyer was winding things up with Nasha. It was basically a he-said, she-said situation, and although the prosecutor had managed to cast some aspersions as to Dean's truthfulness, Brandon wasn't sure that would be enough to convince the jury that Nasha was speaking the truth.

Nasha closed her eyes and fell silent, as if trying to remember the night correctly. She mumbled, "No, I can't remember anything strange in particular."

"Thank you." The prosecutor waved a hand toward the judge. "No further questions, your honor."

When the defense attorney didn't jump in to cross-examine Nasha, the prosecutor was able to begin his closing arguments. Brandon felt he presented things well, and that evidence seemed to weigh against Harlan.

When the defense attorney followed up with his closing argument, he took on a condescending tone with the jury, as if he needed to explain and reinterpret what they had seen. The older lady next to Brandon shifted in her seat, and he could almost feel waves of irritation coming from her and the other jurors. He wasn't positive, but it seemed a strong possibility they might vote to convict.

The prosecutor made his final rebuttal, which really clinched things in Brandon's mind. Maureen Wells was planning to turn her husband in for his underhanded schemes, so he had to kill her to protect his interests.

A lunch break was called, after which the jury would convene to discuss their verdict. Brandon glanced around as he stood to follow the other jurors out a rear door. Nasha and her marshals must have made a beeline from the courtroom, because they were nowhere in sight.

He knew most jurors had been grabbing their lunches in town, so he decided to make an exception on the last day and eat at his favorite cafe, The Happy Poet. He enjoyed their hazelnut latte, as well as their bistro-style sandwiches laden with fresh avocado and sprouts that were reminiscent of his years in Arizona.

After texting Ma to let her know the plan, Brandon jogged out to his car. Sensing something different about the courthouse, he glanced over his shoulder, stopping short when he caught sight of a Bell 407 helicopter sitting atop the building. The helicopter would be quite similar to the Bell 412 he'd flown for river tours in Arizona. He remembered hearing a chopper outside just a little before Nasha entered the courtroom, although he hadn't realized it was actually landing. The marshals must have flown her in.

He got into his car and took off for The Happy Poet. By

the time he walked in the cafe's blue French door, his mouth was watering for one of their green goddess turkey clubs and homemade jalapeno kettle chips. Once he placed the order, he strode into the dining room. He glimpsed the male and female marshal sitting at a table. Nasha sat in the booth next to them, talking with the prosecutor. A heavy gold bangle on her wrist clanked against the table as she set her glass down. For a brief moment, her eyes flitted to Brandon's, and she gave a slight nod. Of course she recognized him from the courtroom, but when she gave him a curious second glance, he guessed that she must be struggling to remember the first time they'd met.

Fighting the urge to go over and refresh her memory about the youth group rafting expedition, Brandon slid into a seat by the window with his back to Nasha. The judge had stated a couple of times that jury members were not allowed to talk with anyone from the courtroom, and he didn't want to break the rules and jeopardize anything, especially at this late a juncture.

Blowing a cloud of steam from his mug, he had to wonder if Nasha would ever recall their Arizona meeting...and he couldn't stop hoping that she would.

8

As she took a sip of the French onion soup that had finally cooled, Nasha tried to listen to the prosecuting attorney as he rehashed the events of the trial. However, Nasha felt it was pointless to try to guess which way things would go.

The bearded redhead had broken up her boredom when he came into the cafe, looking even taller and more gangly in the low-ceilinged room. She met his eyes and once again felt the certainty that they'd met before. As Mr. Keaton droned on, she let her mind wander. Maybe the juror hadn't had a beard when she saw him before, or maybe he'd worn different clothing. She tried to picture him in different outfits. Police uniform, scrubs, skateboarder...she giggled at the last one, then sat up straighter as she envisioned the man in a helmet.

Of course. That was it.

She'd met him before, all right, only it was in Arizona. And she'd been at her very worst—her most vulnerable—going along on a youth group outing she never should've said yes to.

The pastor at the church she'd been attending had done a

series on spiritual gifts, saying you could only know which ones you possessed if you tried them out. So when the youth group leader, Jeff, had asked her to accompany the teens on a whitewater rafting trip, she'd prayed about it and hesitantly agreed.

The moment she'd climbed into the van with the boisterous teens, she'd known it was a mistake. She wasn't up on the teen vernacular, and she wasn't prone to joking around, like Jeff was. Plus, on the drive over, it seemed like Jeff was hitting on her, and she wasn't interested in him in the least. He was the kind of white-toothed charmer who always got the girl, which was precisely why she disliked him. She'd spent the rest of the van trip looking out the window and wishing herself a million miles away.

By the time they reached the rafting site, she was edgy, to say the least. However, their rafting guide seemed to know what he was doing, and he was so tall, the teens couldn't very well ignore him. She couldn't recall his name now, but she did remember how his calm demeanor made her feel he knew what he was doing.

Cutting into the thick layer of cheese that topped her soup, she dipped her spoon in and brought it to her lips. As she sipped at it, she felt a slight flush creeping into her cheeks. Now she remembered how the redhead had managed to get her onto the raft that day, just when she was about to make a bolt for the van. She'd been fumbling with her helmet, furious at herself for agreeing to come along, when he had stepped closer, his long fingers brushing hers as he adjusted the straps. "You can do this," he'd said.

Just four simple words, but something about the way he'd spoken them—as if he didn't have a doubt in the world she could do it—had convinced her. He'd helped her into the safest part of the raft, and once they got going, his eyes had drifted her way every time they hit a rough patch. By the time they had disembarked, even Jeff had noticed, making some snide comment that maybe she'd want to spend a little more time there and catch a ride home with the captivating tour guide.

She split her roll and buttered it, watching the tall man's back. His hair had a slight variation to its dark copper shading, bringing to mind the flames of a fire. Yet he seemed docile, even relaxed, flying in the face of the stereotypical hot-tempered redhead.

Then again, she didn't really know him.

By now, both Leah and Butch had followed her line of sight and realized she was watching the juror. As another group of people entered the cafe, Leah raised her eyebrows at her, as if to ask if everything was okay.

Nasha gave a slight nod and refocused on her lukewarm soup, taking an indifferent sip. She still had very little appetite and knew she wouldn't until the trial finally concluded.

Hopefully today was going to be the final day. She looked at the redhead's back, wishing she could beam her thoughts into his brain. *Please convict him*, she'd beg.

She needed to be free of the prison Harlan Wells had put her in.

On the drive back to the courthouse, Bruce and Leah spoke in low voices in the front of the car. Nasha pretended to watch the scenery, but she gathered that they were debating whether or not to keep her in the courtroom until the verdict was read. While she hated the idea of sitting anywhere near Harlan Wells, she also wanted to see the look on his face when he was convicted of murdering his wife.

If he was convicted, she reminded herself.

Hopefully Dean hadn't managed to cast significant doubts in the jurors' minds about whether or not she'd told the truth. It had seemed her testimony was every bit as crucial as the FBI had decided it would be, given how Harlan had tried to have her killed before he went to trial. She idly wondered if the FBI had undercover people positioned somewhere in the courtroom, but she doubted it. They had trusted the U.S. Marshal service to protect Nasha, and so far, so good. None of Harlan's henchmen had showed up at the bed and breakfast, despite Mrs. Ellicott's rather loose lips.

True, Leah had mentioned that Bruce was talking with an FBI agent at the courthouse this morning. Nasha wondered what that was about, but maybe they were simply making a plan as to how to get her out quickly if Harlan happened to be declared innocent. Her stomach churned. If Harlan was acquitted, she'd become a target again.

As the car pulled directly up to a side entrance at the courthouse, Bruce got out to clear the way for her. Leah motioned for Nasha to follow him. After she did, the female marshal quickly fell into step directly behind her.

Nasha turned and whispered, "I hope you can get back to your family soon."

Leah's thin face was serious, her blue eyes dark. "And I hope the same for you."

Bruce led them upstairs. Nasha held her breath to see where she would be waiting—in the side room or in the courtroom itself. Bruce motioned her toward the courtroom doors, taking a moment to speak briefly with the bailiff. He was an older man who didn't seem too spunky.

The courtroom wasn't filled yet, but Harlan Wells was already situated at the defense table, talking with his attorney. Before he could catch sight of her, Nasha dropped her gaze to the floor tiles, following Bruce's large feet toward a back corner of the courtroom seating area. Leah sat down on the other side of her, so she was securely flanked by her marshals.

The seconds seemed to tick by in slow motion until the judge finally called the court to order again. As Nasha waited, she studied the jury, who had all filed in. The tall, redhaired juror sat in the same third seat on the front row, and he looked like he was lost in thought. The kind-looking older woman sitting next to him glanced out into the courtroom, her eyes lingering on Harlan Wells. Did the woman believe his story? Another thin man in the back row was staring her way with a scowl on his face. She hoped he just had a bad case of indigestion.

"All rise," the bailiff croaked, and the courtroom stood to attention. The judge gave a long talk to the jurors about their responsibility to come to a unanimous verdict. He emphasized the importance of being convinced beyond reasonable doubt that Harlan had pushed his wife to her death before rendering a guilty verdict. Nasha began to feel nervous. Although the prosecution had brought in experts who'd maintained that Maureen's injuries were consistent with being shoved down the stairs, the defense had brought in their own experts who had declared that her injuries could have been caused from taking a swing at her cheating husband.

Who would the jurors believe?

Nasha watched as the twelve jurors headed out a back door to deliberate in the jury room. Everything she could say or do had been done. It was in God's hands. She closed her eyes tight, breathing a prayer that God would help them come to the right verdict, which had to be *guilty as charged*.

9

Brandon sensed the jurors were all restless. Some nibbled at stale cookies the court secretary had dropped off for them. One man tried to figure out how to work the tiny coffeepot, only to give up when he discovered there were no filters for it. The older woman Brandon had sat next to in the jury box poured herself a paper cup of water from the dispenser and settled into the seat beside him. She must feel comfortable around him.

One boisterous, red-faced man said, "Well, what does everyone think? Should we get a show of hands right off the bat? Y'all think he's guilty?"

A younger, curly-haired woman frowned. She had a protective mom vibe about her that somehow reminded Brandon of Molly. "We should go about this the right way," she said. "Honestly, I felt the experts were all over the place, so how do we even weigh what they said?"

Several nodded, murmuring their agreement.

An older man in a flannel shirt piped up. "Now, listen here, I've worked on the railroad all my life, and I'll tell you that sometimes they just say what they want you to hear. I'm talking about both sides. So the bigger question is this: *who do we think was telling the truth*?"

The curly-haired mom said, "The girl—the med student. I believed her."

Another woman nodded. "She was scared, that's for sure."

The red-faced man bobbed his head. "And that Dean guy —he was lying through his teeth. I know we have to disregard what was said, but my neighbor's kid was on drugs and he had that same look to his eyes."

A lean man who'd positioned himself in a chair near the window cleared his throat. "We can't talk about that," he said.

Brandon felt a wave of apprehension. So far, everyone had seemed to be on the same page in believing Nasha. The man in the corner seemed a dark horse.

One wizened man stood, shoving a hand in his pocket to withdraw a pack of cigarettes. "I need a smoke break," he said.

"Is that even allowed?" the curly-haired mom asked.

The man shrugged. "I'm not sure." He headed toward the door that went into the hallway and gave it a sharp rap. "I'll see if the bailiff is outside where he said he'd be."

Sure enough, the bailiff spoke to the man, giving him the go-ahead for a smoke break before closing the door behind him.

"So much for that," the railroad guy said, biting into a cookie. "The judge said we can't talk about the case unless we're all in the room."

Brandon decided to make a suggestion. "When that guy gets back from his smoke break, let's talk about Harlan Wells' testimony."

He was surprised to see that when he talked, people leaned in to listen. It was as if they were seeking a leader of some kind, and for whatever reason, he fit the mold.

He had assumed that the curly-haired mom would guide their discussion, but she seemed more than willing to let him take over. Brandon didn't want the red-faced boisterous man to take control, because he'd struck him as far too flippant. If the jurors wanted Brandon to come up with a plan and build unity, he'd step up to the plate. At this juncture, it was hard to believe that twelve people from all walks of life could agree on anything, but he had to believe a unanimous verdict was possible.

The slim man in the corner shifted in his seat. For just a moment, his eyes met Brandon's. Those eyes were somehow calculating—and determined. Why would a randomly picked juror be so determined?

Brandon cast a discerning eye around the hodgepodge of jurors. Most of them looked to be in the fifty to seventy-year-old range and wore wedding bands. He suspected the prosecution would've chosen the married people, guessing that they'd rule against a man accused of killing his wife.

But why had *he* been chosen? Maybe the defense had assumed that a bachelor whitewater guide wouldn't view Harlan's affair as anything all that bad.

He grinned. They couldn't have been more wrong. He'd always been convinced of the sanctity of marriage, which was why he hadn't settled down yet. He wasn't willing to *settle* at all. He knew God would bring the best one into his life at the right time, just like he had done for his parents and for his sisters.

The smoking juror returned and the bailiff shut the door. Taking a quick glance at the wall clock, Brandon decided they needed to stop wasting time.

He settled back into his wooden chair, which was fairly uncomfortable. "So...what did you all think about Harlan's testimony?"

Nearly two hours had passed by the time Brandon took a moment to glance at the clock again. Almost every one of the jurors had spoken up and explained why they'd felt Harlan was not believable. They had also discussed each of the witnesses at length, sharing their impressions of the experts.

As far as Brandon could ascertain, most jurors were leaning to convict.

The soft-spoken railroad worker put a fine point on the pervading feeling in the jury room. "As a manager, I've seen my share of Harlans. They do harm to our community with their bad dealings. They come in with their money and they expect things to be done their way. I feel like Harlan thought he could get off with a slap on the wrist. He was trying pretty hard to squeeze out those three tears when he talked about his wife, I can tell ya."

The curly-haired woman said, "And did you notice those guards that have to stay right with the med student? I wonder why that is?"

Brandon couldn't stay silent. "I have a feeling they're U.S. marshals," he said.

The older woman by his side gasped. "But why would she need those?"

The red-faced man boomed, "Why, witness protection, my dear. It's in all the movies. That poor girl must be in danger somehow."

"By Harlan Wells," the curly-haired woman breathed. She looked up, her green eyes wide. "Someone's tried to hurt her, and I'm betting it was Harlan himself."

"But why wouldn't they tell us?" the smoker asked.

"They probably couldn't, for some legal reason or another," the curly-haired woman continued. "Maybe it didn't have a direct bearing on this murder case or something."

Brandon was glad the jurors were leaping to the same conclusions he had. That curly-haired mom was sharp.

It seemed to be the right time to call for an initial vote. The jurors didn't have any paper, so Brandon supposed there was no way to keep things anonymous. Besides, people needed to be able to explain themselves if they voted against the group.

"Okay," he said, leaning in and resting his arms on the table. "I think we could try a vote, just to see which way everyone's leaning. Like the judge said, there are only two possible verdicts: guilty or not guilty. Let's start with guilty. Everyone who believes Harlan Wells is guilty, raise your hand."

Slowly, people started raising hands. Brandon slid his own hand up, then took a long look around the room.

Only one person's hand wasn't raised, and it was no surprise to Brandon that it was the slim man by the window. The look on his face was inscrutable.

The red-faced man stared at the slim man. His voice irritable, he said, "Would you care to explain yourself, sir?"

The slim man's voice was gritty. "I believed her best friend," he said. "Emily, I think her name was."

He was actually referring to the woman who'd been so flirtatious with Harlan from the stand.

"Are you kidding me?" one woman asked, her voice incredulous. "That woman seemed...well, no offense, but she seemed a little loose to me. Did you see the way she looked at Harlan? I feel like something else was going on there."

The elderly woman next to Brandon gave a fierce nod. "Shameless," she murmured.

Brandon agreed, but he watched in silence to see which way things went. Would the thin man push back?

The man simply shrugged. "No skin off my teeth what you think about her," he said. "I don't think Mr. Wells killed his wife, is all. And I don't want a murder conviction on my head if it ain't right, you know?"

The jurors went back and forth with the thin man—who told them his name was Glenn—for nearly half an hour, during which time the smoker took another break, further holding up the voting process. After another not-so-subtle reminder from the bailiff about the time, Brandon knew they had to come to a decision.

He asked for a second vote. Once again, every hand raised to support a guilty verdict except Glenn's. This time, Brandon wasn't the only one watching in complete befuddlement. They had rehashed the trial so many times, with each time pointing more and more toward Harlan's guilt, yet this man continued to place his trust in the flirty best friend's testimony above all else?

As if reading everyone's minds, Glenn said, "I'm not changing my vote. Didn't you listen to the judge? I can't vote guilty if I don't believe beyond a shadow of a doubt that he murdered her. I'm voting not guilty from now until the cows come home, and nothing's going to change my mind." He folded his arms across his chest and sent a challenging look toward the red-faced man, who was now glistening with sweat.

True to form, the red-faced man sputtered, "It'll be on your conscience that you let this killer go, then."

Glenn turned his head to the wall as if ignoring everyone.

Brandon winced. There was nothing he could do at this point. The curly-haired woman looked at him. "Looks like we have to call it, then. We can't come to a unanimous decision, despite how nearly *everyone* feels about it." She shot a withering gaze toward the oblivious Glenn.

Brandon nodded. He knocked on the door, and the bailiff agreed to tell the judge that they were unable to reach a unanimous verdict. The judge instructed the jury to choose a foreman, and the curly-haired woman nominated Brandon.

He agreed, signed the forms, and before he knew it, the jury was called back into the courtroom.

As he sank into his squeaking chair for the final time, Brandon shot a look at Nasha. Her dark head was down, almost as if she expected defeat. He wished he hadn't said yes to being the foreman. He'd have to read the verdict that would make her life more miserable than it probably already was.

But there was no time to think about it. The judge gave a few brief words, then said, "Will the jury foreperson please stand?"

Brandon slowly rose to his feet, surprised when his chair only let out a brief squeak.

The judge continued. "I'm told that the jury has been unable to reach a unanimous verdict. Is this correct?"

"Yes, your honor," Brandon said.

The judge proceeded to instruct the jurors that they were to convene one more time for further deliberations, to see if they could possibly arrive at a unanimous verdict. He stressed the importance of coming to a consensus, explaining that if they could not do so, he would have to declare it a hung jury, also known as a deadlocked jury. This situation could lead to a mistrial.

Disgusted to even think about Harlan Wells going to a mistrial, Brandon trailed the others back into the jury room. When everyone had taken a seat, he tried to gather his thoughts.

In the interim, the curly-haired woman turned to Glenn, giving him an unflinching stare. "Are you sure there wasn't even *one* testimony that would make you doubt Harlan's innocence?"

As if to drive the point home, the man pounded a fist into his hand. "Of course there were things that made me doubt he was innocent, lady. But nothing *proved* to me that he was guilty, at least not beyond doubt. Besides, like I said, I think that the wife's friend was telling the truth," he maintained.

The curly-haired woman shook her head as if astounded someone could fall back on such faulty reasoning. Brandon was shocked himself, but he was determined to give things another try.

"What was it that convinced you that the best friend—uh, Emily—was being honest?" he asked, hoping to open dialogue with the puzzling man.

Glenn sat up straighter, as if ready to explain. "She knew the couple better than anyone else," he said. "And women have intuition, so she'd know if he was good to his wife or not."

"He admitted to having an affair on his wife," one woman practically shouted. "How on earth could he be truly good to her? He didn't give a flying fig about her."

The women in the room all chorused their agreement, along with most of the men.

The railroad man said, "And woman's intuition? Good grief, do you know how many women don't see squat when it comes to slimeballs like Harlan? My own sister married one; I should know. I tried to tell her a hundred times he wasn't any good, but she wouldn't listen."

Glenn shot him a sulky look. "That's your story. Might not be the same in this case."

Brandon sensed things were spiraling into chaos, and their time was ticking. "Let's have another vote," he said. "Everyone for guilty, raise your hand."

Unfortunately, although eleven people raised their hands, they were once again thwarted by Glenn, who kept both hands squarely planted in his lap. Brandon could see no good reason for the man to remain adamant in his not guilty vote, but he had to respect it.

"Alright, I'll tell the bailiff." Brandon reluctantly headed

for the side door and gave it a knock. It didn't take long for
the jury to be recalled to the jury box. The entire scenario
played out again, only this time, the judge said that due to the
deadlock of the jury, he was declaring a mistrial for Harlan
Wells. The attorneys were to call his office the next day to
agree on a date for the new trial.

Judge Stowers dismissed the courtroom. Harlan Wells
gave his lawyer a high five, shooting a self-satisfied smile at
the jury. Brandon watched in disgust, desperately wishing it
had been a different outcome. He finally allowed himself to
turn his attention to Nasha.

The lady marshal sitting next to Nasha had pulled her
into a hug, so Brandon couldn't see her face. But from the
shaking of her upper body, he suspected she'd started
sobbing.

He had a sudden impulse to go over and offer her his
condolences, but he assumed that would be against the rules
somehow. Instead, he stood to join the jurors who were
quickly slipping out the back door. Only the curly-haired
woman lingered in her jury chair, and she gave him a glance
that spoke volumes. It was obvious that she felt the outcome
was totally unacceptable, too.

As Brandon took a step toward the door, a gunshot tore
through the air. It took him a split-second to process what
he'd heard, but when he did, he jumped toward the curly-
haired woman, taking both of them to the floor. As
screaming ensued, several other shots rang out. When the
shots stopped, he rolled off the woman, who promptly
curled into a ball, and he peered above the base of the
jury box.

Three armed men had infiltrated the courtroom, and they
all wore black ski masks. Two of them stood guard in front of
the marshals, their guns raised. The male marshal was
bleeding profusely from his neck and making noises that

surely meant he was dying. The female marshal didn't seem injured, but she was staring in horror at her downed partner.

The other armed man was pulling Nasha toward him, his pistol aimed at her head. Casting a frantic look around, Nasha's terrified eyes met Brandon's for a split-second. Her look seemed to implore him to help. Then she was yanked into the hallway.

Brandon took a second look around the courtroom, knowing he'd have to move fast to save Nasha. Harlan Wells was still seated. Unlike the lawyer crouched on the floor next to him, Harlan didn't seem overly concerned. Brandon was fairly certain the judge had exited earlier...but where was the bailiff? He'd have a gun.

Twisting around slightly, Brandon looked toward where he'd last seen the bailiff. His heart skipped a beat when he caught sight of the older man's uniformed pant legs and shoes as they protruded near the side of the courtroom. The gunmen must have picked him off first.

Determined to get to Nasha in time, Brandon began to crawl backward toward the jury box exit, hoping he could evade the attention of the intruders standing sentinel in the back. When the huddled juror sent him a warning glare, curls tumbling into her eyes, Brandon held a finger to his lips. He had made up his mind—Nasha needed help, and he was going to get to her, if it was the last thing he did.

He could hear the female marshal begging the gunmen to let her go so she could get her partner to the hospital. As one of the men barked out a muffled reply, Brandon took his chance and darted straight into the open door of the jury room. Most of the people must have gotten out before the shooting began, because the room was empty.

He hesitated before stepping into the hallway, where the men in the courtroom might see him. Where would Nasha have been taken? The courthouse guards would have surely blocked the front entrance...unless the gunmen had already killed them, too. Still, it seemed unlikely the attacker would drag Nasha along at gunpoint all the way to the parking lot in hopes of making a getaway.

A desperate female scream interrupted his thoughts, and he felt sure it was Nasha. It came from the direction of a doorway in the hall that had a keypad on it.

He inched out of the jury room, hugging the wall as he moved to the keypad door. It hadn't closed completely. Glancing down, Brandon saw that the thick gold bangle Nasha had worn at The Happy Poet had blocked the door from latching.

Smart girl. If she could just keep her head, he might have a chance to reach her in time. And now he knew exactly where they'd decided to take her for their getaway—to the helicopter on the roof.

10

Nasha took another desperate look at her masked captor. The man was so much larger than she was. He must be at least six foot three and he was built like a linebacker. But some gut instinct had warned her not to get into the helicopter with him, so she'd let out a loud scream in the stairway.

"Yell again and I'll put a bullet in your pretty head." The man yanked her arm tight and steered her out the door toward the whirring chopper. She could feel his hot breath on her neck. Nearly stumbling across the regular pilot, who lay sprawled on the ground near the helicopter, Nasha bit back another scream. Another man sat at the controls—this one unmasked—and he gestured for them to get in quickly.

When she balked, the big man moved his pistol from her side, shoving it against her forehead instead. She shuddered at the feel of the cold metal, but told herself to rein in her fear. She couldn't faint like she did in the ER. That day it had saved her, but today, it would likely get her shot.

"Ladies first," the man shouted above the noise of the whirring blades.

Nasha opened the back door of the helicopter and

climbed into the rear seat. She automatically reached for a headset like she'd done on her flights with the marshals, but the man jumped in behind her and grabbed it from her hands.

"Not for you," he shouted. He yanked his mask off before settling the headset over his own ears. He spoke sharply to the pilot, and in a moment, the helicopter began to lift off.

Panic seized Nasha. The man and the pilot didn't care if she saw their faces, which could only be a sign of their deadly intent. What if they planned to shove her out of the chopper? It would be simple enough to fly over a river and push her out. But the Greenbrier river would be far too shallow and her body would be found quickly. Maybe they planned something else, like shooting her and tossing her body over a mountain. If that happened, her parents might not get closure for years, because it would take forever for someone to find her in the dense woods. She shivered.

The man next to her reached into the back for something. Out of the corner of her eye, Nasha caught sight of someone rushing toward the rear of the chopper.

The next moment, the door opened and the man next to her gave a tiny yip of surprise before thudding onto the ground below. The chopper was already rising, but not before someone's long-fingered hand wrapped around the seat base and he started climbing on board.

Nasha couldn't believe her eyes when she saw the redheaded juror struggle into the seat next to her. What had inspired this grand gesture of heroism, she couldn't imagine —but she was more than happy to follow the rafting guide's lead.

Brandon got into the seat and latched the door as silently as possible. It was hard to believe he'd made it this far. The thug who'd been guarding Nasha was both taller and heavier than he was, but somehow he'd managed to grab the man's ankle and yank him from the chopper. Must've been the element of surprise, or maybe he'd had some heavenly help.

Climbing aboard was easier, since he'd done plenty of rock climbing in Arizona, and heights didn't scare him. So far, the pilot hadn't realized he was on board—he must not have heard his partner's surprised squeal—but if he looked around, it would be difficult for Brandon to hide.

He turned toward Nasha. Her lips were tight, but she managed to offer him a weak, appreciative smile. That was a good sign—she wasn't going into shock, even after all she'd seen today. Her marshal friend had been shot in the neck right in front of her. It would be difficult to wipe that gruesome image from her head.

Brandon slid from his seat to the floor, crouching behind the pilot's chair. Using hand gestures, he indicated that he was going to try to overtake the pilot. Nasha's eyes widened, but she nodded.

Brandon looked out the window. They were now high enough that if something malfunctioned or the chopper lost control for a moment or two, they wouldn't crash. Like all his river tour pilot friends, he'd been trained to safely land a helicopter in many different circumstances, even if the engine cut out.

But what could he do to disable the pilot? If he pulled the man from his seat, he'd definitely fight back. They didn't have time for that.

It seemed there was only one option, and it was something Brandon didn't feel he was an expert at—brute force. He'd have to down the pilot with one move.

Thankfully, it hadn't been too long ago that he'd gotten a

few pointers in that regard from his brothers-in-law.
Following the annual McClure July fourth picnic in the
backyard, Ace and Zane had started horsing around, showing
off their fighting techniques. Katie joined in too, since she'd
taken several classes, but she was no match for the men and
bailed out quickly. Although Ace was relatively new at self-
defense strategies since he'd only been a cop for a few years,
he held his own against Zane, a seasoned Marine. They
watched in awe as the two muscled men tackled each other
like pros.

Knowing he could use a little work in the manly protector
department, Brandon had tentatively approached the two
warriors and asked for tips. Ace teased him a little, but Zane
instantly took him seriously, showing him the best ways to
punch, block, and defend himself against knife and gun
attacks.

Now Brandon tried to relax his arms, recalling how Zane
had explained the rear naked choke hold, which would
ideally knock someone unconscious. It seemed incredible to
think he was capable of doing such a thing with only his
body strength, but Zane had sworn it was a proven technique.
He'd even warned Brandon not to use the move unless he
wanted to take someone down fast.

The only thing was, because it involved both his arms,
he'd have to slip one arm beneath the man's jaw and pull him
sideways off the seat. Only then could he lock his grip and
perform the choke maneuver.

Would it work? He had no idea, but he also had no time
to waste. The pilot was bound to look around soon.

Without overthinking things, he turned to face the pilot's
seat and braced his knees. Sliding a flattened hand under the
man's throat, he pulled over and up, then grabbed his own
bicep to tighten the hold. He squeezed the man against his
own chest, then felt him go limp in his arms.

As the pilot's hand slipped from the collective stick that maintained altitude, the helicopter dropped. Brandon dragged the man from his chair and shoved his lolling body onto the passenger's seat. He slid into the pilot's chair, letting his hands and feet fall naturally into place on the sticks and pedals. Veering left, he flew away from the tree-covered mountain ridge they'd been careening toward. He looked around, trying to get his bearings.

Just ahead, he could make out the wide green expanse of a golf course. He was fairly certain it was The Greenbrier Resort, where Molly worked as a wedding planner.

He turned to Nasha. "Can you tie him up somehow?" he shouted.

She paled, but nodded. "I'll try."

He needed to land the chopper as soon as possible, before the pilot woke. The Greenbrier golf course was as good a place as any. He'd call Molly as soon as he touched down and ask her to let the management know why a helicopter was sitting on their green. He couldn't remember if the Greenbrier maintained its own security force, but with the resort's clout, he was sure the police would get to the scene on the double.

Nasha fumbled at his side with a long piece of twine she'd found somewhere. "Tie his hands behind his back," Brandon instructed. "Then try to tie his feet with something."

She gave a quick nod and pulled the pilot's hands together.

Focusing on the flat grassy strip that had come into view, Brandon began to make the small adjustments that would set them down easy. "Small inputs!" his pilot instructor had always preached, and it was true, especially in an area where people might be milling around, like the golf course. He never ceased to be amazed at the sensitivity of the helicopter controls.

As the chopper whirred to a stop, a golf cart came racing up. The trussed-up pilot groaned and opened his eyes, which sent Nasha scurrying into her seat in the back.

After Brandon explained the situation, a couple of golfers stayed with the pilot while another called the police. Brandon helped Nasha climb out of the chopper, but her legs nearly gave way, forcing her to lean on him heavily. He marveled at the feel of her slight body beneath his arms.

One of the older golfers noticed her distress and offered his cart, so Brandon gently helped Nasha into it. Taking it slow, he drove for the main resort building, hoping to catch Molly there. His sister would know just what to do for the worn-out witness at his side, and maybe Ace could help him think of a way to protect her until the marshal service found out about the courtroom shooting.

11

Nasha could kick herself for being such a weakling. After the redhead had so chivalrously helped her out of the chopper, she'd nearly toppled over against him. She was a *med student*, for Pete's sake. She should be accustomed to gory things.

But nothing could have prepared her for watching the brutal way Bruce had been shot. As blood poured from his neck, she and Leah had shared a look of disbelief. It was a fatal wound, and there was no way Bruce would survive it.

Then the man with the gun had rushed her out to the chopper. What had his plan been? She still couldn't bear to think of it.

Trying to take her mind off things, she allowed herself to focus on the redheaded juror, who was carefully driving the golf cart.

"As you know from the courtroom, my name is Nasha," she said. "Please tell me your name, so I can properly thank you for jumping aboard that helicopter."

"Brandon McClure," he said. His voice was mellow and deep. He seemed relatively relaxed, using only one hand to drive.

She shifted to face him. "Thank you, Brandon. I'm glad you knew how to fly a helicopter—on top of your whitewater rafting skills." She smiled.

The cart slowed as his eyes met hers for a moment. They were a greenish gold color, some indescribable cross between moss and honey. She couldn't seem to look away from them.

"You remembered," he said, grinning. "It took me awhile to recall where we'd met, but I finally did. May I ask what you were doing out in Arizona?"

"Witness protection," she said. It was the first time she'd spoken of it to anyone except the marshals. Now that she'd opened up, the story began pouring out of her. "Harlan's goons tried to kill me twice when I was here. The FBI decided that they needed my testimony to try to get him for good, so they put me in witness protection until the trial. My name was Ruby Burns." She twisted her hands in her lap, still despising the name.

His eyes played over her features. "You look much more like a Nasha than a Ruby." He stretched his legs, speeding up a little as they approached the main resort building. "Forgive my asking, but what now? Harlan's going to a mistrial, so does that mean you're still in witness protection?"

She felt trapped, like a butterfly under glass. Maybe she'd never spread her wings again. Maybe she'd be dead to the life she once knew.

"I'm sorry—I didn't mean to upset you," he rushed on. "I'm sure it's awful. Isn't your dad a doctor in town? I think my mom's gone to him."

Wiping a rogue tear from her cheek, she nodded, her eyes fixed ahead. "Yes, my father is an allergist in Hemlock Creek, just like his father was. I'm not sure what specialty I want to focus on yet, but I've been on rotation here, and I also did one in Arizona."

He pulled to a stop near the side entrance. "I'm glad you

were able to continue your education even while you were out west." He got out of the cart and gestured to the white glass-paned door. "Okay—let's go in this way. My sister actually works inside."

Nasha felt a surge of apprehension. She'd only just been introduced to Brandon, and now he wanted her to meet his sister after she'd been through such an ordeal? "Okay," she said hesitantly.

As if responding to the misgivings in her tone, Brandon walked over to her side and gave her a reassuring smile. "Don't worry—my sister's very understanding, and I figure she'll help us figure out what to do next."

Nasha followed him inside, past the chocolate shop and the designer stores lining the gallery. He led her into a vibrantly colored room that featured oversized wedding photos of celebrities like Jackie Kennedy and Grace Kelly.

"Have a seat here, if you don't mind," he said, gesturing to a green palm-print settee. "I'll see if she's in." He walked back to a private office adjoining the large room. Nasha tried to relax as she heard voices murmuring inside.

She had just noticed the ornate, fake wedding cakes on the back table when Brandon strode back out. Nasha caught her breath as she recognized the tall woman with auburn curls walking out behind him. It was the wedding planner she'd met at the bed and breakfast—the one who'd immediately noticed Nasha's state of distress.

"Ruby!" Molly said, rushing toward her.

She stepped into Molly's warm hug, then pulled back. "Actually, my name is Nasha. I was in witness protection when we met. That's why I was acting so weird."

Molly's eyes were soft. "Brandon says you got into some kind of trouble in a helicopter—something about a shootout at the courthouse? What on earth happened?"

Brandon looped an arm over his sister's shoulder. "How

about let's have something to drink or eat first, sis. Nasha here has been through a lot."

"You have, too," Nasha said.

Molly jumped into action. "Of course. Now, you just sit down right here and I'm going to get you both some coffee and food. And Brandon, did you say the police are coming to get that guy from the helicopter?"

He nodded. "Yeah, but I'm not sure if Ace will be coming with them. While you're getting the food, I'm going to give him a call."

"Sounds like a plan." Molly walked out, impossibly steady in her high-heeled boots.

Brandon took a seat near Nasha and pulled out his phone. He didn't elaborate on who Ace was, but in no time he was talking to the man, giving him a brief rundown of what had happened in the courtroom and on the helicopter. "Okay, so you're on your way here?" he asked. "We're in the wedding planning room. We'll stick around until you get here."

As he hung up, he turned to Nasha. "That was my brother-in-law, Ace Calhoun. He's a police sergeant, and I figured he'd be one of the ones called to the scene here. He's on his way. We just need to sit tight and wait for him." His gaze traveled to the open door as Molly returned.

Two teacups were balanced in her hands, and she had a paper bag pinned beneath her elbow. After offering the cups to both of them, she set the bag on the side table nearby. "There's cream and sugar in both coffees," she said. "I know it's not Dr Pepper, bro, but you can get some soon enough." She pointed to the bag. "I grabbed a couple of club sandwiches to go—there should be paper plates in there, too." She settled on a turquoise chair nearby. "What's going on?"

While Nasha pulled out the plates and arranged their sandwiches on them, Brandon gave a brief explanation to his sister. By the time Nasha had managed to drink some coffee and eat half a sandwich, a policeman walked into the room. From the large gun on his belt to his impressive superhero build, Nasha had to guess this was none other than Ace.

"Hey, bro," Brandon said, jumping up. "Ace, this is Nasha Patel, the witness I was telling you about. Nasha, this is my brother-in-law, Ace." He sat down and polished off his last bite of sandwich. "Can you tell us what the next step is?"

Ace dragged a seat over and joined their small circle. His blue eyes were kind. "First, I'd love for you to tell me what you can about what happened today, Nasha."

"I will, but first, do you know anything about my marshals?" Nasha asked. Had Bruce somehow survived? And where was Leah? Nasha had no idea where she was even supposed to stay tonight. Surely she wasn't supposed to return to the bed and breakfast alone?

"Of course. I'm happy to explain," Ace said. "Now that the courthouse is secure, we've been in contact with the U.S. Marshal service. Unfortunately, they said that one of your marshals was killed on the scene, but the other one—the woman—is doing fine. However, she's going to have to be debriefed, so they recommended we find a safe place for you tonight until they can step in with a fresh crew tomorrow."

Nasha didn't want a fresh crew; she just wanted Bruce and Leah back. But it was only fair that Leah would get sent home to recover from what happened to her partner.

She knew the answer would be no, but she had to ask. "Would it be possible to stay with my family tonight?"

Ace shook his head. "I'm afraid not, Miss Patel."

Brandon jumped into the conversation. "I've got a great idea—she could stay at our house. No one's going to come looking for her there."

Molly nodded. "Good thinking. Although I'd love to ask

Nasha to stay with us tonight, my stepdaughter Lola will be coming over later, and I can't risk her safety."

Ace looked at Brandon. "Actually, staying at your mom's place isn't such a bad idea. There's plenty of room. Maybe Zane could come over and we could take turns keeping guard. I'm sure the marshals will show up pretty early in the morning."

"But aren't you on duty tomorrow?" Nasha asked, feeling guilty at the idea of asking these men to stay up all night to protect her.

Ace turned a movie-star brilliant smile on her. "Protecting people is what Zane and I do—each in our own ways, of course." He gave Brandon a nudge. "And given that chopper takeover, it looks like Brandon's also stepping into a protector role here."

Brandon's cheeks colored under his freckles. He took a fast sip of coffee.

Ace slapped a palm against his knee. "Yes, ma'am. I believe we'll move forward with the plan to take you to the McClures'. Brandon, please give your mom a call and make sure that's okay." He gave Nasha a probing look. "Do you feel ready to talk about what happened?" he asked.

Nasha wished she never had to talk about Harlan Wells or his murderous thugs again. Hadn't she already gone above and beyond the call of duty when she'd decided to testify, which had already placed her life in jeopardy three times?

Yet she had to help the police track down the men who had shot and killed her faithful marshal. Although she hadn't seen the faces of the masked men who'd stayed behind in the courtroom, she had seen her abductor's face. Hopefully, it would be a matter of time before they could track him down. And they'd already handed them the pilot.

She looked at Ace, who was waiting patiently for her answer. "Yes, I'll talk," she said wearily.

Brandon set his coffee down and wrapped a comforting arm around her shoulder. "I'll help you," he said. "Don't forget I saw your kidnapper's face, too."

Ace nodded. "And the pilot is getting booked as we speak."

Brandon's eyes were warm as they met hers. "They'll get these guys. And in the meantime, we'll keep you safe."

12

Ace told Brandon it was best if he and Nasha left with Molly, instead of in his police cruiser. That way if anyone was watching the police to see if Nasha came to the station, they'd be disappointed.

Brandon suggested that they cover Nasha's face somehow so she wouldn't be recognized. Molly set to work asking around until she found a scarf Nasha could borrow. She helped Nasha wrap the thin navy scarf around her head and the lower part of her face. Following Molly's suggestion, Nasha tucked her arm under Brandon's as if they were a couple and followed him out to Molly's car. Molly came out a few moments later so it wouldn't be obvious she was joining them.

It didn't take long for Brandon to pull up to Ma's house. He wished Nasha could see it when the roses along the front fence were in full bloom. The frost had come earlier than usual, so the flowers had died off. At least the trees in their backyard still had some nice leaves on them.

As he'd guessed, Ma had been watching out the living room window. She opened the door before they even had a chance to get out of the car. Knowing Ma, she'd likely torn through the house like a cleaning whirlwind the moment he'd called to ask about Nasha staying over.

As Molly headed over to Ma and gave her a hug, Brandon got out and went around to open Nasha's car door. By the time he got there, she'd already opened it and was stepping out.

"I'm sorry," she said. "I didn't realize you were coming around—"

She'd left the scarf wrapped around her face, so he couldn't see if she was smiling or not. "No worries," he said. Maybe most women opened their own doors these days—it *had* been quite a while since he'd dated. But his mom had raised him to be a gentleman, and it was a hard habit to break.

Nasha followed him up to the porch. As he introduced her to Ma, she pulled her scarf down to reveal a tentative half-smile.

Ma didn't hesitate to wrap Nasha in a big hug. "Why, hello there. My name is Esther Sue McClure, and we're pleased to have you visit. I know your daddy—he is *such* a good doctor. He got me all fixed up that time I had that terrible reaction to pineapple. Turns out, that wasn't my only later-in-life allergy." Ma took a long look at Nasha. "But honey, you don't want to hear about my problems. You have big enough ones of your own. I'm so sorry you had such a terrible day. Brandon told me a little on the phone. Now you just come on in and make yourself at home."

She led Nasha into the guest room. Molly trailed after them and said, "Nasha, I know I'm a lot taller than you—so is my sister, unfortunately—but we'll find some clothes for you to borrow while you're here. I'm sure I have capris and some smaller shirts and pajamas you could wear. I'm going to head back to work now, but I'll bring some things over around six thirty." Molly turned to Ma. "And don't worry about supper. Zane and I will spring for pizza and wings tonight. Ace said he plans to come over later, so maybe I'll ask Katie if she wants to drop in, too."

Ma nodded. "Thanks, sweetie. I'll make a salad," she offered.

Brandon leaned against the wall in the hallway, proud to see the way his family worked together in a pinch. He'd been away for many years, but he'd been drawn right back into the tight-knit circle of his mom and sisters. He'd need to look for his own place soon—after all, he didn't want to be one of those guys who hung around and mooched off his parents—but then again, Ma was getting older and he knew she appreciated having someone in the house to look after her.

Nasha told Molly thanks, then turned to Ma. "Would you mind if I just closed my eyes a little bit? I feel pretty exhausted."

Ma gave her a knowing look. "Of course you are, hon. You've been through too much. You go take a rest." She placed an arm on Brandon's elbow and steered him toward the kitchen. "Don't you worry about a thing," she called over her shoulder.

Ma asked Brandon a few questions, probably hoping he'd share more details on Dr. Patel's daughter. Knowing he'd have to explain things later when the rest of the family showed up, Brandon held off on answering, saying he needed to take a little rest himself. Once he closed the door in his room, he found his senses were still on high alert after his helicopter hijacking. He couldn't stop musing on Nasha's situation. The marshals were coming for her tomorrow, which probably meant they'd shuffle her right back into the witness protection system.

So far, he'd barely allowed himself to contemplate the undisguised terror on her face as she'd turned to him in the courtroom. She'd watched her marshal get shot and killed, then one of the gunman had forced her up to the waiting helicopter. The abductors had probably planned to get rid of Nasha in such a way that the police would never find her. If her body wasn't found, Harlan would go into his mistrial with another chance at being exonerated.

Harlan Wells was more than bad news. Brandon was convinced he was not only a dangerous criminal, but also a ruthless murderer—and one who'd managed to escape conviction today.

Brandon let out a huge sigh. It was no mystery why the jury had wound up deadlocked. It only took one juror—one man who dug in his heels, obstinately clinging to a flimsy story from someone who'd likely been trying to impress Harlan with her loyalty. It didn't make any sense. Had Glenn been bought off somehow? Had Harlan leaned on him? If so, who on earth would Brandon mention his suspicions to? The mistrial had already been called. Regardless of whether a juror had been tainted, there would be no do-overs of Harlan's initial trial.

Brandon pictured Maureen's best friend, Emily, as she'd shared her testimony of Harlan's exemplary behavior toward his wife. Her every hair had been in place and she'd obviously spent a lot of time perfecting her makeup. Maybe she'd even hired someone to do both. Who was to say that high-maintenance Emily wasn't ingratiating herself to Harlan, maybe even hoping to shove the mistress out of the picture so she could become the second Mrs. Wells. That way, she could wind up controlling whatever money Harlan ended up with—maybe even his dead wife's.

Brandon frowned. Given the shape of Harlan's bank records, it would be Maureen's money that would keep him afloat at the end of all this, if he went free.

The tantalizingly rich smells of pizza and wings finally drifted under his doorway. He jumped up, ready to join Nasha for a meal and see how she was doing.

13

Nasha blinked awake in the dark room, disoriented. She smelled pizza. It took her a moment to realize she was in the McClures' guest room and Molly must've arrived with supper.

Feeling for a lamp, she bumped her phone off the bedside table, lighting up the screen. She grabbed for it, shocked to see it was already six forty-five at night. She'd slept for over an hour. She rolled from the bed, wishing she had time for a quick shower before she ate. The chopper blades had kicked up crazy amounts of dust, and she was certain quite a bit of it had whipped into her hair.

But Esther Sue McClure didn't seem the kind of hostess who would pay much attention to her guests' hair. In fact, she'd given Nasha such a genuinely welcoming hug, it had reminded her of her own mom.

Nasha flipped on the overhead light, running fingers through her hair in front of the dresser mirror. She wasn't going to dissolve into tears, although she surely felt like it. Ace had said that marshals were coming in the morning, which meant she was still in witness protection. Of course, it was for good reason—there was no way they could let her return to her family when Harlan's men were still determined to take her out.

If she could just hold out long enough and outlast Harlan's murderous plans until the mistrial was over...maybe then it would all be over and she'd go home.

She strode toward the door, fresh determination filling her. Despite the uncertainty of her situation, she could at least try to enjoy her brief time with the McClures. It had been ages since she'd eaten a family meal, and the friendly murmur of voices in the kitchen had an irresistible pull on her. Possibly because she knew Brandon was among them.

Sure enough, Brandon jumped up from the table the moment he saw her and pulled out a chair. "Glad you joined us," he said, pushing the chair in once she'd sat down. "I wasn't sure if I should wake you, but Katie said to let you sleep. Katie's my youngest sister," he added.

Nasha's eyes traveled to the freckled, red-haired woman Brandon gestured toward. Katie's long hair was pulled into a ponytail and her bright green eyes were steady on Nasha's face. Her white, paint-splattered T-shirt and holey jeans stood in stark contrast to her polished sister Molly, who was demurely sipping a glass of tea next to her.

"Nice to meet you, Nasha," Katie said. "I'm a librarian, so I'm the nerd in the family. Ace is my husband—he's finishing up at work now and he'll be over in a bit. He said you looked pretty shaken up this afternoon."

"I was," Nasha admitted.

Katie pushed the half-empty pizza box toward Nasha. "Please, help yourself. We're not formal around here."

Esther Sue pointed to a couple of take-out boxes. "You want barbeque or hot wings, hon?"

"Barbeque, please." Nasha took the proffered container and helped herself to a couple of wings before glancing around the table. A man she hadn't met yet sat near Molly at the head of the table. He had a dark blond beard and watched her with a thoughtful gray gaze. He looked rugged, like one of those homesteaders on the Alaskan shows she enjoyed.

"I'm Zane Boone, Molly's husband," he said. Although his voice was kind, he only offered a half-smile, the kind that said he'd seen more than his share of pain in the world. Nasha couldn't meet his serious eyes again, sensing he'd pick up on her suppressed feelings of helplessness.

She looked back to Brandon, suddenly craving his cheery disposition and spontaneous nature. "I hope you got some rest, as well. You did so much to help me today."

"Yeah, bro, it's time to spill all the details on the chopper rescue mission," Katie chimed in. "Ace and Molly already got to hear your story."

Brandon took a long drink of his iced Dr Pepper and leaned back in his chair, his feet stretched under the table. He shot Nasha a questioning look. "You mind if I tell them?"

Nasha shook her head. "Please, go ahead."

Brandon launched into a blow-by-blow account of what he'd seen and done after the trial. When necessary, he'd look to Nasha to fill in her side of the story. He praised Nasha for the way she'd left her bracelet behind as a breadcrumb for would-be rescuers, then he lightened the atmosphere by chuckling about the wart on the kidnapper's nose and the utterly befuddled look the pilot had given him before he'd blacked out.

As Nasha watched Brandon in his element, waxing on about what now seemed more like a grand adventure than a harrowing near-death experience, she began to realize that her life didn't have to feel like a never-ending, grim series of events. Yes, she'd been in serious danger in the helicopter, but she had also *escaped* that danger, thanks to Brandon's help. Maybe it was all in how you framed things.

On the whitewater trip with Brandon, she'd assumed that he must not be afraid of death, but maybe it wasn't that simple. Maybe he simply had the unique ability to look death in the face and laugh. It wasn't that he wasn't afraid—certainly, he seemed to have feared for her safety in that helicopter—but he had come to rescue her anyway.

Molly wiped her lips with a napkin. "I hate to cut things short, but we need to get back since Krista—that's Lola's mom, Nasha—drops off Lola for a few days."

"I'm so sorry if I kept you," Nasha said.

Zane stood and gave Esther Sue a hug. He turned back to Nasha. "You didn't keep us at all. Krista's not usually on time." He frowned. "She's not thrilled with how easily Lola took to Molly, so she likes to make us wait."

Molly wrapped her arm tightly under Zane's and gave him a peck on the cheek. "I don't mind. I got you *and* I get to spend a lot of time with your sweet girl. I'd be a sore loser if I were her, too."

Katie gave an unpretentious snort-laugh. "Molly, the day you lose to any woman is the day I start getting manicures and facials on the regular."

Nasha found their banter amusing. She'd always wanted a sister. Feeling someone's eyes on her, she turned and caught Brandon unguarded. His intense green-gold look sent a wave of warmth through her body. She fumbled with her paper plate, and by the time she met his eyes again, he'd adopted his typical easygoing grin. "Need some help?" he offered.

"No, but thank you," she said. As she walked over to the trash can, she realized that at this point of her life, she could actually use all the help she could get. And Brandon and his family had already stepped up to make sure she stayed safe tonight. She could never express her gratitude to them for coming alongside her in some of the darkest moments she'd ever experienced.

About an hour after Zane, Molly, and Katie left, Ace arrived. Nasha watched as he grabbed leftover pizza and wings before settling on the couch with Brandon and her.

Esther Sue bustled about, pulling blankets and pillows from a hall closet. Unsure what she was up to, Nasha turned a questioning glance toward Ace.

He finished a bite of pizza. "Zane and I are taking shifts in the garage apartment next to the house tonight—kind of like an overwatch duty," he explained.

Esther Sue stuffed the bedding in a large bag. "Katie used to live there before she got married. It's a mess now, but Zane said it'll give them the best vantage point if anyone pulls in our driveway tonight. I'm going to head over and set things up for the guys."

"Do you need some help?" Nasha offered.

Esther Sue smiled. "No, hon, but thank you. Zane told me you weren't to go outside at all. We have to stay on the safe side, in case anyone's watching us." She headed out the front door.

Brandon turned to Nasha. "I'll be staying in the house with you and mom. I've got Dad's nine millimeter in case I need it."

Ace waved his chicken wing toward Brandon. "You sure you know how to use it, bro?"

Brandon's eyes flashed. "Probably nearly as well as you do. I've been hitting the shooting range with it ever since I got home."

"Good to know. I trust you." Ace gave Nasha a discreet

wink, obviously amused at Brandon's vehement reaction. His phone buzzed, so he wiped his fingers thoroughly and picked it up.

"Yes, she's doing well. Would you like to speak to her?" After a moment, Ace mouthed the words, "It's your marshal," and handed his phone to Nasha.

"Hello?" she said hesitantly, unsure what marshal she was speaking to.

"Nasha, this is Leah. It's so good to hear your voice."

Nasha heaved a thankful sigh. "And yours! Are you okay? Where are you?"

"Don't worry about me—I'm going to be detained a little longer. But I just wanted to check in and make sure you're all set for tonight. Sergeant Calhoun told me he has everything under control, but do you feel safe there? I don't want you feeling anxious."

Nasha glanced around the cozy McClure living room. "I do," she said, meaning it. "It's the next best thing to my home." She took a deep breath. "Leah, do you know if I'll have to stay in witness protection until the next trial?"

There was a pause on the other end before Leah spoke again. "I'm afraid so, given the attempted abduction by Wells' men. The FBI is actively questioning the pilot who took over the helicopter to see if they can prove that Harlan hired him, but they've had no luck yet."

Nasha fell silent.

Leah spoke softly, as if trying to console her. "But I'll be right there as we introduce you to the new marshals."

Nasha leaned forward on the couch, dropping her voice. "Will I go back to Arizona?"

"We can't discuss that on the phone, and besides, it hadn't been decided yet. For now, I want you to try to relax and get some sleep. I'll see you first thing in the morning, okay?"

Nasha wanted to ask Leah how she was doing in regard to

Bruce's death, but that was something they could talk about in person. "Okay, will do. Thanks for calling." She handed the phone back to Ace.

Brandon's eyes had scarcely left her face. "I'm so sorry," he said. "I know nothing has worked out the way you'd hoped."

Feeling undone by the news she had feared was coming, Nasha stood. She couldn't meet Brandon's sympathetic gaze for long. "I...I think I'll go take a shower," she said. "Thank you all for looking out for me. I'm truly grateful."

Ace nodded and Brandon said, "Let me know if you need anything," to her retreating back.

The only thing she needed was to see her family again, and, like everyone else, there was nothing Brandon McClure could to do about that.

14

Brandon watched as Nasha glided noiselessly down the hallway. She was so despondent, and he had no idea how to help. She was clearly missing her family dreadfully. He was unsure if getting her to talk about them would make things easier or worse for her.

As Ace returned from dumping his trash in the kitchen, Brandon lowered his voice and asked, "If Katie were in this situation—like the one Nasha is in, where she can't see her family—what would you do to make her feel better?"

Ace gave him a knowing look. "So, let's see...you're likening your relationship with Nasha to my relationship to my wife?"

Brandon colored. "Stop answering my question with a question."

"Just clarifying the terms here, bud." Ace grinned, rubbing a hand through his black hair. "Well, let's see. You know your sister is pretty tough—she doesn't wear her emotions on her sleeve—so she wouldn't necessarily come to me with her deepest concerns. I'd probably need to get her alone so we could talk for a while...kind of pull things out of her, you know?"

Brandon gave a slow nod. Unlike Ace and Katie, he and Nasha barely knew each other. Sure, he'd saved her life, but even if he could finagle some time alone with her, there was no guarantee she'd open up at all. He might even intimidate her into clamming up even more.

"Okay, thanks," he said. "I'll think about it."

Ace crossed his ankle over his knee and leaned back in the couch. "You do that." Lowering his voice, he said, "But, as an aside, she fits in well with your family. Your mom seems to like her."

Ma liked nearly everyone, but Brandon didn't point that out. However, his sisters also seemed to like Nasha, and that had to be a good thing.

He knew he couldn't hide his interest in Nasha for much longer. But how could he set about dating someone in witness protection who'd likely be whisked away from Hemlock Creek in the morning?

Brandon stayed up late on the couch, trying to focus on an old Humphrey Bogart movie. Nasha had only emerged from her room once to get a glass of water, and the weary look on her face told him she wasn't up to talking.

Ma had gone to bed early, after making sure Ace was all set up in the apartment. Brandon knew that he should be able to sleep easy with Ace and Zane staggering their overwatch duty all night, but he couldn't calm down enough to get to sleep. He retrieved the gun from a locked drawer in Dad's old desk, checked and loaded it, and tucked it under the couch. At least he'd be ready, even if he finally drifted off to sleep.

Shots woke Brandon, and he sat up in a daze, trying to place where they'd come from. The motion sensor light on the front porch had been triggered, so he pulled back a small portion of the curtain and looked toward the driveway.

Sure enough, a small car had parked on the edge of the drive. A man was hunkered down behind the car's passenger door. Brandon could barely make out that he was holding a long gun—maybe a shotgun. It was trained on the garage apartment.

Brandon hastily retrieved his pistol before calling 9-1-1. He desperately hoped Ma and Nasha didn't wake up, which might add to the confusion. He needed to keep his head.

After sharing his address and what was happening with the emergency operator, Brandon looked at the time. It was nearly five in the morning. That meant Zane was on duty in the garage apartment. More than likely, Zane had his sniper rifle trained on the intruder, pinning the man down behind his car door. That would explain the shots and the man's fearful pose. Brandon took a closer look at the small car's tires. One was starting to sag into the driveway, which meant Zane had likely shot it out.

Unsure how to help since Zane seemed to have the situation under control, Brandon headed into the hallway. Nasha's door was closed.

A slight breeze whipped around his bare legs. He should've worn PJ pants instead of shorts. Had Nasha opened a window, even though the heat was running?

He edged closer to her door, but didn't feel air escaping around it. The breeze was definitely coming from somewhere else in the house.

Tracing the steady airflow, he crept into the kitchen.

Flipping the light switch, his attention was immediately drawn to the back door, which had been left ajar.

As he rushed toward it, gun at the ready, a muffled cry sounded from the backyard.

They had broken in and they had taken Nasha.

Shoving his feet into slippers by the door, he burst into the backyard, turning on the porch light as he did so. He had to get to her. He was certain this time they'd have no compunction about eliminating her quickly.

He caught sight of a man dragging her toward an SUV that had been hastily parked near the clearing in their back woods. The attackers had cleverly flanked the house. While Zane had been preoccupied with the man in the car, another one had broken in the back way and figured out where Nasha was.

Brandon sped up, knowing he was the one who'd dropped the ball. While he was watching the front window and calling 9-1-1, someone had taken Nasha—practically dragging her out under his nose.

As the man began to shove Nasha into the back of the vehicle, Brandon shouted, "Stop!" He aimed the gun at him.

When the man turned, Brandon saw too late that he was carrying a pistol of his own. He hit the ground, but not before he felt a bullet whiz past his shoulder. He looked down, relieved to see he hadn't been hit.

Another man jumped from the SUV and raced toward him. Brandon fumbled to raise his gun, but before he could get a shot off, the man stomped his hand to the ground, forcing him to drop the weapon.

"Get up," the man demanded, yanking Brandon to his feet. He brandished a long knife. "And no funny business."

With his blade tip pointing at Brandon's back, he marched him over to the SUV. The other man hastily zip-tied Brandon's wrists. The knife-wielder then shoved Brandon into the back seat, where Nasha sat in a slouched position, probably trying to make herself as small a target as possible. She, too, was wearing zip ties, and her hands were positioned in her lap.

The driver started the SUV and roared off onto the side road. Brandon hoped that Zane noticed the commotion, but he was pretty certain he was focused on the man in front of the house. The police still hadn't arrived, because it had only been a matter of minutes since he'd called them.

"I'm sorry," Brandon whispered to Nasha.

She blinked back tears, nodding.

"Shut up back there," the man in the passenger seat said. He turned to his partner. "Listen, now we're gonna have to get rid of both of them. They both saw us."

The driver shook his head. "I told you we should wear masks, but you didn't listen. I'm going to have to ask the boss what to do next."

The passenger turned irate. "What if he won't pay? He promised a lot for the chick. I need that money. Let's just go to the drop-off point. He's supposed to be there, right?"

The driver reluctantly agreed and continued whizzing along the winding road. As they climbed in altitude, Brandon realized they were heading toward a secluded park with steep mountain overlooks. It was obvious they were hurtling toward their doom.

Desperate, he tried to gauge if he'd be able to wrap his zip-tied hands around the passenger's neck so he could pull back and choke him. He doubted he could pull off that trick without getting one of them shot. It wasn't worth risking Nasha's safety.

Katie had once told him she'd watched a video showing how to break hand zip ties if they were in front of your body. She'd gone on to demonstrate the technique and had shocked him by breaking hers. He would need to thrust both arms downward at the same time and let his bent knees snap the ties.

Would he be able to make such a large move without attracting their captors' attention? It seemed unlikely. He'd have to err on the side of caution, biding his time until he had some kind of advantage over them...if that moment ever came.

15

Nasha clenched her teeth as they whipped around the mountain curves, hoping she didn't get carsick. Then again, maybe if she puked, the driver would slow down. She glanced over at Brandon. His narrowed gaze was fixed on the men in front and his lips were thoughtfully pursed. Hopefully, he wasn't plotting some risky escape move. While she appreciated that he had once again stepped into the crosshairs to save her, she feared he was going to pay for that choice with his life.

Ace and Zane's overwatch plan had been good, but they'd only been able to monitor the front and side of the house from their garage perch. The hitmen must have scoped the place out—they'd known just where to park in the McClures' wooded backyard to allow them to break in the back way.

Nasha wondered how they'd found her. Had they followed Ace back from work and guessed he'd sheltered her with his family? Or had they somehow traced a call? There was no telling, and it didn't matter, anyway.

Nothing mattered anymore.

She focused out the front windshield on the road ahead,

trying to avoid feeling worse. Although she'd grown up in these mountains, she still occasionally got carsick. "Could you please crack my window?" she asked, desperate to quell her nausea.

The driver's response was quick, his tone unyielding. "No."

As Brandon's gaze shifted to her, his face immediately registered alarm. She probably looked white as a sheet. "She only asked you to crack it. She's getting carsick," he prodded.

Reluctantly, the driver cracked both back windows. Nasha gasped at the fresh air, knowing it was the only thing standing between her and losing whatever supper was left in her stomach.

Brandon was relentless in his quest to help her. "Hey, man, could you slow down some? She's really looking green around the gills. You want your car smelling like vomit?"

Grunting, the driver let off the gas. Nasha clenched her stomach with her zip-tied hands. She swallowed repeatedly, hoping to ease her sickness by making her ears pop. The rapidly changing altitude was hard to adjust to.

"Thank you," she mouthed to Brandon.

He gave her a serious nod.

She couldn't tear her gaze from his unusual eyes, which contrasted so nicely with his freckles and red beard. Those eyes were fixed on hers now, and they were filled with sadness and—could she dare hope?—some kind of unspoken longing that seemed to match her own.

If she had to die today, she could think of no better companion to have at her side than Brandon McClure. Why he had made so many heroic attempts on her behalf, she couldn't understand—perhaps it was just who he was. But she knew one thing. If things would have turned out any other way and they'd been allowed to return to their old lives, she would have told him how he lifted her spirits and made her feel like the very best version of herself every time they were together.

She finally turned away, taking in a deep, steadying breath of fresh air from the open window. She seemed to have gained some equilibrium and was feeling somewhat better. At least she wouldn't have to die carsick.

Because she knew one thing from the hard glint she'd seen in her hitman's eyes.

She was going to die today.

Brandon wasn't surprised when the driver pulled off into the secluded park's entrance. He didn't want to entertain the possibility that they might walk Nasha and him out to a high ledge and shove them over the edge, but he had to be realistic. There was no one to save them now, unless "the boss" the men had spoken of—whom Brandon assumed was Harlan Wells—told them to stand down in their murderous mission.

Fog cloaked the area as they pulled to a stop in a remote parking lot by the woods. The passenger jumped out and brandished his gun, forcing Nasha and Brandon to get out and stand by the SUV door. The driver checked to make sure no one was around, and after determining they'd go unnoticed, he led them down a misty path to a small picnic table area in the woods.

Brandon waited for Nasha to sit down on the picnic bench, then he situated himself as close as possible to her. His worst fear was that they'd force him away from Nasha and dispose of them separately. He wasn't about to let that happen, even if it meant getting shot in the process.

Thankfully, their captors didn't scold him for sitting near her. Instead, the driver repeatedly checked his phone, giving sigh after sigh as he did so. "Why isn't he here? I know this is the right place. He said he'd be here."

The passenger shoved his gun in the back of his pants. "He'd better not stand us up, after all the risks we took. Now we got two jokers to get rid of instead of one."

"So far, he's always been good on his—" The driver left off mid-sentence as a car pulled up next to his SUV. "That's got to be him," he breathed. "You stay here with them and I'll tell him what's going on."

Brandon watched as the driver headed over to meet the man who'd hired him. He felt no surprise when Harlan Wells stepped out of the parked car. As the men started talking, the hitman with the gun stood stock-still, focused on the parking lot as he tried to listen in on the muted conversation. Brandon was surprised by the feeling of Nasha's bound hands as they slid onto his arm and clung to it. He leaned closer to her, hoping to block her nervous gesture from the gunman.

They didn't have to wait long. Harlan stalked toward them, a familiar smirk on his lips. "Well, well, well. If it isn't the most annoying little witness I've ever seen and her runaway jury backup." He turned to Brandon. "Who even *are* you? Didn't you get the jury memo? I wasn't convicted."

"You should've been," Brandon spat out, still trying to block Nasha, who hadn't moved her hands from his arm. "Did you buy off that Glenn guy or what?"

Harlan laughed. "Glenn has some gambling issues. My sister runs a chain of video gaming parlors and Glenn's a regular at one of them. I found out he'd raked up some serious debts. And I know someone in the county clerk's office who also had some things she wanted kept secret, so she helped me make sure Glenn was one of several people I got onto the jury pool."

So Harlan Wells really did feel like he controlled

Hemlock Creek, and for good reason. He was more than happy to exploit the dirty secrets he'd found out, even to the point of tampering with due process.

Brandon wanted to say, "You won't get away with this," but he knew that was just hot air. The sad truth was that Harlan likely *would* get away with it, just like he got away with murdering his wife and hiring people to kill Nasha.

Nasha abruptly removed her hands from Brandon's arm, and her clear, unfaltering voice echoed in the foggy woods as she faced Harlan head-on. "You know what? I'm not afraid of you anymore. You're a weak and despicable man," she said.

Brandon was pleased to see Nasha's newfound courage, even if it only came as she was literally staring down the barrel of a gun. At least she could die knowing she'd done the right thing in speaking up and trying to bring Harlan Wells to justice.

And he could die knowing he'd given his life to protect such a brave woman.

Harlan grinned. "I'm sorry that a pretty little thing like you couldn't come around to my side. My mistresses don't care what kind of business I'm in. They just like the power and money I give them."

"That's not power." Nasha was clearly undeterred.

Harlan's eyes narrowed behind his designer glasses. He whirled toward the gunman. "Just get rid of both of them. I don't care how you do it, just make sure it's not traced to me. I'll give you double what I promised before." He strode off toward his car.

As the gunman forced Brandon and Nasha to stand, three loud cracks ripped through the air. Harlan dropped to the pavement. Trying to determined where the shots had originated, Brandon scanned the parking lot and caught sight of two well-hidden armed men taking cover behind a dumpster. They both wore makeshift pantyhose masks.

"Help me!" Harlan moaned, writhing on the ground.

Harlan's hitmen were obviously caught off guard. "Well? Go get him," their driver barked. "Otherwise we don't get paid."

"Then you cover me," the passenger demanded, handing his gun to the driver. Before he even made it to the parking lot, four more shots rang out in quick succession. Both of Harlan's hired henchmen fell to the ground in lifeless heaps.

Brandon didn't wait around. Grabbing Nasha's hand, he took off into the woods behind them, hoping the fog would obscure the shooters' aim. Another shot rang out, this time closer to them. Nasha couldn't match his long strides, so he scooped her into his arms and kept up his pace until he came to a rocky cave area.

"We'll hide here," he said breathlessly, setting her back on her feet. "I've been here a few times. There's a cave that has a small entrance, but it lets you out in a wide spot lower down the mountain." He grabbed her small hand. "You'll have to stick close to me though, since it gets dark in there."

He took a moment to manipulate his tall frame through the narrow opening. Nasha was so tiny, it was easy for her to slip in after him. Gripping her hand behind him, he made his way forward, knowing it was a nearly straight trek to the wider exit below. It was a good thing he'd spent a lot of his free time hiking in the area.

Realizing they could now access their phones without fear of getting shot or knifed, he stopped. There was nowhere to sit so his knees could break the zip ties, but Nasha could retrieve the phone for him. "Could you reach into my back pocket and slide my phone out?" he asked.

She carefully did so, gripping it in her tied hands. He turned and held his hands out, taking the phone and pressing his finger against it until it unlocked.

The phone sprang to life, its harsh light unnatural in the

dark cave. He'd gotten several calls and texts, most of them from Zane.

He scrolled down his contacts and called Master Chief—his contact name for Zane.

After pressing the speaker button so they could both hear, he breathed a sigh of relief when he heard Zane's phone ring on the other end. He'd worried they wouldn't have cell reception, but they must not have gone deep enough in the cave to lose it yet.

His brother-in-law picked up quickly."Where are you, brother?"

"In a cave up at Alexander Park—you know the narrow one we found last year?"

"I know it. You both okay?"

"We are, miraculously. But we might have armed guys after us. I'm not sure—I haven't heard any more shots. I think we ditched them." He went on to briefly explain the shootout in the parking lot.

Zane sounded unperturbed, as if armed gunman were a regular part of his day-to-day existence. "Okay. Don't worry—Ace is here with your mom. The police arrested the guy who was trying to break in. But I'm sorry it took me so long to realize that someone else broke in the back and got both of you."

Brandon was just grateful someone knew where they were. It was only a matter of time until they were rescued. "Dude, no apologies. I saw you pinning that guy down out front. Thank you."

"I'll be there before you know it," Zane promised, his voice gruff with obvious emotion. "You two stay in there. I'll come to you." He hung up.

In the light of the phone, Brandon saw Nasha's smile of relief. "You have a great family, Brandon." She placed a hand on his arm. "And you're a great guy, too. I wanted to thank you for coming after me—again. You didn't have to do that." Tears pooled in her eyes.

He was touched by her humility. "Nasha, listen...I'm not sure what's going to happen next or what just happened in that shootout back there. At this point, I don't know if Harlan is dead or alive." He laid the phone on a nearby rock, then took her small hands in his own. "I want you to know that if you have to testify again, I'll be right there with you this time around. Now you won't have to be the only witness."

She gave a gasp, awkwardly swiping at tears that started to wet her cheeks. "But why do you always try to help me?"

Instead of giving an immediate answer, Brandon squatted down. Raising his arms overhead, he slammed them down over his bent knees. After three tries, his zip ties snapped. Nasha's eyes widened, but she continued to watch his every move in silence.

He stood and took a step closer to her. Slowly and carefully, he wrapped her in his arms, pulling her into his chest. As her sobs intensified, he patted her soft hair. "Because you've needed me," he murmured. "And I've realized that I need you, too."

16

By the time Zane got to them and called into the cave, Nasha had borne her soul to the redhead seated by her side. In the pitch darkness, they'd laughed over childhood memories, shared their teen angst about finding the right career, and had just started telling embarrassing stories about their siblings. When Zane's voice echoed down to them, she actually hated to hear it.

"Y'all doing okay? Should I come in?"

Brandon helped Nasha to her feet. "No, we'll come to you."

He edged around Nasha, turning on his phone light to lead them out. It didn't take long before they emerged into the overcast day, which still seemed blinding.

Zane stood waiting for them, a rifle slung onto his back and two pistols holstered on his pants. He clapped Brandon into a hug. "It's so good to see you." He nodded at Nasha, his gray eyes warm. "And you."

"What's going on out there?" Brandon asked.

Zane motioned for them to follow him, and to Nasha's surprise, he headed back toward the parking lot. "Harlan's dead," he explained. "So are the guys you watched get shot—the ones who brought you here, right?"

"Right," Brandon said.

Zane was maintaining a quick pace, making it hard for Nasha to keep up. "A couple of officers came here with me and are searching the woods, but so far, there's no trace of anyone else lurking around," he said. "Are you sure those masked guys followed you?"

Brandon shrugged. "Not really. We just heard that follow-up shot and took off running." He stopped to push a low-hanging twig aside so Nasha could pass by without getting scratched. "It's possible they shot Harlan a third time, to make sure he died. But isn't it weird that they showed up to kill Harlan and his goons?"

Zane stopped and turned. "It's not weird, actually. That marshal, Leah, showed up just before I left."

Anxiety filled Nasha. Were the marshals already arriving to take her back into witness protection?

Zane continued. "When I told Leah what happened to you all, she took a couple of minutes and filled me in. As it turns out, Harlan called the FBI last night, promising to turn on *his* boss if they'd give him a reduced sentence. He insinuated that he works for some big fish they'd been trying to catch for a long time. I think she said his name was Leo something...Moreau, that's it. Like the movie *The Island of Dr. Moreau*."

"But what's that have to do with anything?" Brandon asked.

"Leah's hypothesis is that the masked men who shot Harlan and your abductors were Moreau's men. Harlan overstepped his authority by planning to make a deal with the Feds. Got too cocky, I guess. He should've known that Moreau guy likely had his phones tapped—shoot, he probably suspected Harlan would turn on him."

"So Harlan Wells is dead," Nasha said, trying to process things. "But why did Leah come over? Am I going back into witness protection?"

Zane's serious eyes met her own, and she felt she might have to sit down to hear the bad news. For some reason, they were going to keep her—

"Oh, no," he said. "You'll be out now. I'm sure there will be paperwork and things but..."

He continued talking, but Nasha didn't hear a word. She was out of witness protection. She was no longer in danger. She could see her family again.

She gave a joyful jump, right into Brandon's open arms.

She was going home.

Two weeks had passed since the harrowing day at the park. Nasha still couldn't believe she was back at her parents' house, even making plans to resume her medical rotation in Lewisburg. Leah had called her a couple of times, just to catch up. They'd talked about meeting up in the park so her brother could meet Leah's stepson.

Tarek, who had indeed grown quite a bit and lost a couple of teeth as well, grinned at her across the dining room table. "Tell me about the cave again," he said, his eyes bright.

Mom patted his hand. "Not now, dear. We're visiting with Brandon tonight."

Brandon smiled over his Tandoori chicken. "I'm happy to tell you about it, Tarek—maybe I could even take you to see it someday, if your parents say it's okay."

As Brandon launched into a vivid description of the cave, Nasha glanced over at her parents. Her mom had a few white hairs she hadn't had last year, but other than that, she looked contented. She kept looking at Nasha as if she couldn't get enough of having her around. Her dad had already taken her aside earlier in the week, telling her he was proud of the way she'd come through all her life-threatening experiences. He said she seemed bolder in making decisions and more prepared to become a doctor now.

Esther Sue McClure had also called Nasha, asking her if she wanted to come over for Sunday dinner. The whole family would be there, even Zane's daughter Lola. Esther Sue hinted that Molly and Zane might share a special announcement at the meal—one that would make her a grandma—and she said she hoped Nasha could share the moment with them.

Nasha smiled as she thought of the McClures. What a loving, tight-knit family, just like her own. And now Molly and Zane were going to welcome a new little member of the family.

After dessert, Brandon slipped out to his car for a moment. When he returned, he carried a bouquet of full peach roses, which he awkwardly handed to Nasha.

"Aw, thank you, Brandon," she said, standing to find a vase for them.

Brandon turned to her parents. "I wondered if I could speak to you both, Mr. and Mrs. Patel," he asked.

Nasha froze in place.

Brandon threw a quick look at her, as if gathering up his courage. "I, uh—Nasha mentioned that she hoped to have your approval before dating someone again. I really respect that idea, and I wanted to ask your permission if I could start dating your daughter."

Nasha sat back down, flabbergasted. In the cave, she'd talked to Brandon a little about her failed relationships, and she'd mentioned that she'd realized how important her parents' approval was in her choices of dates. She'd had no idea he was taking notes.

Dad gave Brandon a thoughtful look, but Mom jumped right in. "Of course we give our permission, Brandon."

Dad cleared his throat. "Yes. You've saved her life so she could return home to us. We are very grateful. You are a good man, and you certainly have our permission."

Mom smiled. "We can see that you two have a great connection. Nasha is even talking about going whitewater rafting sometime. It's good to see her enjoying herself more."

Nasha turned to Brandon, and he met her steady gaze. She carefully set her roses on the table. "I guess I've learned that I can handle more than I thought." She leaned closer, arms outstretched, and Brandon folded into her hug. She mumbled into his chest, "And I'm looking forward to having a lot more adventures with you."

AUTHOR'S NOTE

I thoroughly enjoyed bringing the McClure family to life in the three-book *Hemlock Creek Suspense* series. If you're looking for more West Virginia-set action (including more scenes at The Greenbrier Resort, more appearances by the mysterious Leo Moreau, and the story behind Brandon's favorite country band, Carolina Crush), be sure to check out *The Barks & Beans Cafe* cozy mystery series. This is a clean mystery series that both teens and adult readers are enjoying, and it features siblings Bo and Macy Hatfield. West Virginia is my home state, and it truly is wild and wonderful—I hope you get to visit it someday.

And if you enjoyed this book, be sure to tell your reader friends about it. One helpful way to do this is to leave a review of the book at online retailers or review sites. You can find out more about all my books and sign up for newsletter updates, giveaways, and book deals at **heatherdaygilbert.com.**

-Heather